I0651361

Legh Knight

Tonic Bitters

A novel. Part 2

Legh Knight

Tonic Bitters
A novel. Part 2

ISBN/EAN: 9783337052508

Printed in Europe, USA, Canada, Australia, Japan

Cover: Foto ©Andreas Hilbeck / pixelio.de

More available books at **www.hansebooks.com**

TONIC BITTERS.

𝔄 Nobel.

IN TWO VOLUMES.

By LEGH KNIGHT.

VOL. II.

LONDON:
CHAPMAN AND HALL, 193, PICCADILLY.
1868.

[*Right of Reproduction and Translation reserved.*]

TONIC BITTERS.

CHAPTER I.

It was well for Effie that she had not long to brood over her new sorrow. At the end of May Walter began to sicken with the whooping-cough; and soon every other thought was swallowed up in anxiety about the children. Walter, always delicate, was very seriously ill, and even the strong Davie, and merry little Freddie were speedily prostrated. Effie had the entire charge of these three, for when the baby of a year old was attacked Hannah was fully occupied with her. After a month of wakeful nights and anxious days all fears for the boys were at an end; but little Bessie was still in a precarious state, and Isabel, who had been the last to take the cough, and had been attacked by it with less violence than the others, did not regain her strength as they did. The long summer days passed on, and the boys again raced and shouted in the garden, but the little girl

still lay in her aunt's or her nurse's lap, and seemed
to have no part in the exuberant life around her.
Jessie had avoided the nursery entirely during the
children's illness, as she complained that their violent
coughing made her head ache ; and now that Effie
was so engrossed with Isa as to neglect her usual
care of the boys, their mother declared that a most
unnecessary fuss was made about the child, who
had only become fanciful through over-indulgence.
Harold was deeply concerned to see his little favourite
so unlike her bright self ; but childish ailments were
a mystery into which he never attempted to penetrate ;
and he supposed this extreme weakness was no more
than the natural consequence of the whooping-cough.
He made no secret of a strong prejudice against
doctors ; and Mr. Rogers, therefore, after giving a few
simple directions as to the treatment of the children,
had not obtruded visits which he knew were not
desired.   But when Isa's prostration took the form
of an intermittent fever, which still more reduced her
strength, Effie insisted that the doctor should be again
summoned.   Harold, frightened by her evident alarm,
no longer scorned Mr. Rogers' advice, but intercepted
him on his way from the nursery, and with trembling
lips asked his opinion of the patient.   That opinion,
gently as it was given, sent him in dread—almost in
despair—to his child's side.   And there those two
remained, day after day, and night after night, watch-

ing the gradual ebbing out of that life of three years.
Effie had no hope from the first, but Harold would
not see the truth, and Mr. Rogers admitted that, in
the case of a child, recovery was always *possible*.
Perfect quiet was enjoined, so the other children and
their nurse were removed to a distant room.

The weather was so intensely hot that, although all
the windows were open, the little sufferer lay gasping
for air. There seemed some hope of relief when,
after a more than usually oppressive day, distant
thunder gave promise of a change. Relief was near
at hand for one of the party in that still room. Isa
had been terribly restless all day, but at night had
fallen asleep quietly in her father's arms. She slept
on, undisturbed by the storm, and Effie, utterly worn
out, lay down on the sofa. A louder peal of thunder
roused her from a fitful sleep, to the consciousness
that it was time to give some nourishment to the
child.

" I am sure she is better," whispered Harold, as
Effie knelt down to pour the wine between the little
patient's lips. " See how calmly she is sleeping."

" Oh, Harold! I am afraid she is worse," Effie
half cried out, as she looked at the child's face. She
jumped up and ran to fetch Hannah. The nurse was
quickly in the room. She saw the truth at once.

" Better give her to me, sir," she said, when she
had bent over little Isa for a minute.

"Why?" asked Harold, fiercely, in a hoarse, almost loud voice.

"She is going, sir," replied the woman.

"Going?" he repeated, in the same tone. "What do you mean? Not dying? Effie!" he almost shrieked, "she is not dying?"

"Hush, dearest Harold! You will disturb her. Give her to Hannah."

He obeyed mechanically; and then, instead of looking at the child, fixed his eyes on Effie's face.

"Yes, she is going to rest," murmured Effie, as Hannah laid the tiny little form down on the bed. "See how peaceful she looks."

"It is not true!" cried Harold. "You are mistaken. I will send for Rogers." He was hurrying to the door, when Effie laid her hand on his arm. "Harold, dear, come and look at her. All her suffering is over now."

"It is impossible!" he cried, again; "it cannot be. It *shall* not. Isa! my darling! my darling!" The unhappy father threw himself on the little corpse in such an agony of grief, that the two women drew back awestruck. Suddenly he started to his feet again. "Hannah! run as fast as you can and fetch Mr. Rogers—go this instant, I say!" he cried, as the girl hesitated.

"It is a swoon," he added, when the nurse had left the room. "It must be a swoon." He knew

better, however. After looking at the little face for
a few minutes, he turned again to Effie. "Effie, I
cannot bear it!" he shrieked. "It is too much—too
much. My beautiful little girl! My darling! my
little Isa! Why should I lose her? I *will* not bear
it!"

"Hush, Harold! Oh, don't! You must not speak
so. It is God's will."

"God's will!" he repeated, with awful bitterness.
"If there were anything but a blind chance to rule
the world, do you think *that* innocent would have
had to suffer and die, and worn-out sinners be left to
cumber the earth? And what have *I* done to deserve
such a grief as this? If there were a righteous Judge
above us, why should I, who have always done my
duty, be afflicted, whilst wicked men are spared?"

"Oh Harold! dear Harold! think how happy it is
for Isa to be taken away from all the evil of the
world, and to be free for ever from sorrow and sin.
And may it not be in mercy that this grief is sent?
May it not——"

"Mercy!" interrupted Harold, in the same fearful
tone. "Mercy, to rob me of what was dearer to me
than my life! Mercy, to take from me the only
creature that ever loved me! No! If there *is* a God,
He is not a God of Mercy!"

Effie burst into tears, and fell sobbing on her
knees beside the bed. She remained so, stopping

her ears to Harold's awful words, till Mr. Rogers
came. Then she escaped from the room.

How different it felt outside! It was just dawn. The
thunder had ceased, and a gentle rain was moistening
the parched air. With a sensation as if she, too, were
parched, and needed the refreshing shower, Effie
hurried into the garden. Harold's awful blasphemy
was ringing in her ears ; but something in the morning
air brought back to her mind a very different scene,
seventeen years ago, when her father had led her,
then a child of six, to the new-made graves of her
brothers and her little sister, and had told her of the
happy life to which they had gone. What a contrast
between his words and Harold's! Where was the
faith now which her father had tried to instil into his
children's minds? She had tried to offer Harold
some religious consolation ; but she had felt at the
time that hers were mere parrot-utterances. She
knew that her heart was almost as unbelieving as
Harold's. She had rejoiced that little Isa was taken
away from the sorrows of this world, but she had no
faith to make her rejoice in the child's entrance into
a better world. Her religious professions seemed to
her a hollow mockery now. Her good works were
powerless to comfort her in this hour of trial. There
was no comfort for her anywhere—was there truth in
anything? Her father's faith—was there truth in
that? His prayers for his children—what had they

availed? His teaching—what fruit had that borne?—
Harold an atheist, — Gerard a sensualist, — Jessie
heartless, — herself faithless! Which of them had
not lost all joy in this life, and all hope in another life?

Effie did not know how long she had been meditat-
ing thus, when the back gate bell rang, first very
gently, and then louder. Concluding that it must be
the milkman, and that the servants were not yet up,
Effie went slowly to the gate. There stood—not the
milkman — but Gerard Yonge. In her painfully
excited state of feeling, Effie's first impulse was to
throw herself sobbing on his neck, as she had done in
many a childish grief. She managed to subdue that
impulse; but she was incapable of any other effort, and
stood looking at him without saying a word.

For a few minutes Gerard was as much overwhelmed as she was; but at last he got out the
question, "How is the little girl? I came to ask,
when I thought no one but the servants would
be up."

" She is dead," answered Effie, calmly, feeling quite
unable to say more than the bare fact.

" Dead!" repeated Gerard, turning even paler than
he was before. "Poor Harold!" he covered his face
with his hands, leaning against the gate-post; and
they both stood perfectly silent for some minutes.
Then Gerard said, abruptly, " How is he?"

The horror of that scene swept over Effie again at

the question. "Oh, Gerard!" she cried, "it is awful!"

"His grief?" asked Gerard, in a whisper.

"Yes;" and she shivered.

"Effie, how *you* have suffered!" said Gerard, drawing nearer to her.

His affectionate tone upset all her self-control, and the tears would come, slowly at first, and then so fast that they choked her voice.

"I would give ten years of my life to be able to see him now," cried Gerard, impulsively.

"Will you come in and see him?" asked Effie.

"I dare not," replied Gerard. "He would not see me. He would only think it an impertinence. No, it would be of no use. Do you think it would?"

"Perhaps not," said Effie, remembering how hard Harold could be.

There was another pause, till the sight of a passer-by reminded Effie where they were standing, and she asked Gerard to come into the garden.

"I must, just this once," he said, hesitatingly. "Harold would be very angry, I suppose. But I cannot go away yet. I have come every morning since I heard the baby was ill. I did not know anything about it till I met Joe Butterfield one day last week. How long was the poor little thing ill?"

"Not more than a fortnight, seriously ill—but they have all had the whooping-cough."

"Yes, I heard that. Are the others all right now? Dear old Davie, and Walter?"

"Yes, quite."

"This is not so bad as if it were one of the elder ones. Harold cannot care so much for only a baby."

"She was his favourite of them all," said Effie, sadly. "She was three years old, you know."

"Ah, true," said Gerard, colouring deeply. "I had forgotten how long it is since——" he stopped abruptly. "Poor dear old Harold! When did the little girl die?"

"About three o'clock. What time is it now?"

"Six. I suppose I ought to go. Effie, I am so glad I have seen you. Take care of yourself. By-the-by, how does Jessie bear this?"

Effie started. No one had once thought of the mother. "She does not know," she whispered.

Gerard's sigh sounded like a groan. "Poor Harold!" he said again.

"You will catch cold in this rain," he cried, suddenly, after a long silence. "How selfish of me to keep you here! Good-bye." He held her hand for a minute before he turned away towards the gate. He walked a few paces, and then came back again. "Effie, does Harold know about that night?" he asked, looking very much confused.

"No," said Effie, decidedly. "No, I think—I hope not."

"Thank you," he cried. He half turned away again, and said, in a low voice, "What a beast I made of myself!"

Effie did not speak.

"Effie!" he exclaimed, vehemently, "indeed I am not a drunkard. That horrid affair was all accidental. It served me right for being such an impertinent fool as to venture there. Joe Butterfield persuaded me to go—in fact, he *dared* me—and I was idiot enough to brave it out. My courage failed me at last, and I tried to fortify myself with Mr. Butterfield's wine; and then, when in spite of that I felt utterly ashamed of myself amongst you all, I was fool enough to turn to the poisonous stuff at the Falcon, and so—but it is absurd to be trying to excuse myself—such a thing as that cannot be excused. And you were so kind to me, Effie!"

Still Effie did not speak.

"You were very much disgusted, I suppose?" asked Gerard, wistfully.

"I was very—oh, Gerard, it *was* terrible."

Gerard covered his face with his hands again, and gave a kind of sob.

"I am glad Harold does not know. Did George see anything?"

"No, I think not," answered Effie. She did not consider it necessary to say that Clara had.

" You believe that I am heartily ashamed of myself, Effie."

" Yes," said Effie ; " I thought you must be. I thought you could not be so changed."

" And you believe I am not a drunkard ?"

, " Oh, yes."

" You will believe the best of me always ?" he asked again.

" Yes, always, if I can."

" You have heard all sorts of bad things of me, I suppose."

" Not much."

" Did you hear that Clara Monro refused me, and that I quarrelled with George ?"

" No," said Effie, with a start.

" That was the reason Joe Butterfield thought I dared not show my face in Gateshill—he found out about it, somehow. It all happened two years ago now. Everything happened more than two years ago," he said, mournfully. " I am forgetting again, and keeping you out in the rain. Good-bye. God bless you, Effie." He pressed her hand once more, and hurried away. Effie went slowly in.

She felt equal to anything now, even to seeing Harold. He was sitting alone by the little bed. His face looked set and bitter, and did not change in the slightest degree when she entered.

" Harold, Jessie does not know yet," she said, presently, in the hope of rousing him.

"She will not care," he answered, in a hard, cold tone, which made Effie shudder.

"Shall I tell her?"

"As you like. *I* will not. I will not see her indifference. My child! My child! I have no one left now!" he cried, suddenly, again throwing himself on the little form.

Effie left the room, and went to her sister. Jessie was sleeping soundly, and Effie was forced to stand and admire the beautiful picture. Certainly it was difficult to imagine any creature more lovely than the woman who lay there, with a face as fresh and innocent-looking as that of a sleeping child. Presently she stirred, and then slowly the long dark eyelashes parted, and a look of sleepy wonder came into the soft brown eyes.

"Effie! how you startled me! Where's Hannah?"

"It is not quite Hannah's time to come yet, dear Jessie. I came to you because—because poor little Isa is much worse."

"Worse!" said Jessie, turning a little pale, and speaking fretfully. "Then why don't you send for Mr. Rogers? What can *I* do?"

"No one can do anything, I am afraid," said Effie, sadly.

"What nonsense! You are so full of fancies about that child. But I wish you would keep them to yourself. It is enough to make me seriously ill to have you waking me with that mournful face."

" My tidings are more mournful than my face, Jessie—Isa is dead !"

. "You are trying to frighten me, Effie !" cried Jessie, looking really startled.

Effie did not answer.

" How could you be so unfeeling as to tell me so suddenly ?" exclaimed Jessie, after a moment's pause ; and she burst into tears.

" Auntie !" cried Walter's voice on the stairs ; and Effie hurried out to tell the three boys that their little sister was gone where she would never be ill any more, but would be happy for ever. Freddie, who had regarded the whooping-cough as a most unwarranted interference with his enjoyment, imme- diately put in a claim to go there also, and was only induced to give up the idea by being reminded that if he went away there would be no one to teach baby to walk. That point settled, Effie returned to her sister, whom she found more composed.

" I can't see Harold !" said Jessie, wiping her eyes.

" He is quite broken-hearted, Jessie."

" Yes ; I knew he would be. He cared for Isa much more than for any of us. In fact, I think he only cared for her in all the world."

" Oh, Jessie ! he is such a good husband !"

" Yes, of course he does his duty. But it is many years since he has loved me—that is very evident now. If he loved me he would not break his heart at losing any one but me."

"Jessie, do not be unreasonable now."

" Of course. *I* am always unreasonable. No one has any sympathy with *me*. All your pity is for Harold. You don't seem to think that poor dear little Isa's death is any grief at all to her mother. Harold may break his heart—but *I* am to be reasonable."

Effie saw clearly that there was no hope of that at present, so she left the room. About an hour later Jessie's bell rang, and Effie went to her. She had been crying a great deal, and looked really unhappy ; but she had not forgotten self in her grief.

" Effie," she said, " of course I cannot be expected to get up after such a shock, but I should like some tea—my mouth is so parched—and I think I could eat an egg, and a little toast. I shall be ill if I do not manage to take nourishment now there is this strain on my feelings."

Poor Effie left the room utterly sick at heart.

The husband and wife did not see each other for some time. Jessie continued to treat herself as an invalid, remaining in her room for the greater part of every day, and Harold shut himself up in his studio till he had followed his little girl to her grave. After that he returned to his usual mode of life, and then he and Jessie could no longer keep apart. They met very coolly. Harold repressed all signs of emotion, and Jessie, although she had herself dreaded to see her husband, resented his having avoided her.

This was the commencement of a sad change in the relations between them. In spite of Jessie's frequent outbreaks of temper, they could never hitherto have been considered an unhappy couple. Harold had always appeared almost blind to his wife's faults, and hardly less devoted to her than in the early days of their marriage. But little Isa's death seemed entirely to have altered her father's character. The bitterness which had made his grief so terrible to witness did not pass away with the first burst of agony, as Effie had hoped it would, but acted like poison on his once sweet nature, making it hard and morose. Hard even towards the children, morose to all but Effie. To her, who had been the devoted nurse of his lost darling, he was unfailingly gentle and tender, watching to gratify her slightest wish, and lavishing on her all the fond attention which he formerly paid to his wife alone.

The lamentable results of this conduct were not difficult to foresee. Jessie grew daily more jealous of Effie. This sentiment was soon no longer a fitful emotion, dissipating itself in a few passionate words. It became her daily and hourly feeling, brooded over when she was alone, and, still worse, openly manifested to her husband and sister. Effie's life was rendered utterly miserable. She had no longer any pleasure in Harold's society. Ever since the night of little Isa's death he had inspired her with more fear than affection ; and, much as he had been tried, she could not excuse his present coldness towards his wife. His excessive kindness to her ever since the rupture of her engagement with Gerard had always vexed her, as conveying a tacit reproach to his brother, and now it still more annoyed her on Jessie's account. Even her intercourse with the children had become painful, for out of it there arose constant cause of displeasure to their mother. With Jessie herself there was no possibility of maintaining peace. Her every word gave offence, and her mere presence seemed to irritate her sister beyond all power of self-control. It was a terrible position, and, after all her nursing and watching at the time of the whooping-cough, it was more than her health and spirits were equal to sustaining.

One afternoon, after a more than usually trying scene with Jessie, who had gone away declaring that either she or her sister must leave the house, Effie sat, sobbing bitterly, on the floor of the little playroom.

"Effie ! dear Effie ! what is the matter ?" exclaimed an agitated voice, and looking up she saw George

Monro. "I beg your pardon," he added, in some confusion. "The children brought me into the garden, and after playing with them I thought I might venture in by this open window—but, Effie! I cannot bear to see you in such distress. Is there anything I can do?"

"Yes. Oh, Mr. Monro, find me some work to do far away from here!"

"From Gateshill?" asked George, looking terribly puzzled and distressed.

"Away from this house—away from—oh! I ought not to tell! But I cannot bear it any longer, and you and Clara are my only friends."

"Effie!" cried George, in uncontrollable excitement. "Be my wife. I will take you away from every trouble." Then, lowering his voice to a tone of the deepest tenderness, he added, "I have loved you so long, and so dearly, Effie, that it *must* be in my power to make you happy. I ask for nothing in return, Effie; only give me the right to comfort you —to shield you from trouble." He stopped, and looked at her imploringly.

Effie saw on one side the constant woe, bitterness, and strife of her present home, and on the other, rest, peace, and safety with this good, loving man. She was silent, but her quick breath and changing colour betrayed her agitation. George gathered hope from this, and he began to plead his cause again.

"Remember, Effie, I do not claim any love from you. I only beg you to accept my love—a love that has been growing and strengthening all the years that I have known you. Don't reject it. I am sure—I feel that I could make you happy." He looked eagerly in her face.

"It is a fearful temptation," murmured Effie, dreamily.

"Yield to it, Effie!" cried George, pushing his advantage. "It is a prompting to good; it is not a temptation to evil. I would not ask it for my own sake, if I did not think it would be for your good. Indeed, it is not vanity that makes me think so. I know that I am infinitely unworthy of you, but my love for you is so true and deep, Effie, it is worthy even of you."

"I am not worthy of such love," said Effie, through her still flowing tears.

"Will you take it, Effie?" cried George. "You need not say a word," he added, as she tried to speak, and failed. "Only give me your hand. There, see"—he spoke with vehement eagerness, holding out his hand to her,—"with this hand I give you all myself—my love, my life—it has been yours ever since I first knew you—take it—oh, Effie, only take it!"

Slowly Effie placed her cold, trembling hand upon the open palm before her. Almost before she knew what she had done, she was clasped in George's arms.

At that moment Harold came into the room. George turned towards him, still holding Effie. "Give her to me, Yonge," he said. "I have loved her for years, and she will give me a right to love her for life."

"And what am *I* to do?" asked Harold, bitterly, forgetting everything in the surprise of the moment. It was a painful question from the lips of her sister's husband, and Effie could bear no more. She escaped from the room; and George, shocked and distressed, left the house, as soon as he had explained as much as courtesy required to Harold.

Effie got through the rest of the day, as she had got through many a day, by putting off thought till the night. And even then she did not think, for she was so tired out that directly she was in bed she fell asleep. But her dreams did more than her waking thoughts could have done.

She was in the garden at Pixycombe, hearing again the words of love which she had heard that afternoon; but now, instead of distress and fear, they caused her the deepest joy; for the eyes that looked so eagerly for an answer were not the passionate brown eyes of George Monro, but the kind grey ones of Gerard Yonge. Then she saw Harold, frowning angrily, and menacing Gerard with some danger, from which she only could protect him, and her father's voice cried out, "Take care of him." That cry awakened her,

to lie for some time still enjoying the pleasant feelings
of the dream, and then to fall asleep, and dream
again.

Again she was at Pixycombe—in an arbour which
she and Gerard had made. George Monro was with
her ; she could not hear his words, but she knew they
were the same that he had spoken to her that afternoon. In the arbour it was light and warm, but
outside all was dark and terrible, and in that darkness
she saw Gerard, stretching out his arms towards her,
imploring her to give him shelter. She struggled to
get to him, but George held her fast, and struggling
she awoke.

Next she was in Gateshill Church, but all the pews
were gone, and it was arranged like a foreign cathedral.
At the high altar stood her father, her aunt Elizabeth,
and George Monro, all in priests' vestments. She
was kneeling at the altar of a side chapel before an
image, which was Gerard Yonge. Harold, with
little Isa's dead body in his arms, was moving slowly
round and round the church, shouting out horrid
blasphemies, and Jessie went up to the altar, and,
saying in a loud voice, "Now that Effie is Harold's
wife, dancing is my only comfort," caught hold of
George, and started off with him in a wild galop down
the church, in and out amongst the worshippers.
Then her father came and knelt beside her, and his
priest's vestments turned into a shroud. And her

aunt Elizabeth came up and declared that the image was not Gerard, but his father, Frederick Yonge, and then it turned into Harold, and then into George Monro. And Gerard was kneeling by her side, and the image—still that of George—toppled over and threatened to fall on Gerard, and she jumped up to save him, and so awoke,—this time thoroughly. After each previous dream she had only had a vague feeling of enmity towards both George Monro and Harold, as being in some way opposed to Gerard. Now she gradually became conscious that she had promised to be George Monro's wife, and that to take Gerard's part against him, even in her dreams, was no longer lawful for her. "No! I cannot be his wife!" she cried aloud, starting up in bed, and looking wildly around her.

The cold grey dawn stealing in at the window calmed her a little, and then she lay back to think it all over. Feeling and Reason began to argue together. Reason brought forward George's virtues, his devotion to her, his noble character; contrasted his firm principles, his pure life, his generous unselfishness, with Gerard's weak, self-indulgent nature, and debasing tastes. Feeling would care nothing for all this, but painted vivid pictures of the old days, when Gerard would not have suffered by comparison with George, and argued that if he were weak he had all the more need of friendly support. "But," argued Reason, "he

has scorned that support from me—he will not have
it." Feeling answered, " I can give it without his
knowledge. I can be his friend even if I should
never see him again."—" Can I not be his friend
though I should be George's wife?" asked Reason.
Feeling answered with a shudder, and then Conscience
spoke. " No, I am Gerard's wife at heart—it would
be an awful sin to have any other husband. I could
not vow to forsake every other, and keep me only to
George, for my heart *will* not forsake that other, and
my very dreams keep true to him." Here Expediency
put in a feeble question. " But how can I escape
from my present life except by marrying George?"
Conscience had an answer ready. " What sort of
life would *that* be which could be nothing but a living
lie?"—" But," pleaded Expediency, " as George's wife
I should be led to so much good—I could do so much
good."—" Good cannot come of evil—a false heart
can do no good," replied Conscience, promptly. Then
Feeling had a word to say. " But George has loved
me so long, and I might make him happy." Conscience would not be put off so. " George is true
and honest, and nothing false will ever make him
happy."

The debate was over. Effie got up hastily, and,
standing in her dressing-gown at the high chest of
drawers, which was the only table in her little attic,
wrote the following note to George:—

" DEAR MR. MONRO,

"You must not think that my inconsistent conduct is the result of indifference to your feelings. I cannot tell you how great an honour I should think it to be your chosen wife, or how much I prize your affection. But for that very reason I must revoke the tacit consent which I gave yesterday to what you so generously proposed. I thought then that the depth of my gratitude, and (it is not too much to say) my *reverence* towards you would make up for the absence of other feelings, but I find that it would not be so. I *know* what a wife ought to feel for her husband, and to give you less would be unjust to you, and false to my own conscience. You know why I have no more to give. I truly feel that you deserve any woman's best affections—how could I bear to see you throw yourself away upon a woman whose affections are already spent? Forgive me for having deceived you yesterday. Forgive me for having for a few hours yielded to the temptation to escape from present misery at the cost of your happiness, and my own truth. Forgive me for all, and believe me to be,

"Ever your sincere Friend,

"EFFIE GARNOCK."

Effie despatched this note as soon as the servants were up, and then went to Harold in his studio.

"Harold, you must not think anything of what Mr. Monro said yesterday. I have written to him that there can be nothing between us. He is good, noble—almost perfect, I believe—but I still love Gerard." She said this defiantly—as she always felt defiant towards Harold with regard to Gerard. "I am going to my aunts at Gourock," she continued. "I shall start to-morrow. I have written a letter, which I shall take to Euston Square, and send by the guard of the mail-train. It is much better that I should go," she added, rather remorsefully, as she saw Harold's wounded look.

"Yes, much better for you. Much better to escape from this ill-omened house. You are wise."

"Harold, I would stay if I could do any good. But I only do harm."

"No. You had better go. *You* are free to go."

She was glad that she was free to leave the room then; and she did feel rather like an escaped captive the next morning, when the express train was whirling her northwards.

CHAPTER II.

EFFIE had no intention of remaining with her aunts.
The money her father had left her was not sufficient
to support her in idleness, and she was most unwilling
to be dependent upon the kind old ladies, who would
readily have shared with her their small means.
They were disappointed, but they quite understood
her feelings, when she told them of her wish to take
a situation as governess in a family. Aunt Euphemia
alone would not acknowledge that Effie was right
in desiring to work for her maintenance.

"Hoot—toot, bairn!" said the warm-hearted woman.
"What for should you be fashing yourself about your
wee bit victuals? We'll never miss your keep. And
it's no fit for a weakly body like you—wi' your bit
pale face—to be working yourself into the kirkyard
among fremd folk. Na, na; just bide content wi'
your old aunts, who are wearying for a bairn-like
voice about the house."

But aunt Euphemia yielded when it turned out

that Mrs. Caird, the sister-in-law of her friend
Dr. Lang, was seeking for an English lady to take
the charge of her two younger children. Effie remembered the hospitable stranger who had received
Jessie and herself like old friends when they had
passed through Glasgow eight years before; and she
thought she could not begin work more pleasantly
than by becoming one of that cheerful family circle
in Kelvin Crescent. The necessary arrangements were
soon made, and before she had been a fortnight at
Gourock, Effie removed to Glasgow.

Mr. Caird was one of the merchant-princes of that
wealthy city, and he was as liberal and kind-hearted
as he was rich. In business upright, prompt, and
exact, he was at home an easy, open-handed master,
a yielding husband, and a most indulgent father.
Mrs. Caird was one of those women who can best
be described by the term *fascinating*. A handsome,
bright-faced, clever woman, with cheerful spirits, and
a warm, sympathetic manner. Nothing ever seemed
to escape her observation, and she found something
to interest her in every one, and in every subject
of conversation. Her way with Effie was charming.
She treated her at once as one of the family, gave
her full authority over the children, and congratulated
herself on having secured a friend who would be able
to advise her in matters in which Mr. Caird refused to
interfere. Effie soon found that there were few matters

unconnected with business with which Mr. Caird did *not* refuse to interfere. When she was introduced to him he was the perfection of courtesy ; but he had evidently not the slightest idea that she was anything but a casual guest at his table.

"You remember Miss Garnock, John. She and her sister were kind enough to come to us for one night, eight years ago. You know we were so sorry they could not stay longer. Her sister married soon after—such a lovely girl. Surely you remember, John. We were at the marriage."

"Miss Garnock must excuse my bad memory," Mr. Caird said, politely. "But some of the blame is hers, for having stayed away so long as eight years. I hope you like Glasgow, Miss Garnock."

"I have seen very little of Glasgow. I have been staying at Gourock till now."

"We'll have the pleasure of showing her all our lions. And she has seen very little of the neighbourhood. We must take her to the Trosachs and the Falls of the Clyde before the winter sets in."

"She will be taking fright and hurrying southwards whenever we have a frost. That is what you southerners generally do, Miss Garnock."

"No, I shall not do that," said Effie, rather sadly.

"Miss Garnock has been so very kind as to take

the charge of Katie and Jamie. I am afraid she will
find her office no sinecure; they are quite past my
control."

"You must not heed what their mother says of
them, Miss Garnock. They are very good bairns.
I am very glad to hear that you'll likely make out
a long visit to us. I hope we shall be able to make
you comfortable."

And this, with a daily kind inquiry after her
health and comfort, was the extent of Effie's intercourse with the father of her pupils. The pupils
themselves were a fine merry girl of ten, and a
pretty, delicate, sensitive boy of eight. The other
members of the family were a grown-up son—a
sensible, straightforward young man, who was in
business with his father; three girls between nineteen
and sixteen, and a noisy schoolboy of fourteen. They
were all inclined to be extremely friendly with Effie,
and she soon felt quite at home.

Her pupils were affectionate, warm-hearted children,
and with no member of the family could she find any
fault—except one, and that was a very grave one—
they had no sense of truth. Those who did not
themselves indulge in a habit of prevarication, or
downright falsehood, made light of it in those who
did, and Effie could not get any one to understand
the perfect misery which it caused her. If Mrs. Caird
perceived anything of this sort, she did not appear

in the least surprised or distressed, but would observe
coolly that Helen had such a lively imagination she
really could not be tied to facts ; or that poor Jamie
was so sensitive he was always afraid to tell the truth ;
or that Flora was so funny she could not resist
making up a clever story. In everything else Effie
met with the most ready sympathy ; and if she were
only a little tired or cold she was overwhelmed with
pity and attention. Nothing could be pleasanter
than her position externally. Mrs. Caird was a
thorough lady, and her children and servants naturally
took their tone from her, so that Effie did not encounter any of the petty annoyances which she had
taught herself to expect. Having braced up her
mind to endure slights and rudeness—according to
the conventional idea of a governess's trials—she was
almost disappointed to find that her heroism was
quite uncalled for; and this freedom from personal
discomfort made her all the more sensitive to the
painful moral degradation around her.

In the childish code of morality at Pixycombe a lie
had been looked upon as a disgraceful crime, impossible amongst themselves, and sufficient to put
any other children beyond the pale of their society.
The effects of this early training had produced a
strange inconsistency in Gerard, whose weakness of
purpose and excessive love of approbation often led
him to *act* untruly, whilst he would on no account

speak untruly.   The same code prevailed in the
nursery at Gateshill ; and by common consent in that
house the slightest approach to falsehood was more
severely punished than any other offence.   Effie felt
quite powerless to deal with a fault of which she
had hitherto had no experience.   She soon began
to suspect deceit and treachery everywhere.   Whenever she came upon an undoubted falsehood, she
invariably brought it home to the author, and con-
fronted him or her with it.   The young Cairds were
too good-tempered to resent this ; but it made them
still more untrue, and Effie soon found herself surrounded by a complete network of manœuvring and
deceit.

She was utterly discouraged, and one afternoon
soon after Christmas—when Jamie had perpetrated a
more than usually base piece of trickery, she completely broke down, and cried bitterly, sitting by herself
in the school-room.   How she longed then for the
sound of those dear little voices at home, which had
never given utterance to an untrue word !

She was just thinking sadly of the cruel circumstances which had forced her away from those children,
for whom she had almost a mother's love, and had
placed her amongst strangers, when, looking up at a
slight noise, she saw Harold standing at the door.
Effie forgot all the miserable time before she left
Gateshill, and remembered only that Harold was her

brother. Just now deceit appeared to her the only evil in the world, and Harold at any rate was true. With that thought she threw her arms round his neck, as she had always done in the old happy days when he stood third—and afterwards second—in her world. Harold kissed her affectionately, and then, holding her from him and looking into her face, said, "I have come to scold you, and to take you home."

That word "home" sounded very tempting, but it recalled many things to Effie's mind, and she glanced anxiously at Harold. He looked sad and careworn, but his face had lost the cold, bitter expression which it had for so long after little Isa's death.

"I think you have been punished for running away," said Harold, after a short pause of mutual observation, "so I will not scold you."

"I have been very happy here, Harold—at least —that is—every one is excessively kind to me— but——"

"But—" repeated Harold, gently. "But you are very thin and pale, and look as if you had all this big city on your mind. Now, how soon can you be ready? Can we start to-night, or must we wait till to-morrow morning?"

"To-morrow! Oh, Harold, I cannot leave so soon! It would not be fair to Mrs. Caird."

"I have told Mrs. Caird that I must have you at

once. She is distressed, but resigned. There will be
no difficulty about that."

"But, Harold, I am sure it is best for me to be
away for the present—you yourself agreed that it
would be best."

" Best for you to go for a little change to the aunts.
But if I had suspected your real intentions, nothing
should have induced me to let you go."

"But really I am very comfortable. I would
much rather be here than living idly at Gourock,
though the aunts are so kind."

" And I would rather you should live nowhere but
at home. Your father left you in my charge. Am
I to abuse the trust by letting you slave amongst
strangers ?"

" I do not slave in the least. And you can take
charge of me without keeping me always in your
sight. I am sure Papa would not have wished us to
continue together if we are all happier apart.

" *Are* we happier apart ?" asked Harold. " Are
you happy away from us all ?"

Effie could not say that she was, when her still
tearful eyes said the contrary. " I am happier here
than making misery at home," she answered, at last,
in a low voice.

" *You* do not make the misery at home. It is
miserable enough now you are away. The children
are running wild, and the whole house is in confusion.

Jessie herself complains that you have deserted your duties, and let the entire burden fall upon her."

"I did it for the best," pleaded Effie, penitently.

"I was willing it should be so, as long as I thought you were resting in peace at Gourock. I did not think you would deceive me, Effie."

"What could I do? I knew you would oppose my plan if I told you of it."

"Naturally. I did not learn where you were till the day before yesterday, and I started by the mail at once."

"How did you learn it?"

"I received a letter in which I was reproached for allowing you to be driven from home." He would not mention Gerard, but Effie knew well that the letter was from him.

"How did Gerard know?" she asked, calmly. She was beginning to be angry with Harold again for his continued resentment toward Gerard.

"Some young man from Glasgow—some relation of Mrs. Caird, I believe—has come to London, and he mentioned that you were here."

"Yes, by-the-by, Dr. Lang's son, Mrs. Caird's nephew, has gone to walk the London hospitals."

"Are we to start to-night or to-morrow?" asked Harold again.

"I must see my aunts before I leave Scotland."

"Then we must go to them to-night. I have to

take Bristol on my way home, and the boat leaves the Broomielaw at two o'clock to-morrow. We could go on board at Greenock, if you like."

When Harold looked and spoke as he did now, Effie knew it was useless to oppose him; so she persuaded him to go by himself to Gourock, and made arrangements for her own departure the next day. The Cairds overwhelmed her with expressions of regret at losing her. The children and their mother parted from her with tears, and even the undemonstrative Hugh, the eldest son, took an opportunity of saying, "I am wofully sorry that you are going, Miss Garnock. It is a very selfish sorrow, for I know you must have had a weary time of it here ; but I did hope that with you Katie would have had a chance of growing up with some sense of right and wrong."

Effie was glad to find that one member of the family was aware of the family failing. As she got into the cab to go to the Broomielaw, Jamie ran out of the house, threw his arms round her neck, and whispered, "I'm so sorry about yesterday—I'll no tell any more lees—not the *weeest*," and then ran back. Effie drove off with some hope for this well-meaning, but ill-taught family.

At the end of the long sea-voyage Effie had an unexpected treat in a visit to Pixycombe, after Harold had despatched his business at Bristol. It was nearly

ten years since she had left this happy home of her
childhood—and what a weary ten years it seemed, as
she looked from the pretty churchyard over all the
unchanged scene, and thought of the changes that
had come to her since she last stood by her father's
grave. Then Gerard stood beside her, sobbing in
unrestrained boyish grief, and she had been forced to
control her own sorrow that she might comfort his.
How soon that sorrow seemed to be forgotten! Was
it possible that it was really forgotten—that her
father was forgotten by the boy who had been so
dear to him?

"Who can it be that takes such care of these
graves?" said Harold, when they had been silent for
some time, both occupied with their own thoughts.
"We had better find out, and thank them," he
added.

Effie noticed then that the graves of her family
were distinguished from all around by their well-
tended appearance, and that on her father's lay a
cross of holly, and on her mother's a wreath of rare
winter flowers, now rather faded.

" None of the villagers could have got such flowers
as those," she remarked.

"Good afternoon, Rowe," cried Harold, to an
elderly man, who was passing through the churchyard.
"Can you tell me who is kind enough to keep these
graves in such good order?"

" Well, Mr. Harold, we all did think as it was you and the young ladies. Master Gerard, he pays Widow Kean's boy for weeding, and such-like, but we thought it was you that put it in his head."

Harold turned away, as if he did not care to hear any more ; but Effie did care to hear more, so she asked, " But these flowers, Rowe ? Mrs. Kean's boy did not get them, did he ?"

" Master Gerard brought them to Christmas-time, miss. We did think as he wasn't coming this year. Some of us was to ' The Bells ' on Christmas Eve, and Lee says, ' Wait before Mr. Gerard comes,' says he. And when we left, he says, ' He'll not come now,' he says, and then he shut up. But the next morning, as I were a coming through from the Vicarage, Mr. Snow—he were very late that morning, he were ; he *is* a rare one for lying a-bed—there I see some one a-standing by this grave ; so I says to myself, ' There's Master Gerard,' I says ; and sure enough there he were, standing to the foot of the old master, just where you are, sir, a-making up that holly thing as you see there, Miss Effie. Yes, he comes every year, and puts them flowers on the graves for Christmas. Three years he's been regular, and last year he came to master's death-day, and sits here on the tomb for nigh upon three livelong hours, as still-like as any statter. He were real fond of old master, were Master Gerard."

Effie felt after this that the visit to Pixycombe was well worth three days and nights at sea, as well as the tedious coach journey through bad roads and, in some places, deep-lying snow.

Her reception at home was much more cheering than she had anticipated. Jessie met them at the hall-door with a radiant face. She was most affectionate to Effie, and extremely anxious to hear all about the Cairds, and everything that had happened during the three months her sister had spent in Scotland. But she had not merely to play the part of listener. She, also, had something to tell; and Jessie was never so amiable as when she could communicate any piece of news.

"Who do you think is going to be married?" she asked, when the tired travellers were enjoying their tea. Effie's heart gave a great jump, as she thought, "Gerard," but it grew quiet again as she said, "George Monro."

"Wrong!" cried Jessie. "Not *George* Monro."

"Clara?"

"Yes. But to whom?"

Again Effie's heart jumped, and she said, falteringly, "I don't know."

"Guess," persisted Jessie. "It will be a great blow to you. She has robbed you of an admirer."

"I cannot guess," said Effie, with some impatience.

"Nathaniel Butterfield!" Jessie announced tri-umphantly.

"No!" exclaimed Effie.

"That lout!" cried Harold.

"Clara seems to think him very charming," said Jessie. "She has been here to-day to tell me of her happy prospects. She seems quite satisfied."

Effie could not sleep for wondering at this news. That Clara, whom Gerard had loved, should find it possible to love Nathaniel Butterfield! It was utterly incomprehensible. She could not go to Clara, as she felt shy of seeing George, but she had not long to wait. In the afternoon of the next Sunday she was playing with the delighted children, from whom she had found it very difficult to tear herself to go to church that morning, when Clara arrived, full of her happi-ness. Nathaniel was so good; such a model son and brother; such an honest, upright man of business— altogether so worthy of respect and affection. Effie saw that in every word of praise Clara was mentally comparing her new with her former admirer—greatly to the disadvantage of the latter. Effie also could not help making the same comparison, but not with the same result. Clara's rhapsodies did not moderate her wonder, but they dispelled her doubts. She felt certain that her friend had really conceived a romantic feeling for respectability.

It was not possible for Effie to understand Clara's

state of mind, but it was not so inexplicable as it appeared to her. The Monros had very strong affections, but with them Cupid was not a blind god. Respect was indispensable to the existence of their love. If respect was gone love followed. Clara had experienced this with regard to Gerard. She had suffered much in the experience, and the inevitable result was that henceforward an instinct of self-preservation led her to prefer *respectable* qualities to all others. It was the natural reaction from having once loved where she could not respect. No such reaction was possible with Effie, for her love had no reference to the worthiness of the object loved, but simply to her own capability of loving. She could not understand Clara's choice; but she was better satisfied with it when George had said to her, " Clara will not have a very brilliant husband. But he is a thoroughly good fellow. Clara and I know some things of Nathaniel Butterfield which would shame many a man who professes much more. Not from himself—he is very modest about his own good deeds, but I have heard of them from others. I have no fears for Clara's happiness, though I must own that if *I* had chosen my brother-in-law I should not have made such a sensible choice."

George had met Effie in such a manner as to put her quite at her ease. He was no less cordial than formerly—but it was a more friendly—a less lover-like cordiality. Nevertheless, she thought it more prudent not to resume any of her parish work, but to confine her energies to Prior's Mount, where they were quite sufficiently called for. Very soon everything had fallen into the old train, and Effie was once more the slave, and at the same time the ruler of the whole house.

CHAPTER III.

THE peace which had followed Effie's return was not of long duration. Jessie soon forgot the discomforts attending her sister's absence, and grew vexed that the rest of the household did not forget them also. Harold's improved spirits, and the children's exuberant joy, the smiling satisfaction of the servants, and the polite congratulations of the neighbours were all so much fuel to the smouldering fire of jealousy, which broke out into flame before Effie had been a month at home.

"Have you finished my dress, Hannah?" asked Jessie, meeting the nurse on the stairs one morning, ready to go for a walk with little Bessie.

"No, ma'am, not quite," answered the girl. "Miss Effie said I had better take Baby out at once, while it is fine; she thought it might rain later."

"Miss Effie has nothing to do with it," said Jessie, angrily. "I desire that you do not stir until you have finished my dress."

Poor Baby was carried back to the dull nursery, and her mother went storming into the room where the three little boys were at their lessons.

"I wish to know by what right you give orders to *my* servants?"

"I will come out and speak to you, Jessie," cried Effie, turning very pale, and hurrying to the door.

"No, I choose to speak here. *I* have nothing to say that I am ashamed to say before my children. I desire to know how you dare countermand my orders?"

"I did not know that you had given any orders," said Effie, humbly, hoping to avert a scene.

"You knew that I was particularly anxious to have my dress lengthened for this evening. But of course that was the reason you sent Hannah out."

"I will do your dress this afternoon."

"I do not care about the dress—only I wish to know which of us is to be mistress in this house."

"Indeed, Jessie, I did not know you had anything for Hannah to do, and I thought it such a pity Baby should not be out this bright morning."

"Pray, who has the best right to give orders about Baby? Of course not her mother."

"Of course her mother—but——"

"I *will* come into the room! I will not have the door shut in my face!"

"I did not mean to shut the door in your face—

only— Run away, boys, and have a game in the nursery, it will warm you."

"Stay where you are boys!" cried their mother. "I will not have my children ordered about in my presence."

"If they may not leave the room, *I* must," said Effie.

"You shall not!" shrieked Jessie, quite beside herself with passion, and she set her back against the door.

"Jessie! Do consider the children," whispered Effie.

"Consider the children!" exclaimed Jessie. "It is you who do not consider the children, when you teach them to disobey their mother. Why should *I* consider the children? Do they ever consider me? You make the very servants disregard me. And no wonder, when you give orders as if you were the mistress of the house! I am a mere cipher. But I will not bear it any longer! I have been patient long enough. You have done nothing but insult me ever since you came back. Why did you come back?" she asked, suddenly changing her tone from bitterness to violence.

"Why, indeed!" said Effie, unable longer to command herself, and beginning to cry.

The effect was most alarming: Freddie began to shriek and sob; Davie, crying out, "Auntie! darling little Auntie!" sprang on to her neck; and Walter, doubling his fist, stood before his mother, and said, " You shan't make Auntie cry! Go away, naughty Mamma!"

" This is the result of your teaching!" cried Jessie, still more incensed. "How dare you speak to me in that way, Walter?"

" You shan't scold Auntie!" answered Walter.

"She is a bad, wicked girl! She has taught you to be a very wicked boy."

" Good, dear, darling Auntie!" cried Davie, emphasizing each endearing term with such a violent clasp of her neck that Effie was nearly choked.

" *You* are wicked! You are a nasty, cross, ugly beast—and I hate you!" exclaimed Walter, striking his clenched fist at his mother's face. Freddie's emotion took a fresh turn. He rolled his fat little body off his chair, ran up to his mother, and began kicking her lustily, sobbing all the time.

"Do you mean these children to murder me?" cried Jessie. " You cannot take my place when I am dead. The law will not allow you, I am happy to say. The law knows what treacherous, mean things sisters are—and Harold shall know it. I will tell him how you have taught my children to hate me. Yes, you wicked boys! your papa will punish you." She opened the door, and rushed to Harold's studio, Walter and Freddie after her. Effie sank down on the floor, and she and Davie cried together.

"What does all this mean, Effie?" said Harold, coming in, followed by the children. "I cannot understand Jessie. What does she wish?"

"Harold, let me go away! Let me go anywhere!" answered Effie, slowly rising, with Davie still clinging to her.

"You shan't go away, Auntie! you shan't go away!" shouted the other two boys, throwing themselves on to her, as if they would keep her with them by main force.

"No, Effie, you shall not go away again," said Harold.

. "Then am *I* to go away?" cried Jessie, coming into the room again, like a fury.

"Why should either of you go away?" asked Harold, gently.

"Why? Because I am not mistress in my own house. She makes my servants despise me—they obey her orders instead of mine—and she teaches my children to insult me."

"Boys, go to the nursery," said Harold.

"And they are not to be punished?" exclaimed Jessie.

"Punish Mamma, Papa!" cried Walter. "She made Auntie cry—she is wicked. I hate her!"

"Run away, Walter—go, Freddie. Davie, do you hear?"

"Papa, take care of Auntie," said Davie. "Don't let Mamma scold her."

"Jessie, let the children pass."

"I shall not. They shall not go till they have begged my pardon."

"I do not know yet whether they were to blame. I can do nothing till I understand what is the matter. Can you tell me, Effie?"

"You take her word in preference to mine!" shrieked Jessie, with renewed violence.

"I cannot understand what you tell me. Effie, what is it all about? *You* are calm enough to tell me."

"Not before the children," said Effie.

"No, you are right. Jessie, you must let the children go."

"Oh, of course *she* is right, and I am wrong. You always take her part against me. Every one is against me. I wish I were dead!"

"Jessie!" exclaimed Effie.

"I do. I should be at peace then, and out of the way of you all."

"Why don't you be dead, Mamma, and then Auntie would never cry, and never go away," remarked Walter, most inopportunely.

"There! Even that child knows the truth!" cried

Jessie. "Every one knows that Effie would rejoice at my death. But it would be no good to her. If I were dead you could not marry her—it is against the law."

Harold had turned ghastly white. He made no answer to Jessie's questioning look.

"You would! You dare own to my face that you wish to marry her. You had better kill me at once if you are only waiting for my death. I knew it was so. I knew you cared much more for her than for me. She has stolen everything from me—my husband and my children. I had much better die; there is nothing left to live for. I will go away somewhere, and die."

She turned towards the door, as if about to put her threat in execution, but suddenly turned round again, more fierce than ever.

"Harold, am I to go, or is she?"

"Jessie, I say this once for all. As long as I have a roof over my head it shall shelter Effie. I promised her father on his death-bed that I would be a brother to her. I will. If those belonging to me cause her to suffer I will do all in my power to make amends. This is her home. She shall not be driven from it."

"It cannot be her home and mine. I will not live under the same roof with her. Have you no proper feelings at all?" she asked, turning to Effie. "Can you stay here to make misery between a husband

and wife? Why don't you marry? You cannot
—no one will have you who knows what you are
at home."

Harold turned hastily towards Effie, and, passing
his arm round her shoulders, drew her tenderly
towards him. "Jessie, be silent!" he cried, in a voice
which awed even Jessie. "I will not have Effie spoken
to in that way."

"You dare parade your love for her before my
very face!" shrieked Jessie, shaking off her temporary
fear of her husband's anger, and lashing herself up
into still greater fury. "You are both utterly shame-
less. It is time that I should go. You will be sorry
when you have lost me. You used to pretend to love
me. Your love is soon changed to hatred. But you
will be miserable. You will repent when it is too
late. Yes, hang about her, boys. She has driven
your mother away. She must be your mother now.
Good-bye, Harold. May you never repent having
cast me off." She left the room with a tragical step.

"Harold, go and pacify her!" cried Effie, in alarm.

"No," said Harold. "There is a point beyond
endurance." And he walked slowly to his studio,
where he remained all the rest of the day.

Effie began telling stories to the children, in the
hope of somewhat effacing the recollection of the
drama which had been enacted before them. At
luncheon time Jessie was nowhere to be found. The

servants said that she had been out for some time. Effie grew very anxious as the day wore on ; and when it became dusk, and thick snow began to fall, she went to tell Harold that Jessie had not returned. He looked rather startled, but said nothing. Effie remained in an agony of suspense all the evening ; but at about nine Hannah came in to say that she had received a note desiring her to pack up all her mistress's clothes, and to send them by the bearer— an old man with a cart. This was a satisfactory proof that Jessie was not out in the snow ; and Effie felt no doubt that she would soon come to her senses, and return home. The man had been told not to say where the things were to be taken.

Effie was mistaken. Day after day passed on, and still Jessie did not return. Harold never mentioned her, after he had been told of the messenger who had come for her clothes. On the fourth of these miserable days of anxiety and suspense, George Monro called. His grave face of concern showed Effie at once that he had heard something of what had happened.

"I hope you will not think me an impertinent busybody for what I am going to say, Effie," he began, hesitatingly, after a few unmeaning common-places—things in which he seldom indulged.

"I should never think you that," replied Effie, warmly, her heart leaping at the prospect of getting comfort in her trouble from this faithful friend.

"Your sister is away from home, I believe," continued George.

"Yes," answered Effie, doubting how much he knew, and how much she ought to tell him.

"It is not from mere curiosity that I ask. Do you mind telling me where she is staying?"

"I do not know," said Effie, in a low voice.

"Then I am afraid there is some truth in what I have heard," cried George. "I came to you in hopes of being enabled to contradict the reports which are about. Forgive me for distressing you, Effie; but it is best that you should know."

"Yes; much best. Pray tell me all—and thank you very much for taking the trouble."

"It is said that Mr. and Mrs. Yonge are separated — that they have never lived happily together — that they have not spoken for several months, and that now Mrs. Yonge has left her husband, never to return. You know how everything is exaggerated in a place like this. I would not have repeated all this foolish scandal, which has probably originated in some mistake of the servants; but unless you know what misrepresentations are afloat, you cannot give me full authority to deny them."

"I cannot give you that," said Effie, almost in a whisper.

"You think that I have no right to ask it?"

"No—not that. You are very kind to interest yourself so about us. But—it is true."

"All?" asked George, after a painful silence.

"No; not quite all. Harold and Jessie have not been an unhappy couple. But you must have seen that Jessie has a most violent temper."

"I have seen you suffer under it," replied George.

"Poor Harold has suffered most. He has borne it admirably, but he has been terribly tried. Up to last summer—when little Isa died—nothing seemed to shake his devotion to Jessie. But Isa's death changed him very much, and since then he has not been so forbearing. But it is quite false that they have not spoken for months. There has been only too much said—and too openly——"

"That is it," remarked George. "If servants hear an angry word they magnify it into an irreconcilable breach."

"And now there are not only words, but facts to magnify," said Effie, sadly; "for Jessie has left home, and we do not know where she is."

"Have you no clue at all?"

"Not the slightest. She sent for her clothes, but the messenger was forbidden to say where he was to take them."

"Can your sister have gone to any friend?"

"I don't know of any one. I keep expecting her to return. It is so unlike her to persist in resentment. Her anger is generally so very transient."

" Is she not upheld by some bad advice ?"

" Impossible.   She knows no one intimately."

" Is that so ?" asked George, doubtfully.

" Have you any reason to think otherwise ?"

" Yes ; I think I have. I may be wrong, but it has struck me that Mrs. Price has considerable influence with your sister."

" Mrs. Price !   Who is she ?"

" Do you not know her ?   No, by-the-by, you were away.   But is it possible that you have not heard of her ?"

" Yes, I have.   I forgot.   Jessie told me something about a lady in whom she was interested—to whom Harold had taken an unaccountable dislike— a young widow, is she not ?"

" I am afraid not—I rather think she is separated or divorced from her husband.   I do not think Yonge's dislike was at all unaccountable : a more frivolous, artificial woman I have never seen."

" But how do you think Jessie is influenced by her ?   She has never been here since I have been home."

" She has been abroad.   But perhaps your sister has corresponded with her."

" I did hear something about a foreign letter one day.   How did Jessie get to know this Mrs. Price ?"

" She took Mrs. Mortlake's house in the autumn, and managed to make acquaintance with your sister, s she did with most of the Gateshill people.   She is a very clever woman, and is generally considered very agreeable."

"But how could she influence Jessie? Do you think she was much with her?"

"I believe so. I often saw her here. I believe she volunteered to teach the little boys."

"Oh, yes—they told me a strange lady had given them lessons sometimes. But it is very odd that Jessie should not have said more about her. Jessie is usually so very unreserved."

"Do you not think that is a confirmation of my fears?"

"Yes. Where is this woman living now?"

"I heard a few days ago that she had taken a furnished house at Steadham."

"You are right!" cried Effie. "Hannah said that she thought she read 'Steadham' on the cart that came for the luggage; but I fancied she must be mistaken; it seemed so unlikely that Jessie should go there."

"Shall I call on Mrs. Price, and see if I can get any tidings of your sister?"

"You are very kind. It would be an immense relief to know where she is."

"I will go this afternoon," said George, taking up his hat as he spoke. "Of course, I shall not let Mrs. Price know that my visit has any other object than courtesy towards herself. Do not worry yourself, Effie. We will soon have your sister back again."

Effie did feel immensely relieved now that George
had taken a share in her load of anxiety; but she
could not long share his hopeful views. That
evening Harold had a visit from a stranger, who
announced himself as Mrs. Yonge's legal adviser,
authorized by her to make all the necessary arrangements for a formal separation. Harold shortly
referred him to Mr. Butterfield, and dismissed him.
He had been shown into the room where Harold and
Effie were at tea, and Harold, saying that he had
no secrets from his sister, had refused to grant a
more private interview.

"Oh, Harold, can nothing be done?" asked Effie,
when the lawyer was gone.

"It seems that something is to be *und*one," said
Harold, in a hollow, harsh voice. "Do you remember
that morning in Glasgow, when we took each other;
what was it we were made to say?"

"For better, for worse; for richer, for poorer——"
murmured Effie.

"Till death us should part," interrupted Harold,
with a short laugh. "What a mockery it all is!
Now we are parted—but death has had nothing to
do with it. Death takes those who cannot be spared
—those who are happy and.beloved; but he will not
have those who would be glad enough to see the end
of all this weary life."

His tone was so wretched and hopeless that. it

moved Effie deeply, and, by a sudden impulse, she
came to him and kissed his forehead.

"Effie! Effie! she has broken my heart!" he
cried out, and burst into a passion of grief. After
some minutes he grew calmer, and left the room.
Effie never saw him give way again ; but in a few
weeks he seemed to have aged years, and he fell
back into the bitter, hard temper which he had displayed after Isa's death.

George's visit to Mrs. Price was of no avail, except
in ascertaining the fact that Jessie was living with
her dangerous friend. The lawyers' work was soon
done. Harold made his wife a most liberal allowance,
and professed his intention of increasing it whenever
his own means should increase. After this was
settled he desired that Jessie's name might never
be mentioned in his hearing. The children soon
ceased to speak of her ; and, as Jessie had said, Effie
was now their only mother. George made a point
of keeping up his acquaintance with Mrs. Price, and
thus supplied Effie with frequent news of her sister.
He felt convinced that she was not satisfied with
the course which she had taken, but that as long
as she was influenced by her new friend she would
never acknowledge that she repented of her rash
step. He considered that Mrs. Price's promptings
had alone moved her to that step, and that Mrs. Price
herself was actuated partly by a natural wish to

draw others into her own position, and partly by the desire for a companion to share the expenses of her new house. Effie agreed with him as to the extent of Mrs. Price's influence, when she recalled how, on her return from Scotland, she had been surprised by a remarkable change in Jessie's manner and modes of expression. She saw of what this was the reflection, when George repeated to her some of Mrs. Price's favourite sentiments. It was fearful to think what evil could be brought about by one bad mind.

The extent of the evil became more evident every day. As far as Effie herself was concerned some circumstances soon made it very manifest.

" You will be at the Baldwins' on Friday, I suppose, Effie?" said Clara Monro one day, about a month after Jessie's departure.

" I have not been asked."

" Not asked! Why, I thought they could not do without you."

" It seems they can," said Effie, laughing.

" George!" said Clara to her brother, who was talking with Harold, "Effie has not been asked to the Baldwins' party! There must be some mistake!".

George coloured deeply, and made an incoherent reply. Effie felt sure that the slight was no mistake, and that George knew the cause of it, but she did not then guess what it was.

She *did* wonder when the Butterfields' gave their annual dance, and she received no invitation; but her wonder was changed to something very like horror by a few careless words of Mrs. Samuel Butterfield.

"And you were not asked to the party last night!" exclaimed that warm friend of Effie's, as they met in Gateshill. "I declare it was a shame! I could hardly believe those sisters-in-law of mine could be such scandal-loving prudes. Why, I would not have missed you at any party of mine, if you lived with fifty brothers-in-law."

If Effie had any doubt as to the meaning of this, it was effectually dispelled that evening by the little boys.

"Auntie," said Walter, "can people be better than they ought to be?"

"Certainly not, Walter. If we were always as good as possible we could never be good enough."

"You are very good, ain't you?"

Effie laughed. George, who was present, said, "Yes, very good, Walter."

"Could you be better?"

"No," cried George again.

"Then why does Mrs. James say you are not better than you ought to be?"

"It wasn't that quite, Walter," said the truthful Davie. "She said Auntie was no better than she

should be. Did she mean you are not well, Auntie?
She said if you were better you wouldn't live with
Papa. *Are* you ill?"

George had caught up Davie, and was racing round
the room with him, making a tremendous noise.
Effie felt stunned. The little boys were soon called
to their tea, and then George prepared to leave, but
first he came hastily up to her, and said, colouring
violently, " You must not mind what vulgar gossips
say, Effie. Nobody whose good opinion is worth anything believes a word against you," and he hurried
away.

It was impossible for Effie *not* to mind, and her life
was very wretched. She felt ashamed to walk out,
ashamed even to look at the servants. She would
have given worlds to go away ; but she dared not still
farther aggravate Harold's bitter desolation, nor leave
her sister's deserted children. These children were
the only bright spot in the whole gloomy view, for,
to add to her home miseries, rumours kept reaching
her of Gerard's extravagance and reckless dissipation,
and more than one kind friend amongst the Gateshill
young men opined that he was " fast going to the
dogs."

CHAPTER IV.

"We have come to take you for a walk, Effie," said Clara Monro, coming in by the drawing-room window at Prior's Mount, one lovely evening in June.

"Are you?" returned Effie, listlessly. During the five months of Jessie's absence she had got into a morbid state of feeling which made her shrink from all intercourse with her neighbours, with the exception of the Monros. She was too proud to visit in any house where there was a chance of her being regarded with suspicion; and because she knew that such would be the case with some of the Gateshill families, she took it for granted that it would be so with all. George and Clara would not allow her to shun them; and the more she withdrew from society the more persistently they sought her out. Clara was not to be daunted now.

"I know you have nothing to keep you in, for we met the little boys going to Mr. Rogers' field with their pitchforks and rakes. We are going into the hayfields too. I have persuaded George to think for one evening that no old woman wants him, and to give himself up to me. I shall not have many more evenings for him now," she added, with a conscious look—the look of an expectant bride.

"Then why should you not have him all to yourself? You two would be much better without me."

"Indeed we should not. We always like to have you with us, don't we, George?" turning to her brother, who just then came up to the window.

"Effie knows," answered George, simply, but with such a glance that Effie was glad to escape from the room to put on her bonnet.

It was a great relief to get out of the dull house, with its oppressive atmosphere of disappointed hopes and bitter memories, into the fresh, bright, summer's evening, under the soothing influence of Clara's perfect content, and George's sanguine earnestness. The three strolled along very happily, talking, as they usually did, of George's schemes for benefiting Gateshill in general, and some individuals in particular, and enjoying the sight of merry children tumbling about, and the scent of the sweet, fresh hay. Presently they ceased to talk, and wandered on, in the pleasant companionable silence, possible only between those who thoroughly understand each other. This silence was suddenly broken. As they walked along by the side of a hedge, a woman s voice, quite close to them, said, in a soft, insinuating tone, "Am I the first to whom you have made such vows? Ah, how cruelly men play with our poor foolish hearts!"

Clara burst into a smothered laugh, in which Effie would have joined, had not George's manner startled her into seriousness. He had almost *jumped* at the first words, and then hurried forward, saying quite sternly to Clara and herself, " Come on quickly—don't listen !"

" I wanted to hear what the ' cruel man ' answered," said Clara, still laughing. " He seems rather a tongue-tied lover."

" Perhaps he had expended all his vows before we came within hearing, and had no more ready," suggested Effie. " What a ridiculous woman !" she added ; "she spoke just like the fascinating widow in a comedy."

" The voice was somehow familiar to me," observed Clara.

George continued to look so vexed and so serious that the girls' mirth soon died away, and they walked on again in silence for some time. They had reached a field where the hay-making had not yet begun, and were proceeding homewards by a narrow path through the long grass, when they saw a couple approaching them.

"Here come the lovers!" cried Clara. "I am sure it must be they!"

"The hayfields are much pleasanter than this path—let us turn back," exclaimed George, hastily, and he made a dead halt.

"Have we time to go back?" asked Effie. "It must be getting late."

"I must be home by eight," said Clara.

"And so must I," added Effie.

"It is of no use now!" was George's startling exclamation, in a tone of intense annoyance.

At that moment they had to draw aside to let the approaching couple pass, and Effie glanced up in natural curiosity, as the soft tones which they had heard before were again audible. A little fair woman, not pretty, but very elegant in figure and dress, leaning affectionately on the arm of—Gerard Yonge.

"Good evening, Mr. Monro," said the soft voice. "How you must enjoy this scene of rural happiness and innocence!"

George bowed stiffly, and, suddenly drawing Effie's hand through his arm, walked on at a rapid pace. Gerard had neither spoken nor bowed; but he had turned scarlet, and then white. When they had got out of the narrow path, and were in the hayfields again, George stopped, and released Effie's hand.

"I beg your pardon," he said. "I am afraid I

was very rude and rough; I was hardly conscious what I did."

"Do you know that lady?" asked Effie.

"Don't *you* know her, Effie?" cried Clara. "It is Mrs. Price. I thought I had heard that oily voice before."

Effie could not say anything more, and the others did not. When they left the fields, Clara ran home, and George walked alone with Effie to Prior's Mount.

"I had better tell you, Effie, what you might hear from others," he said, when Clara had left them. "It is reported that Gerard is engaged to Mrs. Price."

This was no news to Effie, after all that she had heard and seen; so she managed to ask with tolerable composure, "Does Jessie see Gerard?"

"Yes; he is frequently there. I believe he went first to see your sister. And I have fancied since then that she has been a little shaken in her determination to remain apart from her husband."

"Do you really think so?"

"I do, indeed. I hope that Gerard's influence would be exerted with that view."

"Perhaps if Mrs. Price is—is going to marry Gerard, she will not be so anxious to keep Jessie with her."

"Probably not. I cannot understand that woman's power."

"She may not be so bad as you think her," said Effie, wistfully.

"God grant she is not, for Gerard's sake!" cried George, as he pressed Effie's hand, and left her.

Going to marry that woman!—attracted by that "oily voice," as Clara had truly termed it, and that vulgarly affected manner! Effie had prided herself on never having felt jealous of Clara, when Gerard's affections had strayed to her; and now, was it jealousy that gave her such a sense of loathing as those insinuating tones rang in her ears, and that figure, dressed in the newest French fashion, floated before her eyes? It seemed as if this only had been wanting to push her misery to that extreme where a turning-point *must* be reached. But it was destined to remain at the extreme for some months.

The beautiful summer wore away sadly. At home there were Harold's dejected looks and bitter words ; abroad there were scornful glances and mortifying slights ; within herself there was an uneasy conscience, a painful weight of responsibility, and an almost hopeless grief for all those who were dear to her. George's visits to Steadham continued at intervals, and he generally reported to Effie how matters were progressing there. The only progress was that he found Jessie daily better disposed towards a reconciliation with Harold, but he thought that she would not take any decided step till her friend was married.

It was not easy to understand what delayed that marriage, unless, as seemed probable, Gerard was embarrassed in money-matters, and did not wish to join poverty on his part to comfortable independence on the part of his bride.

The short winter days had come round again, when, one evening, as Effie was telling the children stories in the dusk, George came in. His visits were always so unceremonious, and had been so frequent since Clara's marriage in July had left him solitary, that the stories were not interrupted till Effie, struck by his silence, stirred the fire into a blaze, which showed her the extreme gravity of his face. Then she sent the little boys away, and asked, " Is anything the matter ?"

" What made you think so ? Is my face such a tell-tale ? Yes, there is something the matter, but nothing to alarm you—rather a cause for hope. Your sister has lost her evil angel—Mrs. Price has eloped."

" Eloped !" cried Effie. " There was no obstacle to their marriage !"

" You mistake me. She has fled *from* Gerard, not *with* him."

" Tell me about it," said Effie, faintly.

George could not very well tell Effie all the details of the story, which she afterwards learnt from other sources.

At about ten that morning George had received a note from Jessie, which Effie now read by the light of the fire :

" Friday morning.

" DEAR MR. MONRO,

"Pray, if you possibly can, come to me at once. I am in the greatest distress, and you are the only friend who can help me.

" Yours very truly,
"JESSIE YONGE."

George started immediately, and found Jessie in a state of terrible perplexity and grief. Two days before, Mrs. Price had gone ostensibly to see a friend at Blackheath. She had been expected back hat day. Early that morning Jessie had been surprised by a visit from a Lady Culmer, whom she knew by sight, as occupying a large house of which the garden adjoined Mrs. Price's garden. Lady Culmer was in violent agitation, and she startled Jessie by asking abruptly, " Where is my husband?" Jessie very naturally thought she was mad, and tried to soothe her. " What have you done with my husband?" she repeated. Jessie assured her that she had never even seen her husband. " Is not your name Price?" she then asked. When told that Mrs. Price had been away for two days, she became still more excited, and exclaimed, " And he has also been away for two days!" This scene continued for some time. Jessie found that her visitor was not mad, but distracted by fear and jealousy. It came out, little by little, that an intimacy had sprung up between Sir James Culmer and Mrs. Price, and that during the whole summer they had been in the habit of walking together in the garden, long after Jessie was in bed. Lady Culmer had watched her husband with jealous vigilance, and had traced his companion home; but she had never seen her so as to recognise her again. On Wednesday morning Sir James Culmer started on a visit to a friend in Buckinghamshire. That at least was the professed object of his journey; but his wife's suspicions had been roused by some means, and she wrote to the friend whom he was to visit, and obtained the information that Sir James was not there, and was not expected there. In the meantime her fears had been still more confirmed by learning that Sir James had been seen with a lady on Wednesday afternoon, dining at the Folkestone Pavilion, previous to the starting of the Boulogne boat. Although Jessie had not had the slightest doubt of her friend before, she now remembered several facts which added to the probability that Lady Culmer's suspicions were not unfounded. In her utter desolation and helplessness she sent for George. Lady Culmer had previously left, quite convinced that, whatever might be Mrs. Price's delinquency, her friend was perfectly innocent, and had been as much deceived by her as any one. The fact that Mrs. Price was engaged to Jessie's brother-in-law was sufficient proof of this.

George's first act, when he was in possession of these particulars, was to go to the house at Black-heath where Mrs. Price was supposed to be staying. As he expected, she had never been there. He then went to the Passport-office, and found that a Lady Culmer—described as small and fair—the real Lady Culmer being tall and dark—had been given permission to accompany Sir James Culmer to Paris. By the time that he returned to Jessie with this information, she had received more positive proof, in the shape of a most repulsive, scented note, written on foreign paper, and posted at Boulogne, in which her, "loving friend, Ellen," informed her that, having hitherto found life "a drear and arid wilderness," she had at last met with "a hope-inspiring meteor," which promised to lead her "to sweetly fertile plains, and richly watered valleys," where her "poor, weary, hungry heart might find a welcome resting-place, and more congenial nourishment" than it had hitherto received. In this hope she had resolved "to sacrifice all—even your society, sweet friend—and to follow the guiding star whithersoever it might lead." She regretted that she should appear false and heartless to one for whom she had "a true sisterly love;" but she hoped he might be consoled "by some fair being, whose happier fate may render his honest but prosaic love more sufficing than it could ever be to her whose life has been one long-drawn sigh from unfathomable depths of feeling."

Jessie, who was perfectly overwhelmed with shame and disappointment, wished to burn this contemptible effusion as soon as George had read it. But he had other work for it to do. There was more work for *him* to do—a most painful task. Gerard was expected at Steadham that evening, to meet his betrothed on her return from Blackheath. Jessie was trembling at the prospect of his arrival, and George determined that it would be kinder to all parties if he were to prevent it. With that view he went to Berners Street, where he found Gerard in his studio. The former friends had not met to speak since the Gateshill ball.

Gerard exclaimed, "George! you are an unexpected visitor. I am so glad I had not gone out. In another half-hour I should have been off to Steadham. I am just putting the finishing touches to a present for Mrs. Price. See what you think of this," he held up a very clever likeness of Jessie, as he spoke fast, and rather nervously.

"It is capital!" cried George. "Did Mrs. Yonge sit for it."

" Yes; she has been down here several times, secretly from Mrs. Price, for whom it is intended as a surprise. I am very glad you think it good. I am going to take it up with me to-night. Do you mind sitting down whilst I put in a few more strokes. I am so glad to see you here, old fellow."

" I am afraid you will not be glad when you know my errand."

" Why ?" asked Gerard, quickly, turning round to look in George's face. " Is anything the matter ?" he added, as he saw the grave expression of that face.

" Yes," answered George.

" Is Harold ill ? Is anything the matter with Harold ?"

" Not with Harold."

" With Effie ! For Heaven's sake, not with Effie !" growing very pale.

" No," said George. " I have come from Stead-ham."

" Ellen—Mrs. Price—is she ill ?"

" Worse than ill," replied George.

" Dead !" asked Gerard, hoarsely.

" Worse than dead."

" Worse ! George, what do you mean ? Do not torture me by this suspense !"

" She is not worthy of you, Gerard."

" What do you mean ?"

"She does not care for you."

"How dare you say that?"

"It is the truth. She has eloped."

"It is false!" He jumped up for a moment, then sat down again, and leaned over the table, hiding his face with his arms. After remaining thus for some minutes he looked up. "I beg your pardon— I did not mean to question your word. Tell me all."

George saw that he suspected all. He told as briefly as he could what he had learnt. Gerard listened quite calmly, though his mouth twitched convulsively, and his face was ghastly white. When George had finished his story, he gave him the scented note. After reading it carefully through Gerard, held it between his finger and thumb in an absent manner.

"May I burn it?" asked George.

Gerard nodded, and when it was consumed he hid his face with his hands as before, and did not move for nearly half an hour. George sat patiently watching him, feeling almost his old affection revive in his deep compassion. At last Gerard raised his head. "I am so utterly ashamed," he said.

"Shame is for the deceiver, not the deceived," remarked George.

"It is not that. I don't care for having been deceived. But that it should have been possible for me to love such a woman! I do believe I loved her,

George. I wonder whether she feels half as much disgraced as I do?"

"I should think from that note that she is incapable of any feeling of the sort."

"That note is horrible!" said Gerard, with a shudder. "But there was good in her. And she had been cruelly treated. She would have been very different under different circumstances." He stared mournfully into the fire for some time, and then went on. "I thought my ' honest but prosaic love,' as she calls it, might have given her a better chance than she has had yet. Her first husband was a brute." He was silent again for some time, and George did not interrupt his sad musing. Presently he began again. "I was a vain and presumptuous fool to think I could help any one up—I need too much help myself. How you would crow over me, George, if you were not a gentleman!"

"I know that I was the worst man in the world to have to tell you all this, Gerard."

"The best man in the world, you mean. It was very kind of you to undertake it. I am grateful, old fellow." He held out his hand; George's heart quite melted as he saw the large tears standing in those affectionate grey eyes.

"Gerard, I think you have the best nature of any man that ever lived," he cried. "I have been very hard upon you lately. I flattered myself that I was moved by righteous indignation, but I am not sure that it was not partly by the meanest and most selfish passion that is known."

"*I* am sure that you were never moved by anything mean or selfish. And you were not harder upon me than I deserved. Are you going? Must you go yet? It will be so dreary when you are gone," he shuddered.

"Miss Garnock knows nothing of all this yet, and I promised Mrs. Yonge that I would tell her to-night."

"Very well, then I won't keep you. Effie is well avenged," he added, mournfully, as he and George shook hands. "What a Nemesis there is in these matters."

"Gerard, you speak like a heathen."

"Yes. I was wrong. I know that, George. I am bad enough, but I am not a heathen. I know it is not a blind destiny that rules over us."

"You know it is a just and merciful Father?" asked George.

"Yes; and George"— Gerard laid his hand impressively on his friend's arm—"I never saw His justice more plainly than now that I am suffering the very same torture that I made Effie suffer; nor His mercy more plainly than now that I have been saved on the very brink of the precipice over which I should have plunged in a few weeks. George! only think if I had married her before this happened."

George could only press his hand.

"I wonder whether Effie would think it an insult if I gave her the picture of Jessie, which I meant for—for that other. Do you think she would accept it?"

"I have no doubt she would."

"Would you mind taking it? It is not large, and very light. The fact is, I am afraid of being left with it staring at me there. It reminds me that only an hour or two ago I was picturing to myself how pleased she would be with my offering, and how intelligently she would praise the work. She is a very clever woman, George."

"I suppose so."

"And she makes one so pleased with oneself. It is such a refined kind of flattery. I knew she was not a—not such a woman as some *we* know, George; but then I had no uncomfortable feeling of inferiority, and it was intoxicating to feel so necessary to her happiness. Necessary! and all the time she was planning how to get rid of me early, that she might go to her 'guiding star!' It is maddening!"

"It is really, Gerard. I can imagine nothing much harder to bear."

"Some things must be harder," said Gerard, musingly. "I had not a very perfect faith in her; and my love for her is of recent growth. Harold must suffer more, for he thinks Jessie has wronged him, and he has loved her all his life."

" I am afraid he does suffer terribly," said George.
" He has grown to look like an old man."

" She believes that he hates her now. Do you think
that is possible ?"

" No."

" But Harold is very hard and inexorable. Poor
fellow ! Poor dear old fellow !"

" He is just, and his wife has done nothing worthy
of *hatred*. If you were to hate that unhappy woman,
one could hardly——"

" I do not hate her—she is beneath it. And
besides, she is so awfully to be pitied. Unhappy,
indeed ! What can be the end of it all ?"

" God knows," said George, reverently, and Gerard
bowed his head.

" Now give me the picture, and let me go."

" You will come again soon," said Gerard, very
wistfully, as George turned into the street. " It is
desolate alone here with bad thoughts. Good night,
old friend."

George repeated to Effie nearly every word that
Gerard had said, and in conclusion remarked, " A man
with a temper such as his can never be very unhappy.
Bitterness is the only real misery."

" You will go and see him soon again ?" said Effie.

" Yes. There is an end now to all estrangement
between us."

" That is one good result of this unhappy affair."

"I hope there may be another good result. I think there will be no difficulty now in persuading your sister to return. She said this morning, in the midst of her grief, 'And I accused Effie of such conduct as that woman's!'"

"Shall I go and see her?" asked Effie, eagerly.

"I think it would be well," said George.

"Then I will go to-morrow."

And so she did, directly after breakfast. As she walked across the wintry fields, over a thin covering of snow, and with a sharp, snow-laden wind blowing in her face, her courage was as cold as the weather, and she felt several times inclined to give up the enterprise. When she was ushered ceremoniously into her sister's presence, her legs trembled so that she could hardly walk; but the servant no sooner mentioned her name than Jessie sprang forward, and seizing both her hands, kissed her affectionately.

"How good of you to come, Effie! I am so dull and miserable, I feel quite ill. I suppose Mr. Monro told you all about that terrible affair. Is not it dreadful that I should have been living so long with such a woman? Effie, do you think I shall be badly thought of for it? What does Harold say?"

Effie did not like to tell her that she had not dared to mention the subject to Harold, so she only said, "It is very dreadful that you should have been so deceived. It is a shocking thing altogether."

"And it is so horrible about Gerard! I am so afraid of his coming here. I could not bear to see him."

"I don't think you need be afraid about him. Mr. Monro left him very calm. His grief is not in the slightest degree bitter."

"Nobody can tell what *my* grief is. I really thought yesterday I never could get over it. I never shall get over it if I stay here all by myself."

This was an excellent opening, and Effie caught at it.

"Why should you stay here by yourself? You had much better come home."

"Do you think I had better ? Certainly, it will be very bad for me to be always alone."

"Nothing could be worse, and we shall be so glad to have you with us again."

"But won't it seem very inconsistent and weak ?" said Jessie, doubtfully.

Before Effie had time to answer George appeared.

"I guessed where I should find you, when I learned you had gone out. I have come to say 'good-bye' to you both. We have had bad news this morning. Harry has been wounded. He was coming home on sick-leave, but was obliged to stop at Malta. I am going to him at once. Mr. Crashawe is most kind in sparing me for an indefinite period. I shall just run down to see my father and mother, and I hope to be far on my way by to-morrow morning."

"I am very sorry," said Effie. "Have you heard from your brother himself?"

"No. A brother officer, who was also coming home, remained with him at Malta, but he will be obliged to leave before long. Harry was not able to write himself. I am afraid it is a very serious matter."

"I hope you will not find it so," said Effie.

"This decides the question for me, Effie," remarked Jessie. "As Mr. Monro is to be away for so long I must go home, for I should be utterly deserted here."

George and Effie exchanged glances of congratulation, and George said, quietly, "Of course you mean to go home now, Mrs. Yonge. It would be impossible for you to do otherwise."

"Do you think so? Then I suppose I had better make up my mind. But how shall I manage? It will be so awkward with the servants and the children."

"I will manage all that," said Effie. "But we will talk it over presently. How soon shall you reach Malta?" to George.

"I hope to be there by Wednesday or Thursday. I shall travel night and day. It will be a great pleasure to me on my solitary journey to think of you as at home again," he said to Jessie.

"Yes. I shall certainly go home. But what do you think I had better do about it?"

"I think you had better write to Mr. Yonge, and send it by Effie to-day."

"Shall I?" asked Jessie, doubtfully.

"Yes, I think so; do not you, Effie?"

"Yes," said Effie. "How does Clara bear this?"

"Poor girl! She is very much cut up. You will try and comfort her, I know."

"I will do all I can for her."

"Now I must be off. I ought not to have lingered here so long. You will write that note directly I am gone?" turning to Jessie. "See, I will put it all ready for you," and he set the writing materials before her. "Now you cannot avoid writing. Good-bye till we meet at Prior's Mount. Good-bye, Effie—God bless you! Wish me 'God speed.'"

"That I do," said Effie, warmly; and the next minute he was gone.

"Do you think I had better write, Effie?" asked Jessie.

"Yes, certainly. And you must make haste, or I shall not be back in time for the children's lessons."

Jessie sat down obediently, and wrote:

"MY DEAREST HAROLD,

"I have determined that I had better come home. I am very dull and wretched here after all that has happened. The shocking discovery made yesterday has shaken my nerves terribly, and I am afraid I shall never get rid of the painful impression it has left on my mind ; certainly not if I remain alone in this house. I hope you will forgive me for having left you for so long. I think now that it was foolish and wrong of me to do so. When I come home I will try to bear things better than I did before I left. As I hope to see you very soon, I will not write more.

　　　　　　　　"Your affectionate Wife."

Effie did not feel quite so sanguine as Jessie as to the effect of this advance, but she took the note boldly to Harold.

"What is that ?" he asked, turning pale as he looked at the address, and speaking very sternly.

"A note from Jessie," replied Effie, quietly. "If you do not read it, Harold, you will prove yourself a great coward."

"I am not that," said Harold, as he opened the note. He read it through without saying a word, and then put it quietly in the fire. Effie stood, waiting for some answer. As he did not speak, but went on reading, she said, at last, "What am I to say to Jessie ?"

"Nothing. And I wish you to remember, Effie, that I desired never to hear that name again."

"Harold ! you are wicked !"

"Probably. But I am not weak."

As he seemed determined to say no more, Effie was forced at last to leave the room, in utter despair. In the evening, however, he said to her, "I have answered that note you gave me, and have sent Boyle with it."

Effie so dreaded the effect on Jessie of that answer, that she went off the first thing the next morning to Steadham. She found Jessie in bed.

"Then *you* have not cast me off, Effie ? I thought every one had. Look at that," and she brought Harold's letter from under her pillow.

> "Prior's Mount, Gateshill, Dec. 21st.

"DEAR JESSIE,

"I am sorry that you are not happy in the position which you have chosen for yourself. I do not know the nature of the 'shocking discovery' to which you allude ; but I believe that you and I have both made the most painful discovery which can be made : namely, that, some years since, we committed an irreparable mistake. You have so openly shown your sense of this, that I do not hesitate to say that I agree in your view of the case. Under these circumstances, it would clearly only add to our mutual misery if we were again to live under one roof. I am willing to make any sacrifice to gratify your wishes, if you desire to change your residence. Should you

prefer this house to any other, you have only to say
so, and I will remove at once. If you wish for the
society of our children, I am ready to resign them.
Pray do not spare either my feelings or my purse.

"HAROLD ARCHER YONGE."

"Is it not cruel?" cried Jessie, as Effie finished
reading this product of Harold's obduracy.

"I cannot believe that Harold will stick to this!"

"He will, you will see. He hates me, I know.
He has hated me almost ever since we have been
married. I am the most miserable woman in the
world!"

"He cannot be so wicked as he tries to make
himself!" cried Effie again.

"He would say it is I who am wicked. He never
will forgive me—I know he never will! See how
hard he has been to Gerard!"

"Something must soften him soon. He used to
be so kind."

Jessie began to sob passionately.

"Take comfort, Jessie," said Effie, kindly. "He
must come to his senses soon."

"I will never go home now!" cried Jessie; "not if
he should implore me to come to him. And I am
never to see my children again, I suppose!"

"Harold says you may have them," said Effie. "I
will send them to you whenever you like."

There was no difficulty on that subject. Directly Effie mentioned it Harold cut her short. " Let them go every day—and for the whole day, if you like. I have said that I will resign them entirely. I am willing to give up my house if that is desired."

" No," said Effie. " Jessie will not consent to that. You will have to endure the thought that you have turned your wife out of her home—for, though she went of her own accord, the separation is now *your* responsibility."

" She may return here in a few weeks, for I am going to Rome."

" To Rome ! To stay ?"

" For some months, or perhaps years. I have a commission to execute. In the meantime, the children belong to their mother—I give up all claim to them."

So the children went regularly to visit their mother ; but Jessie would not remove to Prior's Mount when Harold went to Rome. She said, to Effie's great admiration and delight, that her home was with her husband, and that if she might not be with him she would have no home. She would not remain in Mrs. Price's house, but took furnished lodgings at Steadham.

CHAPTER V.

"What an unusual thing it is to see you at Gateshill so early in the afternoon as this, Mr. Butterfield!"

"Yes, is not it good of him? He came away from the Office two hours before the time to bring me some good news. George is coming home."

"I am so glad!" cried Effie. "Then Harry is much better, I suppose?"

"Yes, his leg is almost well, George says. He writes from Marseilles. They are travelling very gently, to avoid all risk of another relapse."

"You see his recovery was quite miraculous, Miss Garnock," said Nathaniel. "For my part, I had no hopes of him. I did not tell Clara what I thought, for, you see, it would have been no good to set her fretting, would it, Miss Garnock?"

"No, certainly not."

"So, you see, I put the best face on the matter; though I must say I thought George had only gone out to put the poor fellow decently in his grave."

"He says he owes his life to George's careful nursing. He wrote a few lines in George's letter."

"Crashawe won't be sorry to have George back again; and, for the matter of that, we shall not any of us, eh, Miss Garnock?"

"No, I should think there will be an universal rejoicing. Shall we erect triumphal arches and light bonfires?"

"I am sure every old woman in Gateshill would bring some sticks, if she had to go without a fire all next winter," said Clara. "Come, Nathaniel, we must move on. We have got to carry our good news farther. We came first to you, Effie; but, as I have got my husband free for a whole afternoon, I must economise him."

"Is not she looking well, Miss Garnock? George will give me credit for having kept her in such good condition. Don't you think so?"

"Yes, you deserve great credit. Good-bye."

"Why, she's gone already! How quick she is! I never can be sharp enough for her, Miss Garnock. Joe calls us the hare and the tortoise—not very complimentary to me, eh, Miss Garnock? Good-bye."

After Mr. and Mrs. Nathaniel Butterfield had left, Effie sat still in the garden, where they had found her. She was in a meditative mood this afternoon— a mood in which she did not often indulge. The children had all gone to spend the day and to sleep at Steadham—a great treat to them, for now that they were only occasional visitors to their mother they were excellent friends with her. Effie had been alone all day, and it was the 12th of June—a day which always revived old memories, and made her thoughtful, if not sad. On the 12th of June six years ago Gerard had first told her that he loved her; then had begun that two years' dream of happiness, from which she had been so rudely awakened. This was just such a day as that—with threatening clouds and occasional heavy showers. Effie felt restless and oppressed indoors, so after each shower she returned to the garden, in spite of the damp underfoot, and the dripping trees overhead. She could not get that day six years ago out of her mind. Again and again she went over all that had been done and said. Again she saw the gay crowd in the Horticultural Gardens, breathed the sweet scent of the wet flowers, and felt the suffocating atmosphere of the crowded tents. But, more vividly than all this, she saw again Gerard's loving eyes, and heard his earnest pleading words. She could not force into her mind any sense of all that had happened since—it was all a dream, compared with the intense reality of that day.

The visit of the Butterfields gave a turn to her thoughts for a few minutes, but they soon went back into the old channel. There was pleasure in these thoughts as long as she let them dwell undisturbed

upon the past, but it was torture to bring them from
the past to the present. Then and now! Harold
and Jessie then, and now. There was a little comfort there, for Jessie was certainly much improved
of late. But Harold! Then a devoted, happy
husband, living only for his wife and children. Now
hard, bitter, broken-hearted, a voluntary exile from
his home. And Gerard! Then a bright, pure-
minded, loving boy. Now a trifling, self-indulgent,
disappointed man—for the promise of better things
which had appeared in his last interview with George
had soon disappeared again, and more tales than
ever were told of his wild ways. And herself! Then
a confiding, zealous-tempered girl, to whom the
world was ever unfolding fresh beauties and fresh
delights. Now a dispirited, doubting, hopeless
woman, feeling, at twenty-five, already middle-aged.
And for all this change she could find no comfort.
She could help George in his work, but she had not
caught his faith.

"A gentleman wants Master, Miss Effie," said the
cook, interrupting Effie's meditations. "I told him
as Master was abroad, and then he asked, could he
see Mrs. Yonge, or Miss Garnock."

"I will come in," said Effie. "Do not you know
him at all, Cook?"

"No, miss. But then, you see, I don't see all as
comes here."

Effie hurried in, and found a strange young man in the drawing-room ; a most unprepossessing young man, with red hair and weak red eyes.

" You'll not remember me, I suppose, Miss Garnock," he said. " I had the pleasure once of going down the Clyde with you and your sister, in the Gourock steamer."

" Mr. Lang !" said Effie, at once recognising the features of the little boy who had been her fellow-traveller on her first visit to Scotland, and at the same instant recalling what she had heard of Mr. Caird's nephew, who was walking the London hospitals. The thought brought with it the recollection of an unfulfilled intention that some hospitable advances should be made to the young man, in return for all the kindness she had received from the Cairds. The family troubles which had followed so closely on her return from Glasgow had put this intention out of her head. She now felt remorsefully anxious to be very friendly towards her visitor.

" I am so sorry we have never seen you here before, Mr. Lang. You have been in London for some time, I believe ; but my brother-in-law is abroad now, and before he left home he was so very much occupied."

" Pray don't apologise, Miss Garnock. I know the unfortunate circumstances—visitors are *de trop* in such cases."

Effie felt the blood rushing to her face. She interrupted him hastily, with the question, "How are Mr. and Mrs. Caird, and all of them?"

"My father writes me they are all keeping well, thank you. You heard about Helen's marriage, I suppose?"

"No; I did not know she was married."

"They are not best pleased with her choice—in fact, uncle was quite put out about it—so much so that he refused to see her for some time."

"Indeed! I am very sorry to hear that. Mr. Caird is so good-natured that there must have been very serious objections to the marriage to make him oppose it, I should think."

"Well, my governor says it was not so much the marriage itself as the way she went about it that riled the old gentleman. You see, she never told him or my aunt anything about it till the deed was done."

"What was her motive for concealing it?"

"Can't tell, except that she knew uncle didn't approve of the connection. As Hugh says, those girls are all for something underhand. I did not know Mr. Yonge was away," young Lang went on, after a short pause. "I wanted very particularly to see him."

"I am very sorry," said Effie. "Can I send any message to him?"

"No, thank you. It would not be of any use if he is abroad."

" He is at Rome."

" Whew !" whistled the young man.

" Is there anything I can do ?"

" Well, I don't know, I am sure." He considered for a few minutes, and then continued : " It is no affair of my own, you see. I'm thinking Mr. Yonge is not on the best of terms with his brother ?"

" Circumstances have separated them a good deal lately," replied Effie, stiffly.

" Exactly. Well, you see it is about Gerard that I have come now. But I suppose if Mr. Yonge was at home he would not help."

" If his brother is in need of help I am sure he would not refuse it," said Effie, beginning to tremble.

" Well, you see, the fact is, Miss Garnock, Gerard Yonge is in quod."

" In what ?" asked Effie.

" In quod. There are heaps of writs out against him, and he has got nabbed on one of them."

" And what could Harold—what could his brother do ?"

" Well, you see, it is only a matter of 69l. odd ; and I suppose Mr. Yonge would fork out that much to get his brother out of a spunging-house."

" Yes, I have no doubt he would. But how can it be done, Mr. Lang ? And—I don't quite understand about such things—what *is* a spunging-house ? Is it a prison ?"

" Well, it is a prison, and it isn't. But one thing
I can tell, it is a mighty unpleasant place to get into.
And then, you see, the worst of it is, when once a
fellow's caged in that way there's no saying when
he'll get loose, there are always such a lot of snares
ready to catch him again. Now, if Yonge was to get
out for this, he'd likely not be able to say ' Jack
Robinson ' before he'd be wanted again on some other
suit. I know for certain that he's being ' looked after '
for Ridge and Pounce, the jewellers ; he ran a stiffish
bill with them when he was spooney upon that widow,
you know, or whatever she was."

" Then do you mean that it would be of no use if
he were to be released now ?"

" Well, yes ; if he would make himself scarce for a
few months, this run upon him would likely blow
over. You see, it all comes of his having sold two
pictures in the Exhibition : every one's little bill was
ready directly. But, law bless you, there were lots
of things to be settled before tailors and bootmakers
could have their turn. You see, Yonge is a
crotchetty fellow in some matters, and he never will
hear of flying a kite—on his own account, that is.
There never was a softer fellow about helping other
men out of scrapes. Then he's got a most unreasonable
prejudice against the Jews. So, you see, he has just
no chance. When he's flush of the needful he
scatters it about right and left, for all the world as

if he had got Jack the Giant Killer's purse—no, it
wasn't Jack the Giant Killer, it's the other man.
And then, you see, when he is cleaned out he won't
do anything to raise the wind, and so he falls
plump—ha! ha! Not bad that?"

"But I cannot quite understand, Mr. Lang," put in
Effie again, as much bewildered as disgusted by her
visitor's style of conversation, "what can be done
for Mr. Yonge. What did you think my brother-
in-law could do?"

" Well, you see, if any one went with the cash
down, he would be free at once ; and then if he could
be persuaded just to make straight for Boulogne or
Calais, and to lay quiet there for a time, it would be
all right. But he must not show his face in Berners
Street yet awhile."

" If you had the money would you undertake to
manage the rest?"

" Well, you see," said the boy, with a short laugh,
"that's more than my place is worth. You see how
it is. I'm as deep·in the mud as Yonge ; and I'm
not at all sure that if I went to open the bars for
him I wouldn't just get popped into the cage in his
place. I'd risk something for Yonge, for he's a
devilish good fellow, and no mistake, and he has
often pulled me up at a pinch, but I couldn't quite
go so far as that. No, thank you! Not if I knows
it!"

"Has he no friend who would venture anything for him?" asked Effie, indignantly.

"Well, you see, he does not want for friends, but they are mostly in the same boat, which isn't over water-tight, you see, Miss Garnock—ha, ha! not bad that? And there's another thing. You see, Yonge isn't quite heart and soul with any set. He has been having a widish fling lately, and got out with the slow men he used to be thick with, but yet he isn't quite one of us—we are the fast set, you see, Miss Garnock."

"And Mr. Yonge is not *fast* enough for you?" asked Effie, with a suppressed sneer.

"No, not exactly. He has got some old-world prejudices that he clings to as if they were the brightest lights going. But he is a capital fellow for all that. Only it's a bore when a fellow won't go the whole hog. That's the reason not many men in our set would put their heads into the lion's den for him. He was uncommonly kind to me when I first came south, and that's why I am doing what I can for him now."

Effie was glad to perceive one good trait in Gerard's repulsive friend; but she felt quite willing to dispense with any more of his company. So she said, formally, "You may rely upon it that something shall be done immediately to set Mr. Yonge at liberty. I must thank you in my brother's name for the trouble you have taken. Have you had luncheon ?"

" Oh yes, hours ago, thanks. And, by-the-by, I must be off. I am due at Bartholomew's at five. I leave Yonge's cause in your hands, Miss Garnock."

" You may safely depend upon me," said Effie ; and the medical student rose to depart.

" Where is Mr. Yonge to be found ?"

" Well, I am a green ! If I wasn't going to forget that ! Here it is," and he gave her a dirty, tobacco-scented slip of paper. " I wish you success !" And he hurried away.

Effie sat down to think for a few minutes, and then prepared to act. She had soon determined that no one but herself should know of Gerard's disgrace —for to her mind it was deep disgrace. It should never reach Harold's ears if she could help it. Therefore it was essential that she should go herself to " the lion's den," as young Lang had called Gerard's present quarters. The address given was a perfect *terra incognita* to her, and she therefore kept the offensive memorandum—no small test of friendship.

The first thing to be done was to get together the necessary money. She would not draw upon the funds which Harold had left her, as that might have necessitated some explanation to him. Had George Monro been at home everything would have been easy. She could think of no one better to apply

to than George's sister. But then came the reflection
that Clara was not very discreet, and might inadver-
tently betray the secret. Her husband, on the contrary, was discretion itself, and Effie resolved to
borrow of her former suitor.

After a hurried walk up the hill, in spite of a
rapidly gathering storm, she found Mr. Butterfield
in his dining-room, decanting his wine.

" I am very glad to see you, Miss Garnock. I
hope you have come to take a bit of dinner with us.
Clara will be delighted. I am afraid you will have
to put up with pot-luck, for Clara would not let
me ask young Westerton, because she said we were
going to have a make-up dinner. But, whatever it
is, you are heartily welcome to it, Miss Garnock.
And I don't think you are one to be over-nice about
your food, eh, Miss Garnock ?"

" I should be quite contented with ' pot-luck,' Mr.
Butterfield. But I am sorry to say I have not come
to dine with you. I have come for a much less
pleasant purpose. I want to borrow some money of
you."

Nathaniel involuntarily took out his well-filled purse.

" No; I am a more impudent beggar than your
purse will satisfy, Mr. Butterfield. I am quite
ashamed of my errand. But I have had a sudden
demand for 50*l.*, which I cannot well refuse ; and in
Harold's absence I do not know how to get the

money on such a short notice. Knowing your kindness, I——"

"Pray, not another word, Miss Garnock. I am
proud to be of use. Come into my study, and I will
write a cheque. Dear me! the clouds look very
threatening!" he added, as he drew up the blind in
the study. "You had better make up your mind
to stay with us to-night, eh, Miss Garnock?"

"I cannot possibly. I must settle this business
at once. And, Mr. Butterfield, I will not ask you
not to say anything to Clara, but it is desirable to
keep the matter as secret as possible."

"I understand, Miss Garnock. You may trust
me. We solicitors are accustomed to secrets. I shall
look upon this as office business, and I shall not
mention it to Clara, for, as Joe says, ladies are like
teapots—everything comes out at the spout. That
will be right, Miss Garnock, and I am much obliged
to you for having allowed me to do you this little
service. No thanks, pray. Have you an umbrella?
Fortunately, it is quick walking down the hill."

"It would be vain for me to attempt to thank you
sufficiently, Mr.——"

"Hush!" interrupted Nathaniel, hurrying her out
of the house. "I shall tell Clara you came about
the 'Sick Loan Club'—that will not be very untrue,
eh, Miss Garnock?"

Effie, before coming out, had appropriated 20l.,

which she had put aside for the rent, so that she had now only to make the best of her way to the land of bailiffs. As she left the Butterfields' the first vivid flash of lightning almost blinded her, and as she ran down the hill and past Prior's Mount, towards the distant stand where cabs were to be found, the flashes became brighter and brighter, and the thunder seemed to rattle and boom directly overhead. Effie had a constitutional dread of thunder, and yet she never even thought of turning back, and leaving Gerard to his well-deserved punishment, for one more night. She said to herself—and it was in a great measure true—that she was actuated in all this by no feeling but that of old friendship, for how could she have any deeper feeling for Mrs. Price's former lover?

The stand was empty, and before Effie could secure a wandering cab the rain poured down in torrents, and she was wet through. Once fairly on her way, she forgot the storm in terror at the strange adventure in which she was embarked. What scenes should she have to go through? What hitherto unthought-of experiences to encounter?

Nothing very alarming. When her destination was at last reached—the dirty paper having been transferred to the cabman—a few words written on Harold's card soon brought out Mr. Raynes, the proprietor of the establishment, a bland, insinuating man, not over-clean, but not the brutal, cunning-looking Jew whom Effie had expected to see.

"I believe that Mr. Gerard Yonge is detained here on account of a debt," said Effie, as the man took the seat opposite to her in the cab.

"Quite correct, miss. We have the honour of his company. A very pleasant gentleman—very much so indeed, miss."

"Mr. Yonge, his brother, is abroad, but I am acting for him. If I pay the debt will Mr. Gerard Yonge be free?"

"Certainly, miss—for the present. There may be other little matters; but they are neither here nor there—certainly not here. Hem. 'Nathaniel Butterfield,' firm of 'Butterfield and Cheeseman?'—a most respectable firm. Quite satisfactory, miss. 69*l.* 13*s.* 3*d.* is the sum. Quite correct. Very fortunate that I happened to be within. Heavy storm, miss. Will you step in a bit?"

"No, thank you. I am quite sheltered in the cab."

"Then I will send Mr. Yonge. Quite sorry to lose him, I assure you. Afraid he won't return the compliment, though;" and the little sleek man bustled away through the torrents of rain.

About a quarter of an hour elapsed before Gerard came out, followed to the door by his host, with whom he shook hands, and then came slowly up to the cab.

He turned scarlet when he saw Effie, and cried, fiercely, "Effie! What do you do here?"

Effie answered, in the most matter-of-fact tone she could assume, "Harold is away, and I am the only person left to act for him."

"Did he send you?"

"No, he is at Rome."

"What the de—what made you come, then?"

Effie was frightened at his fierce tone—so unusual in him. But she did not flinch.

"Had you not better come inside the cab?" she asked. "You will be wet through. And are you not running some risk by standing here?"

Gerard glanced quickly over his shoulder, with a startled air, and then slowly took the seat which Mr. Raynes had occupied, without once looking at Effie. "Shall I tell the man to drive to Gateshill?" he asked.

"Yes," said Effie, timidly. When the cab had turned she expected Gerard to repeat his former question, but he sat gloomily poking the straw about with his stick, and appeared to have no attention to spare for anything else. Effie began to feel rather angry. She had been thinking over and over again how she could say what had to be said without wounding his pride, but now his apparent ingratitude made her speak out bluntly.

"Your friend, Mr. Lang, says it will not be safe

for you to go to your home. He thinks you might
be arrested again."

"Then it was Lang that betrayed me!" Gerard
cried, suddenly looking up, but instantly averting
his eyes from Effie.

"Mr. Lang came to tell Harold—not knowing he
was abroad—of the trouble you were in. As Harold's
sister, I took upon myself to act for him," said Effie,
in a dignified tone.

"Confound this cab! What a noise there is!
What did you say?"

"That, Harold being away, I took upon myself to
do what he would have done had he been at home."

"Yes, of course, I understand. For Harold's sake."
There was intense vexation in his tone.

"I have brought a 'Bradshaw,'" continued Effie,
desiring to be very cool and practical. "Mr. Lang
advises that you should go to France for a few
months till your affairs are in better order. What a
flash!"

"To France or to the—to Jericho, I don't care
which," said Gerard, recklessly.

"I see there is a train to Folkestone at eight, and
the Boulogne boat leaves at seven to-morrow morning.
You would be out of danger at Folkestone, I suppose,
for one night?"

"Yes, I suppose so," said Gerard, still sulkily.

"Then will you tell the man to drive to London

Bridge? There is only just time to catch the train. Don't you think it would be your best plan?"

"But you—what are you going to do?" asked Gerard, hoarsely.

"I am going home directly I have seen you safe at London Bridge."

"I had better tell him to drive you home at once. I will take another cab."

"No, it is not much out of my way, and it will be safer for you not to change cabs. Besides, there is no time."

Gerard gave the necessary direction to the man. "What an awful night!" he said, as he drew his head in again.

"A very wretched night for you to have to travel in," said Effie, kindly.

"And not at all wretched for *you* to be knocking about in, I suppose."

"Oh, I shall soon be home."

Gerard did not speak again for some time. Then he suddenly passed his hand over Effie's wet skirt. "Did you walk to Cursitor Street?" he asked.

"No," said Effie, laughing. "But there were no cabs on the Gateshill Road stand. Will you see if you can find out any better boats and trains than I could? 'Bradshaw' puzzles me rather."

Gerard took the book from her. "What is to-day?" he asked.

"The 12th of June," answered Effie, calmly, trying not to betray by her voice that she remembered what anniversary it was.

"The 12th of June," repeated Gerard, slowly. He looked at Effie for a moment, the deep colour spreading all over his face, and then took refuge in his favourite attitude—burying his head in his hands—but now, not satisfied with that screen, he buried it almost between his knees. So he remained till the cab stopped at the London Bridge Station.

"Mr. Lang will send whatever you want, I suppose?" asked Effie.

"Yes, I suppose so."

"We are only just in time. There's the first bell. Good-bye."

"Good-bye." He did not offer to shake hands, but turned abruptly away. The cabman was mounting his box to drive off when Gerard came back to the window.

"Effie, I was a brute to be so rude to you about coming. It was very kind—like you. But I would rather have had my right hand chopped off than that you should have been the one to do this for me."

"Good-bye," said Effie, holding out her hand.

"No, my hand is not fit for you to touch, Effie." He rushed into the station just as the second bell began to ring.

Now that the excitement and the necessity for

action were over, the terror of the storm quite over-
powered Effie ; and she arrived at home in such a
state of mental and bodily exhaustion that the cook,
the only servant left in the house, was quite alarmed.
Effie stoutly refused to call in Mr. Rogers, and the
next morning a strong feeling of lassitude and a pale
face were the only ill effects.

A week later Effie had another visit from Alexander
Lang. He came in with the brisk familiarity of an
old acquaintance, and immediately pulling out a large,
greasy pocket-book, produced from it several bank-
notes, and laid them with a triumphant rustle on the
table. "There," he said ; "I'll wager you didn't
look to have your cash back so soon, Miss Garnock."

"Certainly I did not," said Effie. "How does it
happen ?"

"Well, you see, last Wednesday—no—was it
Wednesday, or Thursday? What is to-day ?"

"Tuesday."

"Ah, then it was Thursday. Last Thursday I had
a letter from Gerard Yonge from Boulogne, telling
me to pack up all his painting instruments, and to
send them to him, and to sell off everything else, and
the first thing I was to do with the money was to pay
off this loan of yours. Well, you see, as luck would
have it, one of our men knew a man that was just on
the look-out for furnished rooms like Yonge's, and so
we came to terms in no time; and the other chap

seemed to have heaps of spare cash, and so he stumped
up at once, and like a regular brick, and there's enough
to pay several little bills—though that's a work that
goes horribly against the grain with me. 'Base is the
slave that pays,' say I. But one must make these
little sacrifices for friendship. And now I must be
off, Miss Garnock. I'm sorry to pay you such a
short visit, but I tore myself away from a beautiful
case in the Accident Ward, and I hope to get back
before it is quite done with."

Effie was glad to be able so soon to repay Nathaniel
Butterfield ; but she had a vague feeling of mortifica-
tion that Gerard had been so unwilling to be in debt
to her.

When Effie went the next day to the Butterfields'
she found Clara in great distress over a letter from
George. Harry had become worse on the journey
from Marseilles, and was now laid up at Boulogne.
George wrote in a somewhat constrained manner,
which made Clara fear that he had not told her the
whole truth as to Harry's state. Effie, on her return
home, found that this fear was only too well founded.
George wrote to beg her to break to Clara the news
that Harry had been obliged to suffer the amputation
of his leg. Knowing that Clara's fears went farther
than this, Effie hurried back again with this intelli-
gence, which, as she expected, was a relief instead of
a shock.

The daily bulletin continued favourable ; and in a week George arrived, having left Harry and his mother in the care of Gerard, whom he had met by chance on the quay at Boulogne. He spoke so warmly of Gerard's helpfulness in the sick-room, and of his untiring patience with the invalid, that had he at that moment again asked Effie to marry him she would hardly have had the heart to say "No." But George fully understood the bright glow of delight and gratitude which overspread her face as he continued : "After all, Gerard is a first-rate fellow. We have, some of us, been cruelly hard upon him. It is so easy for those who are free from temptation to condemn those whose susceptible natures expose them to it. I don't know how we can, any of us, sufficiently show our gratitude to Gerard for his goodness to Harry."

CHAPTER VI.

"Hotel des deux Mondes, Paris, May 3rd.

"DEAR EFFIE,

"I expect to be home in about a week. I had a touch of fever at Rome, and my doctor sent me away. I had just finished my job, and I have been longing to see my children. I suppose I shall hardly know my boys after my eighteen months' absence from them. Davie must feel himself quite a man, now that he is in jackets. Kiss them all for me, and believe me to remain,

"Ever your affectionate Brother,

"H. A. YONGE."

Effie hurried off at once to Jessie. "You must be at home to receive him, Jessie," she said, when her sister had read Harold's note.

Jessie turned very pale. "I dare not," she exclaimed.

"I am sure he would be pleased to find you there," urged Effie.

"But if he should reject me as he did before, I could not bear it. It would kill me."

"He would not—I am sure he would not."

"Harold never changes," said Jessie, musingly.

"No," replied Effie; "that is the very reason that I am sure he will forgive you. He must still love you."

"He cannot, Effie. If he had ever loved me, would he have been so angry with me all this time?"

"Yes. It was because he loved you so deeply that he was so bitter in his disappointment."

Jessie began to cry. Effie went on rapidly, "But now, when he finds that you are really all that he once thought you, his old love will come back to you just the same as ever."

"Do you really think so, Effie?"

"I am sure of it."

"But do you think I am so much better than I was? The children are certainly fond of me, now; but I don't think I should satisfy Harold. I never can care about pictures, and that sort of thing. You suit him much better."

"I did not suit him during the wretched year after you left. He was utterly miserable. Jessie, he told me your going had broken his heart."

"Did he, really? Then do you think he did care for me then?"

"I am sure he did—I am sure that he loved you

passionately then—and that he does still. If he had
not loved you he would not have been so bitterly
hurt at your indifference to him."

"My indifference !   Was I indifferent to him ?"

"It seemed like it when you left him."

"Yes. I suppose it did. I suppose I did not care
for him much then. I do not think I am indifferent
now, Effie."

"Oh, Jessie! you really love him now as he
deserves !"

"I don't know about love," answered Jessie, rather
startled by her sister's fervour. "It makes me very
unhappy to think that he is so angry with me ; and
I long very much to see him again. I always felt
safe with him ; and since I left him I feel as if nothing was safe."

"Then you will come back to him, and everything
will be safe again."

"If he would only let me !"

"Try him."

"If I should try—and fail. Suppose he should
refuse to see me. I am sure it would kill me,
Effie."

"He will not refuse. He cannot refuse, if he finds
you at home with the children."

"I wish I could feel as sure about it as you do."

Effie's confidence was rather shaken that afternoon.
When she left Jessie she went to fetch Davie and

Walter from the school in Gateshill, to which they now went every day, and in the village she met George Monro.

"You have heard that Yonge is on his way to England, I suppose," said George, turning to walk with her.

"Yes. I have had a note from him this morning. I have been to try and persuade Jessie to come home to receive him."

"Have you succeeded?"

"I think I shall succeed. She is quite willing herself; but she is afraid of being repulsed again. Of course, that was very terrible for her. I do not wonder she dreads a repetition of it. I cannot forgive Harold for treating her as he did."

"Do you think he would repulse her again?"

"No. I don't think he could. I would not persuade her to risk it if I thought such a thing possible."

"He is very unforgiving," observed George, reflectively.

"Yes. He certainly is. But I am sure he still loves Jessie; and it is two years since she offended him."

"Perhaps he would forgive an offence against himself more readily than——" George stopped suddenly. He seemed to have been speaking more to himself than to Effie.

"Do you think he could hold back any longer if he were to find Jessie with the children?"

"I should not have thought so yesterday—but——"

"But what? Please do not keep anything from me."

"I will not. Read that."

"Paris, May 3rd.

"DEAR GEORGE,

"Don't think that I have cast my resolution to the winds, and have come here to enjoy myself. For some time I have been under a half-engagement to take the portrait of an old invalid lady at Versailles, and I could not resist making that an excuse to come so far with Harry. I still feel as if he were in my charge, and unable to get on at all without me. What a plucky fellow he is, to be bent on going out again after all that has happened! But, indeed, one would hardly think there was anything wrong with his leg, he manages so well. He starts on Thursday for Marseilles, and then I shall go back to Boulogne. I hope to finish my old lady (such a fine specimen of the conventional idea of a French marquise!) by that time, and I have no wish to linger here. I should have left yesterday, but for my Versailles engagement. I have seen Harold, and I would not meet him again for something. I met him first on Sunday, walking in the Bois de Boulogne. He had

two men with him, and I did not care to risk a
repulse before them and Harry, who was with me.
So I only looked full in his face, in hopes that he
would make the first advance. He also looked me
full in the face, and turned very pale. But he
passed without a word or a sign of recognition—so
close that our sleeves brushed against each other.
Yesterday, I saw him again in the Louvre. I thought
I would make one more effort, so I went boldly
up to him, and said something about it's being five
years since we had seen one another. He muttered
a few words—I think they were, ' What if it were ten
times five?' and turned away. In a minute he left
the gallery. The gaiety and brightness of this place
sicken me now, and I shall be heartily glad to get
back to my cell at Wimereux. Harold must be on
his way home, I should think ; but I am afraid there
is no hope of a reconciliation between him and Jessie.
Harry wishes me to say that he has ordered a rocking-
horse to be sent to Gateshill, for Clara's little boy.
I told him I thought the baby would hardly appreciate
his present yet ; but he says a child cannot be too early
taught to ride, and that this promising scion of the
noble house of Butterfield must be trained for a
soldier. What a fellow he is for his profession ! I
wonder he puts up at all with us civilians. How
sorry I shall be to see the last of his dear old limp
to-morrow !

"Remember me very kindly to Mrs. Nathaniel Butterfield, and to all my friends at Gateshill.

"Ever yours,

"GERARD A. YONGE."

"That is rather discouraging, is it not?" asked George, as Effie gave him back Gerard's letter.

"I cannot understand Harold. He used to be so kind and gentle."

"Kindness and gentleness cannot stand the wear and tear of life if they have no firmer foundation than natural disposition," remarked George.

"What would you advise about Jessie?" asked Effie, anxiously.

"What do you think, after Yonge's treatment of Gerard?"

"I think it is now, or never. If Harold comes home, and Jessie is not there, everything will fall into its old course, and the opportunity will be lost."

"You are quite right. I did not think of that. Yes, it will be certainly best to venture—if Mrs. Yonge can muster sufficient courage."

"I believe she will. She sees herself that this is the time for a decisive move, and she is very anxious for a reconciliation. I think a few words from her 'spiritual adviser' would quite decide her." Effie glanced laughingly into George's face, but he did not smile in return. He looked grave and agitated.

"I will say those few words then, as you wish it," he replied.

"I do not wish it, unless you think it best," said Effie.

"I do think it best. But, Effie, if your sister comes home, what will you do?"

"I shall go to Gourock," answered Effie, quickly.

"I thought so."

They walked on in silence for some minutes. They had passed the little boys' school, and were walking along the shady lane in which the house stood. George spoke at last.

"Effie, you have always treated me with so much confidence," he said, "that I am emboldened to ask a question which perhaps I have no right to ask— no right but my urgent need of an answer—Do you still—do you still love Gerard Yonge?"

Effie was startled, and her heart beat tumultuously; but, after a short pause, she said firmly, "No."

"No!" echoed George, rapturously. "But," he added, in a more subdued tone, "he is growing so much worthier of your love—and—Effie! how your face always glows when he is praised."

Effie's face glowed now, as she answered in a faltering tone, "I think that is because—that is— I like to hear him praised because—it justifies me to myself." She finished her sentence hurriedly, almost in a whisper.

"What justification can *you* require?" cried George, fervently.

"For—for caring for any one who is—who is not worthy to be cared for. Oh! it is so dreadful to be—not to be able to help always caring for any one that one cannot respect. The contempt for oneself is so dreadful."

"You mean that you cannot respect Gerard," said George, very gently.

"How can I? I don't mean anything about his conduct to me—that was not his fault—but I do despise him for having been engaged to that woman."

"But you still love him?" asked George, mournfully.

"No, I do not— No, I am sure I do not. Never since that day in the hayfields."

"Effie, you are sure? Then—oh, Effie! That was the only obstacle three years ago. I have not changed since then—I——"

"No, oh no! George, not that!" cried Effie, in great distress. "The obstacle is not removed. I do not love Gerard as he is, but I shall always love the memory of what he was."

"Effie, is my love to be cast away for a memory?"

"George, if you had been married and your wife had died, would you marry again?"

"No, ten thousand times, no."

"I was married—in heart—to Gerard. If he had

died during our engagement, do you think I could ever have married ?"

" No—but——"

" That Gerard—the Gerard who was my husband—*is* dead, but I cannot be unfaithful to his memory."

"It is not only memory, Effie," said George, in a tone of sad reproach. "You still love the living Gerard."

"I do not—indeed I do not. If I were to see him now coming towards us my pulse would hardly be quickened. When I last saw him I felt no more for him than for any mere acquaintance. It would cost me nothing to know for certain that I should never see him again."

"And yet you cling to a romantic dream of what he was ?"

"Yes," said Effie, rather fiercely. "But it is not a dream. It is a reality. You think I was deceived in him—but I was not. I knew all his faults always. I knew always that he might act as he did—in all but one thing—I never thought that he could cease to be a gentleman."

" But," said George, irresistibly tempted to continue this subject, even at the risk of paining Effie, " his conduct to you was not that of a gentleman."

"He was not to blame for that," repeated Effie. " He could not help himself. He wished to do right. And then who could blame his taste ?"

" I could," said George, in a low voice.

" I respect him for having loved Clara," said Effie, going on volubly.   " But to love that——"

" Do not let us speak of her," interrupted George.

" We have forgotten the little boys !" exclaimed Effie.   " Poor children ! how tired they will be of waiting !"

" And there is no hope for me ?" asked George, as they walked hurriedly back.

" Oh, George—dear George !   I respect, and—and love you more than any one in the world.   But I can never marry."

" And you will go away."

" I must.   You know I must."

" Well, I suppose it is best.   When this world is utterly dark, one is driven to seek all one's light from above.   There are the little boys.   And now I will leave you.   Good-bye.   God bless you, Effie, wherever you go."

" If I could but thank you, George !   If I could but express my gratitude for all your goodness !"

" Do not torture me by such a word as gratitude !" cried George, as he hurried off.

Effie had no time either to repent of, or to exult in her choice of a dead memory in preference to a living, loving heart.   She was impatient to get everything settled at once, for, being so near as Paris, Harold might arrive at any moment.   Jessie's scruples as to coming home were soon overcome, and she was installed triumphantly at Prior's Mount two days after the receipt of Harold's note. But she was very unwilling to accede to Effie's other plan. She had forgotten her jealousy of her sister, and could not understand why they should not all live together again. Effie was resolute, however, and, when Jessie had been three days at home, she started for Gourock. Half an hour after she left Gateshill, a note came from Harold to say he should be home at eight o'clock that same evening. Jessie was in a terrible state of agitation and alarm all day; and when eight o'clock was approaching she could bear it no longer, and sent for George. The children were still playing in the garden when George obeyed the summons.

" He is coming at eight o'clock," said Jessie, hardly able to speak with nervous excitement; "and I dare not see him alone."

" I think you ought to make the effort," urged George. " It would not do for any one else to be present."

" Not when we meet, perhaps," answered Jessie, her teeth chattering as she spoke. " But, indeed, you must be here to warn him. I cannot let him come in and find me here. If you do not stay I shall run away before he comes."

Seeing how great Jessie's agitation was, George could not leave her, though he felt certain that his remaining would be unfavourable to the chances of a reconciliation with Harold.

"Will Papa come soon, Mamma?" asked Walter, jumping into the room through the open window.

"What time is it, Mamma?" inquired Davie, at the same moment.

"A quarter to eight," answered George. "Quite time for you young men to come in. Don't tease Mamma, Freddie. She is tired."

"I would rather have him," said Jessie, faintly, as she lifted the little boy on to her knees.

Davie and Walter went to the front window to watch; and the little party remained in perfect silence for half an hour, Freddie having fallen asleep in his mother's lap.

"Here he is! Here he is!" shouted the two boys from the window.

"Go to him," gasped Jessie, looking at George with a ghastly face, and trembling violently.

"Stay where you are, boys," cried George, as he left the room.

"How do you do, Monro? I am glad to see you," said Harold, warmly, as he shook George's hand. "Where are my boys?" he added, pressing on through the hall. "Surely Effie has not sent them to bed."

"The boys and their mother are in the drawing-room," answered George, distinctly.

"Who?" asked Harold, stopping suddenly, and looking into George's face.

"Mrs. Yonge and her children are waiting anxiously for you."

"Come in here," said Harold, in an altered tone, turning round, and walking into the nearly dark play-room. "Did I understand you to say that my wife is in this house?" he asked, confronting George, sternly.

"Yes. She has been longing for your return. But she is half dead with fear that you might not be pleased at her presence here."

"She judged me rightly. I was not aware that she had chosen this house for her abode. I had hoped to see a little of my children—but I will not interfere with her arrangements. Will you be kind enough to ask Effie to write to me at Fladong's Hotel, and appoint some place where I may meet my sons without the risk of intruding on their mother. Good-night."

"Stay, Yonge! You cannot go away like this Your wife is pining for a kind word from you. She bitterly repents of her former mistake, and will implore your forgiveness, if you will allow her the opportunity."

"She has my forgiveness. But we have mutually agreed that it is best we should not meet. You must pardon me, Mr. Monro, if I say that in these matters the interference of an uninterested person is most undesirable."

"I am quite aware that it is so," said George, commanding himself with a great effort. "It was only at Mrs. Yonge's earnest request that I consented to take upon myself to tell you of her being here."

"I am obliged to you for that. Good-evening. You will give my message to Effie?"

"Effie is not here. She is at Gourock."

"Effie gone! And who is to take care of my children?"

"She probably thought that your children would need no care but that of their mother and father."

"Their father is driven from them," said Harold, bitterly.

"Then, if their father deserts them, their mother's care and love will suffice for them," said George.

"Poor children!" exclaimed Harold, still more bitterly.

"Papa! what are you doing? We have been waiting for you so long!" cried Davie, forcing his way into the room.

"My noble little man!" exclaimed Harold, as he looked proudly at his eldest son.

"Papa! I want Papa!" shouted Freddie, in the hall.

Harold took the little boy in his arms, and walked towards the street-door.

"Papa, where are you going?" asked Davie. "Mamma is waiting for you."

"I have got to go back to London, Davie. I will see you again soon. Wattie, my boy, come and give Papa a kiss. I suppose your little sister is in bed? Good-bye, my boys; I must be off now," he added, hastily, as he heard a movement in the drawing-room. In another moment—just as George was persuading Jessie to rush into the hall—he had left the house.

"He has gone!" gasped Jessie, as the street-door closed with a bang; and she sank on the floor, sobbing convulsively.

"You had better go to bed now, boys," said George, preventing the children from returning to their mother. "You will see your Papa to-morrow."

"Mayn't we say good-night to Mamma?" asked Davie, timidly.

"Your Mamma is not quite well," answered George, and the little boys ran upstairs.

"What *shall* I do?" asked Jessie, looking up with a despairing face as George re-entered the room. "I knew it would be so," she continued; "I knew he would not forgive me. He never will forgive me! Oh, George! am I not a miserable woman?"

"It is a great trial, certainly," replied George, hardly knowing what to say. "But I am not hopeless. He will relent yet."

"Never! He will never relent. He will never see me again. And to be so near him! Oh! it was too hard!" Jessie began to sob again so violently that George was quite frightened. He had never felt so utterly unable to offer any comfort.

"To—to hear his voice, and no—ot to dare to go—o to him," sobbed out Jessie. "And the—en for him —for him to— He must hate me to treat me so!" she cried, suddenly checking her sobs, and starting to her feet. "Must not he hate me, George?"

"No, I believe that he still loves you deeply. In spite of his assumed calmness just now he was fearfully agitated. You heard how he hurried away. He could not trust himself to see you."

"Do you think it was that?" said Jessie, wistfully.

"I feel sure of it. Take comfort, Jessie. All will come right in time."

"Do you really think so?"

"I do indeed."

"But Effie was sure it would be all right now."

"Effie is so forgiving herself she cannot believe that any one can be otherwise."

"Harold ought not to be so unforgiving. Is he not wicked, George?"

"We are all wicked when we give ourselves up to our own will. Yonge is not himself now. He is like one possessed."

"Is not it just like that? It is terrible. He used

to be so kind and gentle, and now—oh, he is cruel—
he is wickedly cruel!"

The sobs, which so troubled George, began again.

"You must remember," he said, very gently, "that
you appeared cruel to him once."

"I know—I know!" cried Jessie. "But I have
repented; and you say yourself that when we repent
we are forgiven, don't you? Oh, if Harold is so hard,
how do I know that there is forgiveness anywhere?"
She caught hold of George's arm, and looked in his
face in sudden terror.

"We are told to forgive others because we are
forgiven," answered George, in a low voice.

"Then Harold ought to forgive. Oh, George, tell
him it is wicked not to forgive!"

"He would not listen to me," said George, sadly.

"He thinks he needs no forgiveness," Jessie continued, in a meditative tone. "He *is* very good—
very true, and conscientious, and that kind of thing,
but—is that enough, George? If he should die—oh,
if he should die! Go to him, George—speak seriously
to him. Talk to him as you talked to me at Steadham. You might make him think differently, and
then—then, perhaps, he would forgive me."

"I will do my best, if I have any opportunity,"
said George. "But you would be the one to influence
him if—— "

"How can I, when he will not see me? Oh, I shall

die if he will not see me. I cannot bear it. I must see him. Tell him I shall die if I do not see him." Jessie was becoming very violent again.

"Calm yourself, Jessie. You will see him soon. He cannot live without you. You will be happier together than you have ever been."

"If only I may be with him I shall be quite happy."

"That was not formerly the case."

"No—but then—then,—I don't suppose I loved him then."

"Did you marry him without loving him?"

"I suppose so. Effie thought I loved him enough, but I don't think I did—not half so much as I do now—now that he hates me. Oh, I know he hates me! I know he will never forgive me. And it is all my own fault. It is too much—too much. I shall die! George, I shall die! Oh, save me! I am dying! I am dying!" and the overwrought woman fell down in a fainting-fit.

George called the servants, and, when she was partially recovered, left her in their charge. The next day, when he took the children to see their father, he told Harold boldly that his cruel treatment of his wife had made her seriously ill, and even ventured on some of the admonitions which Jessie had suggested—apparently without the slightest effect. Harold listened coldly, but courteously, till George had finished speaking, and then, without a word, returned to his children, towards whom he was tenderly affectionate. Two days later Mr. Butterfield communicated to Jessie, through the lawyer whom she had employed, that it was Mr. Yonge's wish that his two elder sons should be sent as boarders to the school at Blackheath where he had himself been educated. Jessie acceded at once. She was now really shaken in health, and the care of all the children was more than she could bear. So, as soon as the Midsummer holidays were over, the little boys were sent to their father, to be taken by him to Blackheath.

A week after Harold's return to England Effie had received a note from him, saying that he was about to visit Edinburgh on business, and would come to see her, if her aunts had no objection. Effie had heard from Jessie and from George of all that had taken place at Gateshill, and, after consulting with her aunts, she wrote the following letter :—

"Gourock, May 17th.

" DEAR HAROLD,

"Remembering how kind a brother you have always been to me, it is very hard for me to write what I am afraid will give you pain—and very hard also to deny myself the great happiness of seeing you, after so long an absence. But as long as you refuse to treat my sister as your wife has a right to be treated, I feel that it would not be showing a proper sympathy with her *undeserved* suffering if I were to consent to any friendly intercourse with you.

" Do not think that I defend her conduct in leaving your house—now more than two years ago. I look back upon that—as she herself looks back upon it— as a most ill-advised and unjustifiable step. But she has bitterly regretted it ever since; she is now quite ready to acknowledge her error, and anxious to do all in her power to atone for it.

" You may often have felt cause to complain of your wife's coldness and indifference. I believe most firmly that if you would forgive her now you would never again have such a complaint to make. Harold, believe me—if Jessie never loved you truly in the early days of your marriage, she loves you truly now. Do not spurn her love. Do not leave her to pine in hopeless regret for happiness which she feels that she has lost through her own folly. If you do, how will you be fulfilling the promise which you made my father on his death-bed?

" Your affectionate Sister,

" EFFIE."

This letter had no more apparent effect than George's words. Effie hoped in vain for an answer.

CHAPTER VII.

" EH, Effie bairn, come away, and mix a salad for me. Ye're just the only body in the house that knows the art of it," said Euphemia Garnock, bustling into the room where Effie was sitting with her invalid aunt, about a month after her arrival at Gourock.

" And what for are you so nice about the salad to-day, Phemie ?" asked aunt Elizabeth, when Effie had gone to fulfil her task.

" It's just that long body of a doctor is coming in to his dinner, and you'll no be wishing him to get his cold meat without any green stuff, eh, sister Elizabeth ?"

" I'm not grudging the doctor the best you can set before him ; but what should possess the man to be wanting his dinner now—him that never breaks his fast after his morning meal till seven at night ?"

" I'll no undertake to say," replied Euphemia. " But whenever I met him in the street he just told me he'd be looking in immediately, and would be glad of a bit of dinner."

Aunt Elizabeth's wonder was not at all decreased when the doctor appeared, and sat quietly down to talk, as though he had the whole day to spare, instead of being the busiest man in Gourock. The old lady's active brain puzzled over this riddle all the time the others were away in the dining-room; and the interest of it was still farther heightened when Effie ran laughing back to her, and whispered, "He has begged aunt Euphemia to stay with him over his wine. I am sure he means to ask her to marry him!"

"The man is daft-like enough to-day, but he'll not be so daft as that, bairn," answered aunt Elizabeth.

"I don't think that would be 'daft' at all, Aunt. It would be the wisest thing he could do. Aunt Euphemia would make him a capital wife."

Effie was right. In about a quarter of an hour aunt Euphemia came into the room, looking very much heated, and a good deal amused. The doctor followed, with his usual calm face and manner.

"I will wish you 'good-afternoon,' now, Miss Garnock. I have to see a patient at four o'clock. Miss Euphemia will explain to you the cause of my having taken advantage of your hospitality on this occasion. Good-afternoon, ladies."

"Well, aunt Euphemia, have you accepted him?" asked Effie, as soon as the doctor was gone.

"Why, bless your sharp eyes, bairn! How came you to guess what the man was wanting the day?"

"*Was* that what he was wanting, Euphemia?" cried her sister.

"It just was, then," answered Euphemia, laughing. "Eh, but I had grand work to keep from laughing in the body's face. What for should he be wanting *me* for a wife?"

"Why, Aunt, he could not have a better wife."

"I am no saying that I'd have been such a bad wife to a man, if one of them had had the sense to ask me twenty or thirty years back. I was not much of a beauty then, but I was a comely enough lassie, and no wanting for wits. But for a body to be wishing to marry upon an old gomeril like me—I'm thinking he'll no be in his right senses, puir man!" and the doctor's proposed bride indulged in a prolonged fit of laughter at his expense, in which her sisters and Effie heartily joined.

"But, aunt Euphemia, you have not refused him?" asked Effie, when they had somewhat recovered their gravity.

"Na, bairn. What for should I refuse him? I have aye been in the mind that a woman is never the better for being her lane. There was na one single creature went into the Ark—they were all just two and two—and that's the best way for us all— only it's the way that we canna' all manage to walk in.

I'd na be walking the world a single body the day, could I have met with an honest laddie to gi' me his hand when I was a lassie. And what for should I say 'no' to an honest man that bids me take his hand, though it is ower late in the day to be changing my gait? Eh, bairn, ye'll have your laugh at the old woman ganging to her bridal, when she should be thinking of ganging to her grave."

"I shall laugh for joy, Aunt. I like Dr. Lang, and I think he will make almost as good a husband as you deserve."

That same afternoon Effie had an opportunity of congratulating the bridegroom-elect. Dr. Lang overtook her as she was walking through the village.

"Good-evening, Miss Effie."

"Oh, Dr. Lang! Good-evening. I congratulate you. I am so glad to hear of your engagement to aunt Euphemia."

"I am glad it is settled myself," said the doctor, not quite so rapturously as might be expected in his position. "I have a great respect for Miss Euphemia. In fact, I consider her the most worthy person of my acquaintance, and I have no doubt she will make me a very excellent wife."

"She is a dear, good creature," said Effie. "So thoroughly unselfish."

"So I have understood."

"Aunt Euphemia seems to have been quite surprised at the honour you have done her."

"Yes. I should have been surprised myself last week if any one had told me what would occur."

"Indeed !"

"Indeed I should, Miss Effie. I will tell you how it all happened, if you are walking this way. I have a visit to pay on the Greenock Road."

"I shall be very glad to walk with you," said Effie, greatly amused with these unromantic confessions.

"I had not the slightest intention of marrying again till within the last month. I was perfectly comfortable in every respect. My servants understood my ways, and I had no fault to find with them. But last Thursday three weeks—no, it must have been Wednesday, for it was one of my dispensary days— my housekeeper, Mrs. Campbell, was summoned to attend her husband, who had met with an accident. His illness will likely be very protracted, and I see little chance of her returning to me. She was no sooner gone than everything went wrong. None of my meals were properly served, and my bed was often unmade during the whole forenoon."

"That was very bad management," observed Effie, as the doctor paused.

"Yes, was it not? Mrs. Caird came out one day, and found me in this said state of discomfort, and she persuaded me to return with her to Glasgow for the night. When I was there, she and Caird both spoke very seriously to me on the subject of marrying again, which, they said, would be a great relief to their minds, as they were sure I could not be so comfortable as a single man as I should be with a wife. I would not hear of it at first; but they went on so at me, pointing out to me all the disadvantages of my present condition, and the advantages to be expected from changing it, that at last I was fairly wearied out; and, for the sake of peace, I told them I would do as they wished if they would find me a suitable wife. Well, it seems they had often talked the matter over, for Mrs. Caird had a whole string of lady's names ready at once. I was positively bewildered by the number of them—some that I could not remember even to have seen—so I just begged her to make an orderly list of them, and I would consider of it. Between us we soon got the list down to seven, and your two aunts, Janet and Euphemia, were amongst them. Before I left we had struck out two more, and I had promised to think very seriously of those that remained. On my way home I heard something which made me strike out another, and then only your two aunts and two others remained. That was last Monday week. Well, I turned the whole four of them over in my mind all the week, and on Sunday I called on an old friend of mine in Gourock, and asked her advice on the subject; she was all for your

aunt Euphemia, so that decided me, and I determined to settle the matter the first spare half-hour
I had. To-day I got through a consultation sooner
than I expected, so I took advantage of the opportunity, and I do not at all regret it. This is my
destination, Miss Effie, so I must bid you good evening. Thank you for your company."

Effie hurried home, enjoying the idea of how she
would make aunt Elizabeth laugh at her future
brother-in-law's confessions; and, seeing her other
aunts at their bedroom windows, she went direct to
the drawing-room, full of her subject. A man's voice
arrested her at the door, with a sudden shock, and
there, close to the invalid's sofa, sat Gerard Yonge.
He turned very red as she entered, and then very
pale. She also felt that she turned pale, but with
surprise and confusion, she said to herself, not with
agitation.

"You see I have got a guest, bairn," said aunt
Elizabeth, in an unusually soft tone. " He'll have
been here half an hour—brightening an old woman's
day."

Gerard and Effie had shaken hands whilst aunt
Elizabeth was speaking, and Effie had contrived to
see that Gerard looked thin and old, but that his
expression was much pleasanter, and more like his
former self than it had been for the last five years.

"I have been walking with Dr. Lang, Aunt,"

she said, laughing again as she thought about that walk.

"Has he given you his—what is it?—avuncular blessing?" asked Gerard, looking shyly at her.

"He has given me his avuncular confidence," returned Effie, still laughing. "Aunt, I have such an amusing story to tell you."

But her aunt seemed to have lost all interest in Dr. Lang, and everything connected with him. Her eyes were fixed upon Gerard with a more than usually bright, eager look, and there was a brilliant red spot on each of her hollow cheeks. Effie was quite alarmed at her appearance.

"You are over-tired, dearest Aunt," she said, anxiously, leaning over the sofa.

"No, bairn, no," answered the old lady, rather impatiently.

"I have been boring you, Miss Garnock!" cried Gerard.

"Boring me!" repeated aunt Elizabeth, with a sharp laugh. "Na, laddie, you could na *bore* me— if that new-fangled word will be the same as *wearying*. I would na weary of gazing in your bonnie face, if you would sit there till I am carried to the kirkyard."

Gerard laughed, but there was something so unnaturally excited in her aunt's manner that Effie could not laugh.

" Eh, Effie, bairn, so ye're home again. You'll no be caring now for a walk, Mr. Gerard," said aunt Euphemia at the door, forgetting, in her own excited mood, the awkward relation in which Gerard and Effie stood towards each other.

" Yes, I should like a walk," said Gerard. " I want to see all I can, and I don't know how soon I may have to leave." He gave a quick, anxious glance at Effie as he spoke.

" Are you no coming, bairn ?" asked Euphemia, leaving the room.

" No, Aunt, I will stay with aunt Elizabeth."

Gerard coloured violently, and compressed his lips.

" Go, Effie," said the invalid, imperatively. " I wish you to go."

" Aunt, I would much rather stay with you. I want to tell you something."

" To pleasure me, Effie, will you go ?"

Effie was completely puzzled. Before her aunt spoke she had seen an appealing glance pass to her from Gerard, but he had directly left the room. Effie still hesitated.

" Janet !" cried Elizabeth Garnock, as the elder sister passed down the stairs, " take Effie with you. I wish her to go."

Effie could not resist any longer. Before they got out of the house, aunt Elizabeth's sharp voice was heard again. " Janet, I want to say a word to you."

Miss Garnock went back for a few minutes, and by the time she returned to start off with Effie the other couple were far in advance. Aunt Janet walked slowly, and aunt Euphemia very fast, so that the distance increased, instead of decreasing, till the latter looked round, and, perceiving them, slackened her pace, but not enough to allow them to come up with her.

"I would be glad if sister Euphemia did not carry her years so like a lassie," said Miss Garnock, presently. "I am wishing to speak with her, and she will no heed me if I cry on her at this distance. Run, Effie, and tell her to bide for me."

This was a most distasteful errand to Effie, who felt very shy of Euphemia's companion, but she dared not resist the will of her kind, but dignified aunt. She ran on, therefore, and, arriving breathless, touched aunt Euphemia on the arm.

"Eh, bairn! how ye startled me! Sister Janet is wanting me? And here have I been so taken up wi' this braw young callant that I had no ears nor eyes for any other body. I'm thinking I'd get my pawnies, if I had my desert," and the good-natured woman hurried back to her sister, Effie following close.

"I'm thinking, Euphemia," said aunt Janet, "that it would be a deed of kindness to call for Mrs. Cameron, since we have come so far."

"Yes, sister Janet. But what will we do with Mr. Gerard here? He'll no think it much of a diversion to be calling for a sick body."

"Effie can take him on to the Cloch—the young folks will be all the blither without us."

"I should like to call on Mrs. Cameron, aunt Janet," cried Effie, greatly embarrassed and distressed.

"Another day, Effie. Euphemia and myself will be quite enough company for the poor body this evening."

"Do come with me, Effie," said Gerard, in a very low, and most beseeching tone.

As her aunts had already gone towards Mrs. Cameron's gate, Effie saw no possibility of escape, so she turned with Gerard. Both were silent as they walked slowly along the quiet, shaded road, and heard, without heeding, the gentle waves playing with the pebbles on the beach. At length Gerard asked, abruptly, "What are your plans, Effie?"

"My plans?" repeated Effie, very much startled by the question.

"Yes. What do you mean to do? Where do you mean to live for the future?"

"I mean to live here—always. I am very happy here. My aunts are so kind—and it is so peaceful." There was a weary tone in her voice as she said this, which touched Gerard deeply.

"You have certainly not had much peace hitherto,"

he cried. "You know that Harold refuses to forgive Jessie?" he added, after a short pause.

"Yes. I am very sorry."

"So am I. Sorry and angry too. It is too bad of Harold."

"I think it is. Jessie is very different now to what she was."

"Yes. She used to try Harold terribly. But I believe now she has had a lesson which she will not soon forget. There *are* such lessons, Effie." Gerard gave Effie a strange, eager look as he said this.

Effie bore it with perfect composure. As she had told George, Gerard's presence now hardly quickened her pulse.

"Do you think Harold will ever come round?" asked Gerard, presently.

"I do not know what to think, now. It was very long before I gave up hope."

"*I* have not given up hope yet. Somehow it will all come right, I feel sure. And they will be all the happier for this. Jessie is learning to appreciate Harold, now she has lost him. That is the way." Again that pointed tone and look.

"Just when he is proving himself to be unworthy of her," cried Effie, indignantly.

"He is not himself now, Effie. I have ecclesiastical sanction for saying so," said Gerard, laughing faintly. "But he will come round. You see if he does not. I bet you that in ten years they will be a thorough Darby and Joan."

"I hope you may be a true prophet."

"But in the meantime," continued Gerard, "why should not you go home to Jessie and the children?"

"I am much better here," answered Effie, quickly. "I can do no mischief here."

"Effie! don't speak so. *You* do mischief."

"I do, indeed. When things go wrong I cannot help interfering, and then I get into trouble."

"But you yourself own that Jessie is so different— she would not be jealous of you now."

"She is very much improved, certainly; but ——"

"Do you not believe in reformations, Effie?" in a husky tone. "Do you not believe

"'That men may rise on stepping-stones
Of their dead selves to higher things'?"

"Not much—no, I ought not to say that. I do believe in Jessie's reformation. But I think she is better without me. She is forced to act for herself now, and that does her good. And then it is best for her to have the children to herself."

"You know that Davie and Walter have gone to school?"

"Yes; I am glad of it. Jessie could not have managed them all, especially now that Hannah is married."

"Then you are bent on staying here to distribute

blankets and ladle out porridge?" asked Gerard, when they had walked on in silence for some time. He had seen her do this for some pensioners of her aunts, the night before Jessie's marriage. This remembrance of that far-off time moved Effie much more than his presence now had the power to move her. She could not answer him at once.

"Are you quite determined to stay here, Effie?" Gerard asked again.

"Quite. There is nothing else to be done. You know I once tried taking a situation as governess, and Harold came and fetched me home, as if I had been a runaway child. That was a terrible mistake."

"Yes—as it turned out. But I could never have forgiven Harold if he had allowed you to remain there."

Effie could hardly bear this, for it was spoken in the old tender tone, which had been music to her for so many years. She could not force herself to say a word, but the silence was broken by Gerard exclaiming, vehemently, "Effie! how good you were to me when I was—when I was in that trouble! And at the Falcon that horrid night! How can I ever make any return to you? How can I ever show you how much I—" his voice failed, and he stopped abruptly.

The sight of Gerard's emotion restored Effie's composure. "Those were mere acts of humanity," she said. "No one could have done less for a friend."

"You are the only person in the world who would have done so much for me, Effie. To think of your little white figure gliding in amongst all those tipsy beasts—when I was the worst beast of the lot! And then to see you at that den! Effie! how boorishly I treated you that night! And you were wet through, too! What a night it was! It seemed all a dream till I got to Boulogne. I have no fear of Mr. Raynes now, Effie," he added, with a sudden air of triumph. "I am free. You will never again be called upon to do that 'act of humanity' for a friend." How well Effie remembered that hurt tone in Gerard's voice!

"You mean that you have freed yourself?" she asked, eagerly.

"Yes, I snapped the last rivet yesterday, and came off here directly. Effie, I have been talking to your aunt Elizabeth—she wished me success—she sent you to me now. Will you—"

Effie hastily interrupted him. "You must have been working very hard for the last year."

"I was fortunate in getting plenty of work. And I had an object."

"Were you at Boulogne all the time?"

"Near Boulogne. At a little place called Wimereux. A wretched wilderness, but just the place for me. I could do nothing but work. You will not ask what spurred me on to work, Effie."

Effie was frightened at his earnestness. He seemed to be trying to probe her feelings, and she had not yet probed them herself. She hesitated.

" Shall I tell you ?"

" No—yes—if you like."

" That half-hour in a cab that—that 12th of June. They say that drowning men see their whole past life. I saw mine then. I saw how you had trusted me, and I had deceived you—how, when every one else cast me off, you still believed I was not all bad— and, when I had become almost as bad as they thought me, you were still willing to be my friend— my Guardian Angel—" He broke down again, and Effie was hardly less overcome. " I vowed that your trust should not be in vain," Gerard went on, with a great effort. " Perhaps I might have failed," he added, " as I had so often failed before. But, happily for me, I fell in with George and Harry Monro at Boulogne, and was able to be some help to them. And then — their exaggerated gratitude gave me more hope of myself, and so— Effie! finish the work for me !" He stopped, and stood before her, looking in her face, with anxious, eager eyes.

Effie only shook her head gently.

Gerard went on: " I do not ask for your love—I know that I have forfeited that beyond recall. And

I do not offer you my love—for I know that you have every right to doubt—even to scorn it. But I ask you to consider whether you might not be happier, and do more good as my wife, than as the almoner of your aunts. Effie! you are wasted here, but if you would come to me—oh, Effie! I would strive, as never man has striven before, to make myself more worthy of you—to undo the wrong I once did you—to make up for all that you have suffered."

Gerard's appeal to her for help had almost vanquished Effie, and, though doubtful both of his feelings and of her own, she had been half inclined to yield to the old childish pity for Gerard's weakness. Whilst she hesitated, he had spoken again, and then all was changed. In his generous repentance he would marry her to rescue her from her present dependent and isolated condition, and to atone to her for the past. If she could do *him* good, that was a temptation; but if he was to sacrifice himself to do *her* good, that should never be.

" Effie, would it be impossible for us to be again to each other what we once were ?"

" Quite impossible," said Effie, in a low, decided tone.

" You think me presumptuous for having fancied it could be ?" asked Gerard, with sad humility.

" No, no," cried Effie. " Not that. But what you

propose could not—could not make either of us happy.
Do you believe it could ?"

" Yes—yes. Indeed I do, Effie. I know it would
make me happy. Trust me once more, Effie. Give
me a chance. Give me a chance of redeeming my
character with you. Give me a chance of wiping off
my disgrace in your eyes—in my own eyes. You
do not know—*you* can never know—what it is to
despise oneself—to feel that one has forfeited the
respect of all good men—even all self-respect. You
could save me from this, Effie. If you would stretch
out a helping hand to me I could rise again—I know
I could. But if you will not— Effie! who said,
' Take care of Gerard '?"

Effie was deeply moved. But five years of suffering cannot pass away, and leave no trace. The heart
that is not broken by disappointment, is hardened by
it. All her doubts would once have melted before
Gerard's pleading voice and loving eyes, but she had
learnt, in a bitter school, to distrust that voice and
those eyes. And there was no longer anything within
herself to second their suit—for she believed what
she had said to George, that she no longer loved
Gerard.

" No, Gerard," she murmured, sadly, as soon as she
could command her voice. " It would be of no use.
It is of no use to try and revive a corpse. It is better
to bury it out of sight."

"You mean that all that was once between us is now a corpse."

"Yes. Is it not?"

"I suppose so. You mean that you—that you do not care for me at all, now."

"I care for you very much."

"But—you know what I mean—that you do not love me."

"No."

"No! Oh, Effie, speak plainly. Do you mean that you do, or you do not?"

"That I do not."

"Fool that I have been!" exclaimed Gerard, bitterly; and then he walked on in silence, looking very miserable. Effie felt tempted to disregard prudence and consistency, and to comfort him, at any cost. She was thinking how to set about this work, when he spoke again.

"You have not forgiven me, Effie."

"Indeed I have. There was nothing to forgive. I was as much to blame as you were."

"*You* to blame?" cried Gerard. "But you are sure you forgive me?"

"I forgave you—if there was anything to forgive—directly it all happened."

"Then it is not that that makes you—that made you say what you did just now?"

"No, indeed it was not."

"I fancied, somehow, that *you* could not change." Gerard said this mournfully, not reproachfully; but Effie took it as a reproach, and answered, rather fiercely, "One can do a great deal in five years."

Gerard gave her a quick, scrutinising glance. "I suppose I must not ask if—if there is any one else?"

"No; you have no right to ask that," answered Effie, still fiercely, for she was stung by his suspicion that she could so entirely change as to care for any one else.

"I beg your pardon," said Gerard, and they walked on in perfect silence, till Effie suddenly remembered that they were going away from home, and that it was almost dark.

"We had better turn now," she said; and Gerard turned, without a word.

When they had retraced about half the distance, Effie could bear the silence no longer, and began talking on indifferent subjects. Gerard replied constrainedly, though not sullenly, to all her observations. At the gate of her aunts' house he said, "I cannot come in, Effie. I hope they won't be angry. I could not face any one just now. Good-bye." He held her hand for a minute, without speaking, and then turned abruptly away.

The aunts were not angry, but very much disappointed, at their visitor's sudden flight; and when the others went down to supper, aunt Elizabeth called Effie back.

" You have na said him nay, bairn ?"

" Dear Aunt, what could I say ?"

" Dinna tell me you no longer love yon laddie, Effie."

" Aunt, dear Aunt, I do not love him—not as I did."

" Not love him, bairn! I could look into those bonnie eyes for ever. Not love him, Effie! He is just his father's living image. Frederick Yonge will have been ten years younger than yon laddie when last I saw him, but the eyes, and the voice, and the winsome manner, they are just the same. Oh, Effie, you should na have driven him from you. He would have made you a happy woman, lassie."

Effie burst into tears. She was half repenting what she had done, and now her aunt's reproaches made her still more regret it. And yet, after a night of meditation, she could not make up her mind to reverse her decision. She had taken such pains to cure herself of loving Gerard, and the habit of distrusting him had grown too deeply rooted to be easily cast off.

When, early the next morning, Gerard came to say " good-bye," looking pale and miserable, she was almost shaken again ; but there was no opportunity then for any explanation. He had only a few minutes to spare, and aunt Elizabeth monopolised them.

" You will let me see your face again before I die,

laddie," said the impulsive old lady, raising his hand to her lips and kissing it. Gerard stooped and kissed her forehead, and when he turned to Effie his eyes were full of tears.

"You never displeasured me in your life but this once, Effie," said aunt Elizabeth, when he was gone.

CHAPTER VIII.

AUNT EUPHEMIA'S quiet wedding took place in September; and in the following December another event occurred to change the course of that little household, which had once seemed so far out of the possibility of any change but one.

Effie, sitting at breakfast with Miss Garnock, was occupied with letters from Jessie and the boys, when she was startled by a sudden movement on the part of her aunt, who had also received letters. The old lady had covered her face with her long thin fingers, and presently her whole body was shaken by three or four dry sobs.

"Dearest Aunt!" cried Effie.

Aunt Janet rose, and pushing some papers towards Effie, slowly left the room. The packet bore the post-mark "New York." First Effie read, in a clear, business-like hand:

"MADAM,

"I regret to inform you that my client, Mr. Walter Garnock, died at his residence, in this city, at three o'clock A.M. on the 11th ultimo. He was in the full possession of his faculties, and was surrounded by all the members of his family. He will be much regretted by a numerous circle of aquaintance. His very flourishing mercantile affairs are to be conducted by trustees, until his son shall be of an age to succeed to their management. A promising estate in the West devolves upon the second son. The daughters are also amply provided for.

"I have great pleasure in informing you that, by the will of my late client, I am empowered to invest for the benefit of yourself and your sisters, Miss Elizabeth Garnock, and Miss Euphemia Garnock, in any manner which you may please respectively to direct, the sum of twenty thousand pounds sterling, in three equal shares. Hoping for the favour of an early communication of your wishes,

"I remain, Madam,

"Your obedient Servant,

"WOLFE MASON."

Enclosed was a half-sheet of paper, scrawled over with uncertain characters:

"November 8th.

"DEAR SISTER JANET,

"They tell me that my time here is nearly up. This doom has come suddenly upon me— though I am not a young man. I am leaving five

children, who will want for nothing but good friends.
They are all that children should not be, and they
bid fair to disgrace our name even more than my
father thought David and I did. If I could have put
them under your care, they might have had a chance.
I once thought of asking you to come out to me—but
it is too late now. They must take their chance.
The eldest is a girl of fifteen, and quite ready to take
her part in all the frivolity of all our fashionables
here. I never heard how my father provided for his
daughters, but I have made some mention of you
all in my will, in remembrance of old times. For the
sake of those old times, Janet, will you take pity on
my orphans? I thought I would not ask so much of
you—but a dying man grows desperate. If they are
left to their mother's family there is no chance for
them; their uncles are dissipated blackguards, and
their aunts heartless flirts. I should like to think
they would learn some good. They will be very
rich. There is no good to be got in their life now.
You might make something of them. I know I have
not deserved it of you, but you were always good,
kind girls.

" WALTER GARNOCK."

Effie had seldom heard her aunts speak of this, their
eldest brother. She knew that, after a wild youth,
some disgraceful circumstances had obliged him to

leave Scotland, and that he had settled in America. His sisters had learnt of his marriage with a rich New York beauty, and of his increasing wealth; but they had never heard directly from himself, although they had frequently written. It seemed hardly possible that they should grieve very deeply for one who had given so little proof of any natural feeling; but the warm-hearted old ladies forgot everything but their early days of companionship and love, and mourned for this reprobate exile as though he had been the best and most affectionate of men.

Aunt Janet was prepared to add to her mourning a more striking proof of devotion to her brother's memory.

"Doctor, when will there likely be a ship sailing for New York?" she asked, when Dr. Lang came to condole with his sisters-in-law, the same evening that the news arrived.

"I will make inquiries, if you wish it, Miss Janet," replied the doctor, with a surprised expression.

"I do wish it, doctor, and will be grateful to you."

"She's meaning to take that awfu' journey, doctor," sobbed out aunt Euphemia. "And we'll never set eyes on her again."

"Do your brother's affairs require——" began Dr. Lang.

"My brother has left five orphans, who are needing

a mother's care," said aunt Janet, in her stately manner.

" And you intend going to them ?"

" I am wishing to start by the first ship that sails."

" Had you not better wait till the weather is more settled ?"

" The bairns are desolate in a wicked city," was all the answer.

" You would wish me to make inquiries at once, then," said the business-like doctor. " I will soon return."

These inquiries resulted in the information that a fast steamer to New York would start in nine days. Any one less resolute than Miss Garnock would have been daunted at the idea of so short a preparation for such a momentous change—but she was dauntless. Her whole mind seemed to be occupied with the children to whom she was going, and she had no thoughts to spare for the voyage—no inconsiderable undertaking for one whose travels had never exceeded thirty miles. She made all her arrangements with her usual calm dignity, and even at the last, though her voice failed as she bent over her invalid sister, she never lost her perfect self-possession. Aunt Euphemia and Effie had worn themselves out in the necessary preparations, and they had hardly had time to think of the blank that was to be made amongst them. But poor aunt Elizabeth, lying on her sofa, had time for all sad thoughts ; and when the parting was over, and the brave old lady had left the home which she never expected to see again, then all Effie's energies were taxed to rouse and cheer the bereaved sister. How glad she felt now that she had not been tempted to leave Gourock by Gerard's representation of her life being wasted there! She had never been more necessary to any one than she was now to her invalid aunt, and the old lady was quite ready to acknowledge it.

" What would have become of me if yon bonnie laddie had carried you away, bairn ?" she would say, affectionately.

" You want me more than he does, don't you, Aunt ?"

"I'd carry a sore heart if I were missing you, lassie. But I'll no give in that you were in the right to cast away the love of a good man."

" Aunt, it was not love he offered me ; it was only pity."

" Effie, you have not your ordinary quick sight in that matter. The lad may have had his faults—as which of us has not ? but he loved you well yon day that he came wooing, with his bonnie, bashful face."

Another favourite topic with aunt Elizabeth in these dull winter days was equally distressing to Effie.

" A heavy weight is lifted from my heart, bairn,"

she said one day, soon after her sister's departure. " I am a poor, faithless body to have let it lie there ; but it is no easy to cast all our care where we are bid. and I had aye an over-careful mind."

" What was your care, Aunt ?"

" Just the 'unrighteous mammon,' bairn—just the treasures that the moth and rust corrupt."

" Aunt, how dare you say anything so false ? You never gave a thought to such things."

" Not for myself, Effie. But it has been a sore trouble to me to think that one of those days—whenever I am laid in my resting-place—you would likely have to work for your maintenance—for I know that you would never more be dependent upon Harold Yonge."

" That I would not. But do not let us be dismal, Aunt."

" There is no longer need, bairn. The old body's pelf will not all perish with her, now. God forgive me ! Many's the time I ha' been tempted to blame my poor father's memory for that fashious bit of an annuity, that would rob Davie's bairns of their father's lawful inheritance. But that is over now, and I will carry a light heart to my dying-bed, to think that my bairn will be independent of Harold Yonge, and every other body."

But, before the spring, aunt Elizabeth had a subject for her thoughts which swallowed up every

other consideration. Dr. Lang recommended that
she should undertake a journey to London, to consult
an eminent surgeon, who had been most remarkably
successful in cases of spinal disease. The doctor had
not offered this advice before, knowing that her
means were too limited to meet the inevitable expenses of such a move. The old lady was first
scornful at the suggestion, then half-angry, and finally
excited. The idea once put into her head, she could
not rest till it was carried out, and before many days,
she was as eager as a child for everything to be
settled. Effie was very doubtful of the wisdom of
the step. A cure was utterly hopeless, and the slight
alleviation of suffering which might be gained seemed
hardly worth the risk attending the journey. She
was forced to keep her doubts to herself, however,
after a fruitless endeavour to communicate them to
Dr. Lang, for any opposition in her present excited
state, would have been more injurious to the invalid
than the experiment on which she had set her wishes.
So, with a heavy heart, but with cheerful looks, Effie
went about all the necessary preparations.

Jessie found a suitable, quiet lodging in Park
Village; and the 15th of May was fixed on for the
important start. By the evening of the 14th, aunt
Elizabeth had worked herself into such a fever of
nervous agitation, that Dr. Lang was very doubtful
whether she would be well enough for the journey

the next day—though it was only to be as far as Mrs. Caird's house at Glasgow, where the travellers were to rest one night.

"Bairn, will we bide where we are, and never fash our heads any more with yon great London doctors?" asked the invalid, suddenly.

Effie, to whom her uncle had communicated his fears, caught at the suggestion. "If you like, Aunt. I should like it."

"You are no caring that I would have to give up hope of losing this weary pain, then, Effie?"

"Yes, dearest Aunt, I care very much. But if you dread the journey——"

"I'm no dreading the journey, bairn. What for should I dread the journey, when Janet carried a good heart to her far travels, and went through them, too, with never a let? What for should you think I'd dread the journey, bairn?"

"It is different for you, aunt Elizabeth, not being strong. Aunt Janet is so vigorous."

"I am not such a poor, feeble body as you think, lassie. It is aye the will that does the work, and I have a good will to be eased of my burden. 'A wilfu' woman maun ha' her way,' you know, Effie, so you had best not say me nay."

"Then I may go on with my packing, Aunt. I was just putting in your grand wedding silk."

"I'll never need it more, lassie. You'd far better

put up my shroud—I'll be needing that the sooner of the twain. Ah, Effie, I'm fearing it will be awfu' dreary for you to be left your lane in a fremd road-side inn. I never thought but to have been laid in my ain kirkyard, where my father and my mother are side by side. But there's puir Davie lying his lane in Devonshire, and I'll be laid past like a worn-out garment, in some heathenlike cemetery, or what-ever they call it—where never a body that passes will ken the name of Garnock."

"Aunt, dear Aunt, don't have such melancholy fancies."

"They are not fancies, bairn. It is na for naething that my mind is aye dwelling on one of those uncanny burying-grounds, that are no like our own holy kirk-yard. You'll no let me be laid there, lassie? Gi' me your promise, Effie." The poor old lady caught Effie's arm, and looked in her face with nervous eagerness.

"I promise, Aunt. Won't you come to bed, now?"

"I canna sleep, bairn. Night after night have I lain on my weary bed, and never closed an eye till the bonnie morning light came glinting in at the window. What good do I get of my bed when I canna sleep?"

"That must be Dr. Lang again," said Effie, as the gate-bell rang softly.

"I'll no see him. I am not needing him. I canna' be fashed with him again the night."

Effie hurried out of the room, and at the top of the stairs met Gerard.

"You are surprised to see me," he said, laughing, as he took her hand. "I have come to know if a pair of strong arms will be of any use to you on your journey."

"Let us go into the dining-room. Aunt Elizabeth is——"

"That's no the doctor's voice," cried the invalid. "Effie, is it Frederick Yonge?"

"Go to her, Gerard."

"It is a heavy porter come to move your luggage," answered Gerard, as he went up to the sofa.

Aunt Elizabeth caught his hand with both hers, and sinking back on her pillow looked into his face with speechless content.

"You dinna mean that you are come to bide with us, laddie?" she said at last, in a hoarse whisper.

"As long as you will have me. I shall not leave you, at any rate, till you take possession of Beulah Cottage."

"Are we to possess a 'Beulah Cottage?'" cried Effie, laughing, in her intense relief at the change in her aunt since Gerard's arrival.

"You'll cleave to us all the far journey, lad?"

"You speak as if I were a limpet. Yes, just so.

Like a limpet to a rock," and he gave a quick, conscious glance at Effie, colouring as he met her eye.

"'His mercy endureth for ever,'" murmured the old lady, shutting her eyes, and remaining for a few minutes as though in devout thanksgiving. Three or four tears rolled slowly down her withered cheeks, and then she looked at Gerard again with a bright smile. She was still holding his hand.

" You have come to me the night, laddie, like a good angel, to be my stay and comfort on the way that lies before me," she said, solemnly.

" You will have no more fears about the journey, now, Aunt," said Effie, seeing that Gerard was too much surprised and moved by her aunt's earnestness to have any words at command.

" No, my bairn. My mind is at rest now. Shame on me, for a faithless old body, that I should ever have doubted help would come. I will go to my bed now, lassie. You may cry upon Isabella."

" I think she has gone out, Aunt."

" Can't I take Isabella's place?" asked Gerard.

" Will you?" said aunt Elizabeth, eagerly.

" Is it to carry you to your room? I am an adept at that. I used to lift Harry Monro about like a child, when he lost his leg. And he is twelve times your weight, I should think."

" I am not very heavy," said the old lady, as the

powerful young man raised her gently in his arms, and bore her, lying flat like a baby, into the next room.

"The first painless move I ever had," she said, as he laid her on her bed. " Now, laddie, you will be needing some sustenance after your journey. Effie, we are a pair of clever bodies to have suffered a guest to be famishing whilst we were full of our own matters!"

" I have told Cook to take the tray into the dining-room," replied Effie, quietly.

" Then go away, laddie, and stay your hunger—you will likely have had never a bit in your mouth the whole day."

" I had a capital breakfast in Glasgow this morning. But I'll go now. I suppose it would not be discreet to stay any longer. I might discover that, as Bessie said to Mrs. Mortlake the other day, Effie, before us all, 'You don't look so pretty with your hair in a box.' "

" You'll no be daring to insinuate that I wear a wig, you wicked young pickle," cried the old lady, in high glee.

" If I come in again in half an hour I shall see it hanging by the side of the glass. There's the box it lives in. I am sure that's a wig box!"

" Woe's you, if you meddle with my braw new bonnet. Effie, you'll just be forced to show him the other side of the door. It's no proper that a big callant like yon should be diverting himself with all my bit vanities. Bless the lad! what will he be making of my fine wedding cap? If he is na looking as vain of himself as a bit silly lassie! Effie, you maun save the wee perishable thing from his rash hands; it will just be no fit to be seen after being stuck in that daft-like fashion on the top of all those toozie curls."

Effie could do nothing but watch her aunt's delighted face, as Gerard prowled round the room, and took unwarrantable liberties with all the articles of dress that were scattered about, in readiness for packing. It was more than six years, too, since she had seen Gerard in such a mood as this, and it seemed so like old times that she was almost as happy as her aunt.

"If you dinna cease making free with my wardrobe, I'll just have to cry on the police."

"It is utterly impossible that all these things should go into that box. It's just like Effie to think it could be done. I fancy I see her toiling away at it—black in the face, and pressing her lips together, as if that would make the lid go down. If I put this cap in the box like a good boy, may I come in and see her pack to-morrow morning."

"You have just made awful work of the poor bit cappie."

"What a shame to say so! There's not a frill rumpled! Here, Effie, catch! Now I am going. Good-night. I have not made you ill with anxiety for the best cap, have I?" he said, kindly, as he stood by the bed-side.

"You little know how the sight o' your bonny face, and the sound o' your blithe voice has been even as a new life to me, laddie. I will not be dying by the roadside now, Effie, and leaving you alone amongst strangers."

"Was that what you meant to do?" asked Gerard. "I am glad you have changed your mind. I am not going to stand anything of that sort. Shall I see you again to-night, Effie?"

"You'll no go away to-night," cried aunt Elizabeth. "I would sleep all the better if you were biding under my roof."

"I'll come the first thing in the morning. Before that beautiful silver-grey front is out of its box. Good-night."

"Effie, I thought I was a bit lassie again, and Frederick Yonge was carrying me across a burn. And it was just his very self—the saucy sailor laddie —when yon bonnie face glinted out from under the border of my Sabbath-day cap."

The old lady was full of tender reminiscences of her boy-lover, and fond admiration of his son all the while that Effie was putting her to bed; but ten

minutes after she lay down she had fallen into a
quiet sleep.

"I think you are a wizard, Gerard," said Effie, as
she went into the drawing-room. "My aunt is
asleep already, for the first time for more than a
fortnight."

"I was afraid I might have tired her too much.
She looks very ill."

"Yes. She has been worrying herself so about
this move. I was quite in despair about her this
evening. She had the most dismal forebodings, and
yet she would not give up the journey. But she is a
different creature since you came."

"I am so glad I came."

"What happy inspiration prompted you to come?"

"I thought of it when first Jessie asked me about
the lodging for you, but I was not sure I could manage
it then."

"It was very good of you. Did Jessie inflict on
you the task of getting our lodging?"

"The task was much more in my line than in hers.
I am a connoisseur in lodgings. I think you and
Miss Garnock will be comfortable at Beulah Cottage.
A friend of mine used to live there. Such a cha-
racter, Effie! I should like you to know him.
He was for thirty years a missionary in Borneo,
and now that he has come home on a visit he is
doing much the same work in all the lowest parts

of London. You and he would get on capitally together."

"Have you known him long?"

"Only since last September. But we are great friends."

"You cannot have many interests in common," said Effie, laughing.

"More than you think," replied Gerard, gravely, looking rather hurt. "But we have strayed a long way from Beulah Cottage," he added, presently. "The landlady is great fun. She enjoys an unsubstantiated claim to having fallen from some such giddy eminence as a wholesale shop in the City. You must make up your mind to have her former greatness thrown at you every time you order the dinner, and at every other opportunity. But she is a very good cook, and the furniture and things look clean and comfortable. I hope it will be all right."

"Aunt Elizabeth is sure to think it perfect, as you have had to do with it."

"And you are sure to think it imperfect for the same reason," said Gerard, with rather a tremulous laugh, and a wistful glance at Effie.

"I shall be quite satisfied if we only get there safely."

"You have been worrying yourself, Effie."

"How could I help being anxious? I feel, somehow, responsible for this move, though I have always opposed it. But there seems to be no one but me now to take care of aunt Elizabeth."

" How plucky it was of your elder aunt to start off as she did ! Fancy the old grenadier, with her straight back, going full tilt to break a lance against the Yankees—a gallant Crusader vowed to the rescue of five young Scots, taken captive by the fashionable world of New York."

" You are laughing at her, Gerard."

" Indeed I am not. I honour her immensely. How does she get on with the American connections?"

" Very well. Aunt Janet is sure to get on well everywhere. She gives a better character of the children than their father did. She seems quite pleased with the two boys and the youngest girl."

" Will I clear away the tray, miss?" asked the cook, appearing at the door.

" Have you taken care of yourself, Gerard?"

" I quite forgot it!" cried Gerard, laughing. " I am not hungry. Never mind anything now. It is late—I shall be keeping you up."

" You must take something. Aunt Elizabeth is sure to ask me directly she wakes."

" Will you come down with me, then ?"

When they got down Gerard only poured himself out some wine and water.

" Are you not well, Gerard ?"

" Yes, quite well. Do I look like an interesting invalid ? I had better go now, I suppose. Good-night."

" Thank you so much for coming."

" I came for my own pleasure. I had no idea Miss Garnock would think so much of it. I hope she won't be any the worse for my treatment of her cap."

" Nothing could have been better for her than your treatment of her altogether. She has gone to sleep full of you and your father, instead of all the horrors of the journey, which have lately occupied her mind all night—and all day too."

" What a good thing that I am like my father ! Good-night, Effie."

Gerard appeared the next morning before aunt Elizabeth was ready for him, but not before she had begun to listen eagerly for his arrival. He was very much disappointed to find that Effie had finished all the packing, but he consoled himself by various ludicrous representations of all the processes, such as he imagined them to have been, and so contrived to keep the invalid occupied and amused till it was time to start. Dr. Lang, who came with his wife to see the party off, expressed to Effie his satisfaction at the wonderful improvement in his sister-in-law since the previous evening.

This happy state of things continued throughout

the journey. Aunt Elizabeth seemed quite to enjoy the sail up the Clyde, lying comfortably propped up with pillows on the deck of the steamboat, with Gerard sitting by her side. Those two were so engrossed with each other that Effie would have felt quite solitary had it not been for an occasional quick glance from Gerard, which seemed to claim her sympathy in their amusement. At Kelvin Crescent the invalid held her court in one of the drawing-rooms, which was given up to her use, and quite fascinated all the Cairds, from the impulsive mother down to the timid Jamie. Gerard, also, made such good use of his time that, before they left the next morning, he had become like an old friend of the family.

The railway journey, which had been a terrible bugbear, went forward merrily enough; and when they stopped for the night at Carlisle aunt Elizabeth expressed great indignation against "those fearsome bodies that make such a work about a bit ride at the tail of a kettle." When they reached London the old lady's disappointment at finding it "no so far unlike any ordinary big town," was as amusing as Isabella's firm conviction that every one she saw was either a pickpocket, or the Lord Mayor. Their land-lady came smilingly forward to welcome the travellers to Beulah Cottage, and conducted them into a little drawing-room, with a bedroom adjoining, which aunt Elizabeth declared to be quite perfect.

"I think you will find the hapartments clean, though 'umble, ma'am," said the hostess, with mournful dignity.

"They seem very nice rooms," said Effie.

"I 'ave hendeavoured to give them a better style than is husually found in similar hapartments."

"You see it is such an advantage your knowing how things ought to be, Mrs. Heaton," remarked Gerard, with a mischievous look at Effie.

"Yes, sir, in some respects it is an hadvantage. Though, on the hother 'and, 'aving been haccustomed to move in such a different sphere of life, I am not always haware of what may be required."

She looked at aunt Elizabeth as she spoke, and the old lady's quick sympathies were instantly aroused.

"You'll have seen trouble, I am fearing. Change of condition is aye a heavy cross to bear."

"Yes, ma'am, it is, hindeed. And those who 'ave fallen from a 'igher hestate meet with few who can hunderstand the hanguish——"

"Effie, come and see the rest of the house," whispered Gerard.

But when they had left the room he only asked, "Will the fall of the noble house of Heaton be good or bad for your aunt? If you think it will bore her I will stop the old lady's mouth."

"Perhaps to-night we had better save her from it. But I don't think anything would worry her when you are by. Gerard, how *can* we thank you for all you have done for us? I did so dread this journey, and it has been quite pleasant!"

" I have liked it immensely. Now, to the rescue! Mrs. Heaton, will you be kind enough to tell your servants that Miss Garnock would like some tea? I would not trouble you, only I forget the parlour-maid's name. There is only one unfortunate maid-of-all-work," he added, when the woman had left the room. " But I believe Mrs. Heaton has a vague sense of a butler. You think this will do, Miss Garnock?"

" 'Miss Garnock' will no do, laddie."

Gerard turned very red, and looked at Effie.

" Effie will think I am trespassing on her ground if I call you Aunt," he said.

" Effie has nothing to say in the matter."

"Then we won't care about her," said Gerard, laughing. "Very well, Aunt. Now, I must go."

" Will you no bide for your tea, laddie?"

" No, I must not. Good-night, Aunt."

" You'll come early to-morrow? You will not forget us now you have brought us to your big city."

" No fear of that. But you will be sick of me if I come too often."

" You cannot come too often for me, laddie."

" For Effie, then. She says nothing."

" Effie has no voice in the matter."

"Then I am to come in spite of her. And if she objects we will turn her out. Shall we?"

"She'll not object. Bless you, laddie."

"Good-night, Effie."

"Why should *I* object to your coming, Gerard."

"I thought you might, perhaps. I thought I might be too much for your aunt. You must tell me if I am."

When Effie began to explore, she found, in a pretty little sitting-room next to the drawing-room, various pieces of furniture which had been called hers at Pixycombe, and something else which made her start back with surprise and delight, and after a few minutes run to her aunt.

"Oh, aunt Elizabeth!" she cried, "one of the rooms is hung with portraits of Jessie and the children! Such beautiful water-colour drawings! They must be Gerard's."

"Eh, bairn, you are no wise to set light by yon laddie's honest heart."

Effie did not remind her aunt that "yon laddie" had once set very light by *her* honest heart.

CHAPTER IX.

THE surgical treatment adopted towards aunt Elizabeth was sufficiently successful to satisfy Effie that
the journey to London had not been undertaken in
vain.   Although Mr. Stamper, the surgeon whose
renown had led to that journey, gave no hope of
any radical improvement, he very soon succeeded in
allaying the suffering which had been unceasing for
more than twenty years.   But the constant visits of
her doctor, added to the sudden change in a life
which had been so long unvaried, kept the old lady
constantly in the same unnatural excitement which
had so troubled Effie before they left Gourock, and
this excitement was only to be subdued by Gerard's
presence.   Fortunately, Gerard seemed always to
have time to loiter away at Beulah Cottage—playing
boyish pranks or making ludicrous sketches when
the invalid wanted cheering, and talking gravely
with her when she wanted soothing.   When, at
length, he persuaded her to let him take her portrait,

there was an excuse for a daily visit of several hours. Effie could not understand Gerard. She knew that he had become rather famous as a portrait-painter, and was overwhelmed with professional engagements, and yet he was always at leisure to amuse her aunt. She knew that he had paid all his debts, and was making money rapidly, and yet he lived like a poor man. There was a mystery about him, in spite of his frank boyish manner, and his bright face. Effie constantly caught herself striving to read the riddle, and then felt ashamed of her curiosity.

Her own position towards him was changed, too, in a remarkable manner. From their childhood she had been accustomed to take the upper hand with the easy-tempered boy, and it had been an understood thing amongst them all that Gerard was one who could not be trusted to go alone. Now she began to discover, to her surprise, that he had broken his leading-strings, and had got the upper hand of *her*. There was a manly self-respect about him, in striking contrast to his former weak self-distrust. And, in the same degree, his former inordinate deference to her had given place to a protective, and, she thought, almost contemptuous kindness. In all his conduct towards her now she read an assertion of his independence and, it seemed to her, of his indifference. She could not but acknowledge that

Gerard was changed for the better, but the change did not quite please her.

George Monro was also changed during the year of her absence. He was as warm a friend as ever, but there was no longer anything of the lover in his words and looks. Effie learnt how much she had valued her power over these two men through the vague discontent caused by the belief that she had lost it. And she felt that she had lost more than this. She, who had been used all her life to be necessary to all around her, found now, or thought that she found, no one who needed her. Gerard had superseded her with her aunt; Jessie had taken her own right position towards her children, to the exclusion of the usurper; and George Monro had deposed her from the command over his affections, which she was beginning to regard as her inalienable right. Poor Effie was eating humble pie in Beulah Cottage through all these bright summer days, whilst her aunt and Gerard joked and flirted together, and Jessie came again and again to pour out her lamentations over her husband's continued estrangement.

One day in the beginning of August, when the invalid was taking her afternoon nap in the drawing-room, Gerard came into Effie's little sanctum, and threw himself into a chair, with a tired, vexed look.

"Is there anything the matter, Gerard?" asked Effie.

"Yes; a great deal. I have got to go away. I hope she won't mind it," looking towards the drawing-room.

"Shall you be away long?"

"No; I hope not. Only a few days. It is an awful bore." He was silent for some time, kicking up the corner of the drugget with great energy. "Effie, can *you* manage not to be savage when things go wrong?"

"No—not at all," answered Effie, laughing.

"I wonder how it's done. My missionary friend, Mr. Eden, has learnt the secret. When anything fails that he has been working at for years, perhaps, or all his plans are upset in any way, he only says, 'It was not to be,' or, 'It is best so,' and turns to something else as calmly as if—— Bother this drugget! I have got it all wrong, Effie. How Mrs. Heaton will be down upon me!"

"You have made the drugget suffer for your own annoyance."

"Yes. How soon do you think aunt Elizabeth is likely to wake? I ought not to be loitering here. But I should like to say 'good-bye' to her."

"She never sleeps more than half an hour, and it is nearly that now."

"I hope she won't be vexed at my going."

"She must not make such unsparing demands upon you."

"I like it. I am immensely proud of her liking to have me."

"But you must not hurry over your business on her account."

"I shall be glad enough to get it over, without that. It is a miserable business. There's her voice. Shall I go to her?"

"Don't tell her you are going away just at first," said Effie. But she began to fear Gerard was sacrificing too much in care for her aunt when he sat on with her for nearly an hour.

"I am going out of town, Aunt," he said, when at last he got up.

"You will not bide away, laddie?" cried aunt Elizabeth, taking fright immediately.

"Only a day or two. I have some business to settle which cannot be put off."

"What will I do without you, my bairn?" asked the old lady, who had lately taken to calling Gerard by this endearing term.

"I don't know what I can do without you," said Gerard. "I would give anything to escape going. But it must be done. I have stayed here a great deal too long, and shall have a run for it. Good-bye, Aunt." He stooped and kissed the old lady, and then turned to Effie. "Direct to me at the post-office, York, if you have anything to write about," he said, in a low voice, as he shook hands with her.

When Effie went back to her aunt she found her in tears.

"I'll never win through twa weary days without the sight of his bonnie face. I'll be laid in my grave if he bides away one day longer."

Effie began really to fear that it would be so, when her aunt continued to fret all the evening, and by bed-time was in a fever. Then, Isabella's attempt at carrying her to her room was a sad failure, and the thought of having this to bear all the days of Gerard's absence made the poor invalid still more nervous. She lay awake all night, and the next morning was so ill that Mr. Stamper looked very grave when he paid his daily visit. That visit only made matters worse, throwing the patient into a state of restless excitement, which did not subside all day, and by night had become almost like delirium.

The second morning after Gerard left, Effie received a note from him, saying that he found he could not possibly get through his work under two more days. When her aunt began to calculate how early her laddie could arrive, Effie thought it best to save her from suspense by telling her he could not come that day. She repented that she had done so, however, when the poor weak old lady burst into a passion of tears, and continued for many minutes to sob out, "I'll never see him more—I'll never see him more." She grew calmer after a few hours, and the doctor thought her better than on the previous day; but towards evening she sank into an apathetic state, which alarmed Effie terribly. Mr. Stamper also was uneasy, and when another day had passed without any change he told Effie that, if possible, Gerard had better be summoned, as a chance of rousing the patient. Effie wrote by the next day's post, and on the following afternoon Gerard arrived.

"How is she?" he asked, breathlessly, as Effie met him in the hall.

"Very ill. She does not seem to know any one, and she will not eat."

"Is it my fault—for having gone?"

"Mr. Stamper says it may have been coming on for some time," replied Effie, seeing how miserable Gerard looked.

"Am I to go to her at once?" he asked.

"No. Mr. Stamper wished to be present. He will be here at four with a physician—Dr. North. You had better come and have something to eat."

Gerard shook his head when he saw the tray spread for him.

"I can't eat. Does she speak at all?"

"She has not spoken since the day before yesterday. We cannot make out whether or not she is conscious."

Gerard buried his face in his hands, in his favourite manner, and remained so till the doctors came, Effie having returned to the sick-room.

Mr. Stamper told Gerard that he had long feared Miss Garnock's brain was affected by the spinal disease, but he had not anticipated such a rapid development of the evil.

"Is there no hope?" asked Gerard.

"None, I fear."

"Did my going away do harm, or—or would this have happened without?"

"It must have happened sooner or later. Perhaps it may have been slightly accelerated by her emotion when you left. Shall we go upstairs?"

The poor old lady was lying quite still, with her wide-open eyes wandering restlessly from side to side. She took no notice when Gerard went up to the bed.

"Speak to her," said Dr. North.

"Aunt Elizabeth," whispered Gerard, as soon as he could command his voice, for he was terribly shocked at his old friend's appearance.

She turned her head towards the voice, in a listening attitude.

"Dear Aunt," he repeated.

"What for are you aye crying on Aunt, Frederick Yonge? Ye ken she's awa' to the kirk wi' Davie." There was something awful in these words, spoken in a very high key.

"It is I, Aunt—Gerard. I have come back."

"Ay, Tar, I kenned ye would come back. Ye had aye a leal heart, Frederick Yonge, and ye would na be leaving me my lane—me that loved ye so weel. Ye'd no leave me to dree and die for missing the sun o' my life."

Gerard took one of the restless hands, and it closed tightly upon his.

" You'll never leave me more, Tar ? Gi' me your word that ye will aye bide wi' me."

" Always, dear Aunt."

" What for do ye gi' me ' Aunt ?' Will you be likening me to her that was na friend to puir Davie ? Dinna ca' me ' Aunt,' Tar. What way have I angered you, that I'm no ' Bessie ' the day ?"

" Bessie, dear Bessie !" muttered Gerard, in a voice choked with tears.

" That has the ring o' your ain voice, Frederick Yonge. It sounded fremd to my ears when ye would na gie me ' Bessie.' "

" I have got something for you ; you will take it to please me, Bessie," said Gerard, as Effie put a cup of beef-tea into his hand, signing to him to try and make the invalid take it.

" Eh, mither !" cried the old lady, catching sight of Effie. " I was a wilfu' wean the day, and would na take it to pleasure you. But I canna say na to Frederick Yonge."

She suffered Gerard to feed her like a child, and then lay quiet, still holding his hand. Her eyes had a more settled expression, and she looked almost as if she were falling asleep. The doctors went away, and Effie sat down by the darkened window. Nobody stirred for nearly two hours, when aunt Elizabeth began a low murmuring, from which Gerard just managed to make out that her mind was still occupied with her girlish days. Once she suddenly called out, quite loud, "Mither, dinna let Davie get the taws! It was na Davie, it was Walter. Walter is aye telling lees. Frederick Yonge says sae." If Gerard made the slightest movement as if to withdraw his hand the poor sufferer broke into fretful crying, like a child.

When Mr. Stamper came again, the last thing at night, bringing with him a professional nurse, Effie met him at the door with the question, " What are we to do ? Mr. Yonge cannot move. My aunt will not let go his hand."

The doctor went up to the bed, and said, firmly, " Miss Garnock, you must not keep Mr. Yonge any longer."

" Who'll he be that comes meddling between me and my Tar ?" shrieked the patient. " Mither, bid yon fremd body gang his ways. I'll no be fashed wi' him the day."

Mr. Stamper signed to Effie to speak, and she obeyed.

" Bessie, Frederick Yonge will be ill if you do not let him rest."

" Are ye no weel, Tar ? Gang awa' then, and rest

ye. But ye'll no bide long? I'll just die gin ye
bide awa' fra me."

Effie beckoned Gerard out of the room, and told
him that the doctor wished to be left alone with his
patient for a little while, and that in the meantime
she should make some tea. When they got into the
drawing-room Gerard seated himself by the table,
and laid his head down on his arms, sobbing passionately for some minutes. At last he looked up.

"I cannot go away to-night, Effie. May I send
for my things?"

"I have sent. They are in the front room upstairs.
Dear Gerard, how trying this is for you!"

"What a shame of me to make it worse for you by
—by giving way in this absurd, childish fashion."
He got up and walked about the room, struggling
with his grief.

"I never thought it would be so awful to hear
any one wandering in their mind," he said, presently.
"It gives me a feeling of something supernatural.
And when she takes me for my father I almost begin
to fancy that I am really he. How fond she must
have been of him!"

"Yes. Has she ever talked to you about him?"

"Sometimes; not much. Effie, do you think he
could have—have been false to her—have broken
faith with her?" Gerard's face turned scarlet as he
asked the question.

"No; I don't think so. She was always such an invalid, I don't think he could have felt anything but pity for her."

"No, you are wrong, Effie. I am sure he loved her once. From the little she has told me, and from some letters I have seen, I am convinced that he did love her. But he was very young—and—and—perhaps it is in our blood."

"I am certain there was no engagement between them," said Effie; and then felt sorry that she had let slip words which might sound to Gerard as a reproach.

"Not quite so bad as that, I hope," he observed, quietly. "What can 'Tar' mean? Have you heard that word before, Effie?"

"I will get my father's letters," replied Effie. "They may help us to understand a good deal, and make us better able to answer her."

"It seems very dreadful to be acting a part at such a time!" said Gerard.

When Effie came back the tea was ready, and she gave the packet of old yellow letters to Gerard, saying, "Will you glance through them whilst I give you some tea? How famished you must be!"

"Yes, here it is," exclaimed Gerard, after some time. "This letter is from aunt Elizabeth to—to Daddie. She says at the end, 'Give my love to the

Tar, and tell him we are all wearying to see him at
the Manse.' "

" Here is another," said Effie, who had taken some
of the letters. " ' Give . Tar many thanks for the
bonnie plaid. I'll aye mind him when I see it, and I
will see it all day, and every day.' "

" She used to call my father ' Jonathan,' sometimes," said Gerard. " She says here, ' My mother
bids me say we will look for Frederick Yonge with
you, whenever you come to the Manse. It is but
fitting that David should have the company of his
Jonathan.' These letters are too sad!" he cried,
putting them reverently down on the table.

" Gerard, you will be knocked up if you don't eat
something. At any rate drink this tea."

Gerard put his hand over Effie's, as she gave him
the cup, and said, looking fondly at her, " Poor
little girl! This is worse for you than for any
one."

" Miss Garnock is very restless now," said Mr.
Stamper, coming quietly into the room, and speaking
in the same low tone in which the other two had
spoken. " I am afraid you must go to her again,
Mr. Yonge. This constant fretting excites her so
painfully."

" I am quite ready," said Gerard. " Do you think
she is at all better to-night ?"

The doctor shook his head.

"Is there any immediate danger?" asked Effie, calmly.

"A change may come at any time, or she may last for some days."

"Is there no chance of her recovering consciousness?"

"I think not. The end will probably be quite calm, and will come almost imperceptibly. I will look in the first thing in the morning. Good-night."

Many days and nights passed on, making the only change in that darkened room, and still the Great Change did not come. Sometimes the sufferer would lie for hours holding Gerard's hand tightly, but giving no other sign of life, excepting a regular, unvaried movement of some part of her body. At other times, especially at night, she would talk incessantly, and frequently laugh shrilly—going over scenes of her childhood and girlhood—now contesting some trifling matter with one of her brothers, now pouring out the tale of her love to Frederick Yonge. Occasionally her mind would revert to the sad passage of David's exile from his home, and then she would break out into angry remonstrance with her father, or plaintive lamentations to her mother and sisters. She was always worse after this had happened.

Effie sent for her aunt Euphemia, but her arrival did more harm than good. The sick woman did not recognise her sister, and evinced her usual repugnance to the presence of strangers. Poor Euphemia could do nothing but cry, and her sobs excited the invalid most painfully. At last Mr. Stamper hinted that if Mrs. Lang could not control her feelings she must not enter the sick-room, and then the poor woman sat all day on the stairs, questioning every one who came from her sister.

One afternoon, ten days after Gerard's return, the sufferer had been quiet for some hours, after a more than usually violent night. It was a very warm day, and Effie was sitting by the open window, behind the heavy moreen curtains. Gerard was at his usual post by the bed. Suddenly the invalid asked, " What way is it aye dark, now ?"

Effie drew aside the curtains, and let the bright daylight into the room. The sick woman moved her hands, and began feeling up Gerard's arm.

" This is you, Tar ?"

" Yes, dearest Au—yes, Bessie."

" I'd like to rest in your arms a wee. If ye would let me lay my head on your shoulder I'm thinking I could sleep. I'm weary—so weary."

Gerard sat down on the bed, and, raising the old lady in his arms, placed her as she wished. She lay quite still for a few minutes, and then said, "I could bide this way for aye, Tar. I ken it is your ain sel that holds me, though I canna see your bonnie face."

"You cannot see my face because you are sleepy," said Gerard, quickly.

"Na, it is the dark hinders me. But I'm no feared for the dark, wi' your arm about me. Mither' we are just ganging through the dark valley—Frederick Younge and me— Eh! but wha told me he had gone before? It is na true, is it, Tar? This is you —your ain sel. It was na you that they buried in yon fremd sea?"

"No, no, I am here," said Gerard. "Effie, come!" he added, in a frightened whisper.

Effie did not see much change in her aunt, excepting that her eyes had a blind look, though they were wonderfully bright.

"I'd like to see you, Tar. What for do ye no light a candle?"

"Soon—very soon," said Gerard, huskily.

"I'm wishing it now. I must ha' light. I'll die if ye dinna gi' me light."

"Effie, say something," whispered Gerard, in great distress. "Tell her of The Light—I don't know how—you know what to say."

Effie did not know what to say. She scarcely knew what Gerard meant till, finding she did not speak, he leant over the dying woman, and said, "God will give you light, dearest Aunt. The Lord Jesus is the Light you want."

"A Light to lighten the Gentiles, and the Glory

of his people Israel," murmured the sufferer, catching the word.

" Yes, that is it," cried Gerard, eagerly. " Let us ask Him to give us light. Effie! pray for her."

Effie sank upon her knees, but she could think of no words of prayer. Again Gerard put her to shame. He murmured, softly, half-singing—

> "'Through Life's long day, and Death's dark night,
> Oh, gentle Jesus, be our Light.'"

" I'd no fear the dark, if you would sing me to sleep," said aunt Elizabeth.

Gerard at once struck up, in his rich tenor voice, the beautiful hymn—

> "'Abide with me : fast falls the evening-tide.
> The darkness deepens. Lord, with me abide.'"

When his voice ceased the dying woman began to speak again in her feeble tones.

" Carry me over the burn, Tar. What for do we bide here in the dark, when Mither is there in the light—and David—and— What way are there twa Jonathans. I see him yonder wi' Davie in the light. Are ye no here wi' me, Tar ?"

" Yes, I am here."

" Ye'll no leave me. Ye'll no gang awa' to them, and leave me my lane ?"

" No, never."

" I'd like to go to Davie in the light. But I'll no

leave you, Tar. Haud me fast !" she almost shrieked.
"They're crying on me ! But I'll no gang awa' fra
you. I'll no leave you your lane— I'll no gang
awa'. Eh, but it's bonnie yonder. And there's
Mither, and David, and Jonathan, all in the light.
What for dinna ye take me till them ? I'd like to
be in yon light. I'm feared for this weary darkness.
Haud me closer, Tar. Are ye gone away too ? I
dinna hear ye."

Gerard began to sing again, though his voice was
tremulous, and choked with tears—

> " 'Sun of my soul, Thou Saviour dear,
> It is not night if Thou be near.' "

"The Sun !" murmured the dying woman, so in-
distinctly that Gerard could hardly hear her, and
Mrs. Lang and Effie could only see that she was
speaking. " I see the Sun. It is glinting on Davie,
and on Jonathan's bonny curls. Eh ! I'd like to be
in the sun. There is neither sun nor moon there.
'The city had no need of the sun, neither of the
moon to shine in it——' "

" 'For the glory of God did lighten it, and the
Lamb is the Light thereof,' " added Gerard, when the
dying woman's feeble tones ceased.

" I'm ganging to them, Tar," she began again.
" They're needing me, and I canna say them nay—
David and Jonathan. Ye'll no miss me, for they

told me ye were married upon a braw young bride, and ye'll likely no mind me now. Ye were no to blame—I aye—telled—them—ye were—no to blame. I'm coming, Davie. Tar—ye'll let—me—gang to— Davie— See till him—there—in the light— Dinna haud—me back—fra him. What—ha' ye— made o'—my—plaiddie—the ane—ye—gied—me ? I'm—just—perishing—wi' the—awfu'—cauld. It's a' dark—and—cauld. I—canna—win to—the light. What for — are — ye hauding — me—back ? Let me gang awa'—to the light." The broken, faltering voice ceased, and Gerard bent down to see if the breath had ceased also.

" I'll sleep a wee," were the last words of the worn-out sufferer.

After a long silence, only broken by aunt Euphemia's stifled sobs, Gerard laid his burden gently on the bed, and then knelt down by Effie. The nurse came forward and busied herself at the other side of the bed, and in a short time the doctor arrived. Then Gerard left the room, and aunt Euphemia, finding that all was over, burst into unchecked lamentations, which soon drove Effie away also.

In about half an hour Gerard came to Effie's door with a glass of wine. He was very pale, and his eyes were swollen with tears.

" Drink this, Effie. Have you been lying down at all ? You must be so tired."

"Then what must *you* be?"

"I don't feel tired." The tears came into his eyes again as he spoke. "We ought not to be sorry," Gerard continued, thoughtfully. "She has had such a sad life—and now— Effie, is it selfishness, or faithlessness, that makes it so hard to feel glad that all her pain is over?"

"Gerard, what a comfort it was that you were here! I could not think of a word to say, and those hymns were just what she wanted."

"I could remember nothing but hymns."

"How did you remember them? and just suitable ones."

"Mr. Eden is always singing hymns. I have learnt them of him. Oh, how I longed for him at that awful time! Or for George Monro. I am going to see if I can find Mr. Eden, Effie, unless I can be any good here. Can I?"

"There is nothing to do," replied Effie, sadly.

Gerard turned sharply away. "If I find Mr. Eden I shall bring him to see you. But I am afraid he is not in London. I will go up and tell Jessie first. Good-night. You will go to bed early?"

When Gerard came back, however, he found Effie sitting in the drawing-room with George Monro, who had come to her as soon as he heard what had happened. Gerard turned very red, and started back. "I beg your pardon," he said, rather coldly.

"Don't go, Gerard. I want your advice. You know how she disliked cemeteries. What do you think of Hornsey Churchyard?"

"She would have chosen it, I think."

"George says he will take me there to-morrow. Will you come, too?"

"No—that is, I cannot. I shall be engaged."

"Did you find your friend?"

"No; he is in the country."

"Would the day after to-morrow suit you?" asked George.

"No. No day would suit me. You will not want me. Good-night; I am going to bed."

"I must be going," said George. "Good-night, Effie. Don't forget how *she* gains by your loss. Take care of yourself. I cannot bear to see you looking so pale and wan. God bless you."

Gerard walked out of the room.

"Good-night, Gerard," said George, following him. "You must be quite worn out, too. Few men could do what you have done for the last ten days."

"Few men meet with any one that it is such a— such a pleasure to—to do anything for," answered poor Gerard, nearly breaking down again.

"Good-night. Take care of Effie."

Effie came out of the room as George went down the stairs. "Take care of *yourself*, Gerard," she said, kindly, as she heard George's last words. "You want it more than I do. Good-night."

"Good-night." Gerard took her hand, and held it tightly clasped. "You will care for me a little, whatever happens, won't you, for the sake of those that we both loved?"

"What could happen to make me forget all that you have done, Gerard?"

Gerard dropped her hand suddenly, and turned away, muttering, as he went upstairs, "It is not that I want. There was nothing in what I did. I did it because I loved her."

After the funeral Effie went to Jessie's, but not to remain. She had learnt, by bitter experience, that there was no place for her in her sister's house; and, although Jessie was very kind, and was extremely anxious to make her as comfortable as possible, she could not feel at ease whilst in constant fear that she might, as before, overstep the bounds of her due position. George Monro solved the difficulty as to Effie's future abode by putting it into Mrs. Mortlake's head that a boarder would be a great addition to her comfort, and inducing her to mention the idea to her next-door neighbours. It required a very little farther stretch of diplomacy to persuade Effie that Mrs. Mortlake's house would be just the home for her—so near to all her greatest interests, and yet not amongst them; so free, and yet so far removed from solitariness.　By her aunt Elizabeth's will she had come into the possession of 250*l.* a year, the accumulation of what the old lady had been able to save from her annuity, added to Walter Garnock's legacy. This made her quite independent; indeed, with her few wants, she seemed to herself to be inordinately rich. George helped her out of this dilemma also, by sedulously bringing under her notice all fit objects on which to expend her superfluous wealth.

As soon as Effie was settled in Mrs. Mortlake's comfortable establishment she vigorously recommenced all the works of George's cutting-out which she had dropped at the time of his first proposal. She thought there would no longer be any awkwardness on this account, as it was evident that the feelings which had then actuated him no longer existed.

The change which Effie had noticed in George when she first came to London became more and more marked the more she saw of him. It seemed as if all the individual *man* had been lost in the *priest*, and a rigid asceticism had taken the place of the generous feelings and refined tastes which had once been his. This change made work with George possible, and free from embarrassment, but it took from it all enthusiasm and all pleasure; for he now inculcated work as a duty—a discipline of self—not as a service of love to a loving Master.

Work, however, for its own sake, was a necessity to

Effie ; so she visited and taught under George's direction, and in the intervals played with the children, sympathized with Jessie, and tried to follow the flights of Mrs. Mortlake's mind. Gerard she seldom saw. He was often in the next house, but he never sought her, and when she met him looked grave, and not at his ease. With George he was still less himself, and George's manner to him was cool and reserved, as well as his tone in speaking of his former friend.

Harold's only intercourse with his family, at this time, was that he occasionally appointed some place in London for his children to meet him, and that he always accompanied the two elder boys to and from school.

CHAPTER X.

"How was it arranged that Davie should go with Harold to Ventnor?" asked Gerard Yonge of his sister-in-law. They were sitting alone at the dinner-table, from which the three younger children had just run away.

"Through the lawyers, as usual," answered Jessie, sadly.

Gerard made an impatient gesture. "And he took the scarlet fever there?"

"On the journey, Harold thinks."

"Does Harold write to you?"

"No; only to Walter. Is it not hard upon me?" continued Jessie. "It is four years ago, now, that I offended him. And I have never seen him since."

"It *is* terribly hard, Jessie."

"I know that I did very wrong; but I have surely been punished enough. Do you think he will *ever* forgive me, Gerard?"

"I am sure he will. Something will bring him to

his senses. It is all his abominable pride and obstinacy."

"But he used not to seem proud and obstinate. I always thought him so very gentle. Do you think he has altered?"

"I will tell you what my 'spiritual director' says about him. He says, that when a man has not much belief in anything—in anything but what he can understand—all his natural good qualities become so exaggerated that they cease to be good. For instance: a good-natured man becomes weak and mean-spirited; a firm man obstinate; an honest, conscientious man proud and self-righteous. Do you see what he means?"

"Yes. Is it George Monro that says so? But do you think Harold is really—that he does not believe anything?"

"He may be changed—but many years ago he told me that he neither believed in a Personal God, nor in a future life. I don't mean George Monro by my 'spiritual director.'"

"Who is it, then? Gerard, you are not going to turn Roman Catholic, are you?"

Gerard laughed heartily. "My 'spiritual director' is more like a Quaker than a Roman Catholic," he said. "No; it is Mr. Eden, the missionary I told you about. He is going back to Borneo next week, after three years' rest—and—and I am going with him, Jessie."

"You going to Borneo, Gerard! What do you mean?"

"That I am going to Borneo," replied Gerard, looking straight before him.

"Oh, dear! I am so sorry," said Jessie. "I shall miss you so much. What should you go to Borneo for? I thought you were getting on so well."

"So I am—in the way of making money—but that is not everything, and I cannot stay in England."

"Why? I don't understand."

"I am miserable," he cried, impulsively, getting up and walking to the window. "I stay away, and long to be here—I come here, and long to be away. Now this morning—I knew it was just what I might expect—but—Jessie! you and I are fellow-sufferers. We are both bitterly punished for follies that we have long since repented of. You are worse off than I am, poor Beauty!" he added, affectionately. "Your fault was less, and your punishment is greater. But it will all come right with you."

"And not with you?" asked Jessie, timidly.

"Never! Why do they shilly-shally in this way, Jessie?" he asked, fiercely, turning away again. "Why don't they marry at once?"

"Who?" asked Jessie, in great surprise.

"Effie and—George Monro. I thought at first they were only waiting till Effie was out of mourning; but now—— It is a year and a half since aunt

Elizabeth died. They can have no reason for waiting. However, I shall be safe at Sarawak before I get the wedding-cards." Gerard was striding about the room in vehement excitement, much to Jessie's alarm.

"Gerard, I really don't believe there is anything between them," she said, at last.

"Did you see them this morning as we went into church ?"

"No."

"Of course there is something between them. I have known it for two years and a half. And I have no business to mind it—but I do. Here come the Butterfields!" he exclaimed, suddenly. "I shall escape. I want to see George about some books he has got of mine; I shall go up there now;" and he left the room by one door, as Mr. and Mrs. Samuel Butterfield entered by the other.

Half-way up the hill Gerard met George. The friends looked stiffly at each other. "I was coming to you," said Gerard. "Good old Alp," he added, caressing George's splendid Newfoundland dog.

"Will you turn, and walk with me? I cannot stop. I am going over to Steadham, to a poor man who is dying."

"I only wanted to ask you for those Mission Reports I lent you—Mr. Eden wants them back."

"Must you have them at once? I lent them to

Mitchell at Steadham. I will call for them to-day, if you want them now."

"Mr. Eden is going back next week, and I promised to pack those books, with some other things for him, to-morrow. I am going with him."

"Where?" asked George, stopping to look at his companion, in extreme surprise.

"To Borneo."

"What for?"

"To try a fresh start. Look here, George. You and I started in the same race years ago. The odds were all in my favour at one time. But I tripped, and now you have come in first, and I am nowhere. I beg your pardon for using slang."

"Never mind about the slang. But I don't understand you. What have I to do with your success or failure? It seems to me that our courses are as distinct as possible."

"We have both run for the same prize, have we not?"

George stopped again to look at Gerard's agitated face. "Are you alluding to Effie Garnock?" he asked, rather stiffly.

"Of course I am. I am not blaming you, George. I was a fool, and deserved to lose what I had not the sense to keep. But that does not make the loss any the more endurable."

" Do you mean that you would like now to renew your engagement ?"

" I asked Effie to do so, two years and a half ago, and was refused."

" She refused you!" cried George, rather more joyfully than was kind towards his dejected friend.

" Yes. She told me she did not care for me any longer. I saw how completely I had lost the race ; and I guessed who had won it."

" And you grew desperate ? Was that it, Gerard ? We had all such hopes that you had turned over a new leaf after you were at Boulogne—was that what threw you back again ?"

" Threw me back ? I have been all straight ever since that, George."

" Straight in money-matters, yes ; but—do you feel in your heart that you are worthy of such a woman as Effie ?"

" No, perhaps not. Do *you* think yourself worthy of her ?"

" I am not speaking of general unworthiness. You know what I mean."

" About my conduct to her seven years ago ? I know that was very bad—but don't *you* allow repentance to atone for past faults ? Are you as hard as Harold ?"

" I am not referring to anything that is past. You know that you at present associate with those whom you would not like Effie even to see.

Gerard coloured violently as George looked searchingly in his face. "Yes; I know that," he said, in a low voice.

"And you think yourself worthy of her?"

"I don't think myself worthy of her. But I know *that* does not make me unworthy. George, you have been listening to scandal. That is neither worthy of you, nor of your Office. You might have taken the trouble to sift the reports you heard. Time will prove their truth or falsehood—perhaps, perhaps not. I do not care to clear myself. If you like to think so badly of me, I can't help it. I shall be off in a week, and there's an end of me, as far as you are all concerned. I will go back now. I won't contaminate you by my company any longer." He turned away in strong excitement, and walked rapidly back to Prior's Mount.

At the gate he met Effie and the two boys.

"We are going to try and get warm," said Effie.

"Is it cold? I am quite hot."

"Oh, uncle Gerard!" cried Walter. "Why, it is the coldest day there has been this winter; colder than it was ever last winter. All the ponds are frozen over. We are going to see if there are any skaters."

"May I go with you?" asked Gerard of Effie.

"We shall all be delighted to have you, shall not we, boys? We have just got to go into the village first, but then we are going to the ponds."

Gerard was very taciturn and abstracted till they got

into the fields, and the little boys had run on towards the ponds; and then he said, suddenly, in a hoarse, tremulous voice, "I am going away next week, Effie."

"Away! Where to? For long?"

"'It may be for years, and it may be for ever,'" quoted Gerard, with an attempt at carelessness, which failed lamentably.

"What do you mean, Gerard?" cried Effie, alarmed at his strange manner.

"I am going to Borneo, as a missionary."

"You are joking, Gerard."

"Indeed, no. It is bitter earnest."

"You a missionary!"

"Well, not exactly a missionary; at any rate, not at present. I shall be a kind of secretary to Mr. Eden."

"You mean really to devote yourself to the life of a missionary?"

"Why not? I was to have devoted myself to the life of an English clergyman. There is not so much difference between the two, if both do their duty."

"Then why don't you take Orders here, instead of going so far away?"

"It would not answer my purpose as well," replied Gerard, with forced calmness.

"And you mean to be away for years—never to come back?" asked Effie, faintly—dizzy with a kind of blank horror.

"No; I hope not that. I hope to come back in a few years, for a visit, if no Dyak takes a fancy to my head."

"Gerard!"

"I want to try what change of air will do for the cure of a troublesome complaint I have."

"Are you ill?" asked Effie, glancing anxiously at his pale face.

He answered the glance with a melancholy smile. "Not in body," he said, pointedly.

"Aunt Effie!" cried Freddie, running back, "there is Mr. Monro and Alp coming down the Steadham hill towards the big pond. Let's go to meet them."

"Very well, Freddie. You and Walter run on," Effie managed to say, with some difficulty.

Gerard continued, as if he had not noticed the interruption. "I cannot shake off an imbecile habit of brooding over what might have been, but for my own folly."

As he seemed to expect Effie to speak, she asked, timidly, "Is that your complaint?"

"No; only one of the symptoms."

Effie did not dare to put on Gerard's manner the only interpretation of which it seemed capable; so she tried to give a lighter tone to their conversation. "And you mean to give up your profession?"

"I am sick of my profession—trading upon vanity! Making money which I don't care to spend on myself, and doing more harm than good when I try to spend it on others—and getting misunderstood whatever I do."

" Who misunderstands you ?"

" One that I thought my friend, though I was not very friendly to him."

" Are you sick of your friends, as well of as your profession ?" asked Effie, not knowing what to say.

"Not of all, Effie," he answered, looking tenderly down at her.

" I should think you need not go so far as Borneo for change of air," said Effie, her spirits rather revived by that look.

" I choose Borneo because my doctor is going there, and he recommends me the society of the Dyaks as a wholesome tonic."

" His treatment must be almost as severe as the cold-water cure."

" No, I don't think that, Effie. The first plunge will be awful," his voice failed, and he stopped in great agitation, looking at Effie, with a white face, and eyes full of tears. Presently he went on, his expression gradually assuming a sort of intentness— a far-off look—which Effie had once or twice noticed in him of late. "There must be something very satisfactory in the life of a missionary ; every trifle having the highest possible aim, and the whole thing being a sacrifice of oneself—I don't mean, of course, in such play work as I am going to attempt, but in the real thing."

Effie did not speak, and he continued, dreamily, "Then the end, which they must always look to as possible! There must be something awfully exciting—a kind of solemn delight—in dying as a martyr. And, even if it should not come to that, the whole life is a kind of slow death." He was silent for some minutes, the wrapt expression remaining on his face.

"The idea of my holding forth upon the pleasures of martyrdom!" he exclaimed, suddenly, in a lighter tone; "when I can't even bear a little every-day suffering, and am flying from England to escape some occasional twinges of pain, which seem to me——"

"Pain! suffering!" repeated Effie. "Gerard, you *are* ill!"

"Yes, Effie, I am ill—ill at heart." His almost spiritual look had now given place to one of intense tenderness.

"I cannot understand, Gerard," Effie faltered out. "You speak in riddles."

"I do not want another blow like that I got at Gourock."

"When do you mean?"

Gerard continued, in wild excitement, without regarding Effie's question: "You look so soft and kind that I have been led on to say more than I intended; but you need not fear that I am going again to ask you to 'revive a corpse.' I only want to tell you, Effie, before I go away, perhaps for ever, that by the side of that corpse there is a living thing that suffers, and sometimes groans, as it is doing now."

"Gerard, I cannot understand you."

"Shall I tell you in plain words, Effie? Mind, I am asking nothing. I only tell you that I love you so passionately—so selfishly—that I cannot stay here to see you married to George Monro."

Before Effie could answer, the two little boys came running back.

"Auntie!" they cried, "Mr. Monro is drowned! Alp is swimming about in a hole in the ice, and Mr. Monro's hat, and stick, and books, are by the side!"

Gerard gave Effie a look, which was a perfect epitome of all that had gone before—his ardent love for her, his belief in her love for George, and his yearning for a martyr's death. The next moment he was gone, and when Effie came in sight of the pond he had pulled off his coat and boots, and was walking quickly across the ice. Before he reached the hole the treacherous floor gave way, and he disappeared, breaking so much ice away in his fall that a clear space was opened to Alp. The brave dog, forgetting his own danger, immediately re-

membered his duty. He dived at once, and presently
came up again, holding some one—whether Gerard
or George Effie could not tell—with his head above
the water. All this had happened in less than five
minutes.

"Run, Walter—get help!—the nearest you can
think of!" gasped Effie. "Freddie, fetch Mr. Rogers!"

The boys were off in an instant, and then Effie
could only stand and watch the poor dog's ever more
and more desperate efforts to keep himself and his
burden from sinking. As she stood, there came
across her the memory of that evening when, from
the very same spot, she had thrown her treasures
into the pond. It seemed to her hours before she
was roused by voices, and, looking round, saw several
men with ladders and ropes, and amongst them George
Monro.

"You here, Effie!" he cried. "Is there anything
the matter?"

"Gerard is there—in the water. Save him, George!"
It never occurred to her either to wonder, or to rejoice
that George himself was safe.

"We have a man to rescue instead of a dog!" cried
George to his companions. "Quick!"

They *were* quick. In a few minutes two strong
ladders were lashed firmly together and stretched
across the pond, passing over the hole. A bricklayer
stepped boldly along this bridge, and George followed.

It was some time before they could relieve Alp of his burden, but it was done at last, and then the bricklayer took the inanimate form on his broad back, and walked along the ladder as boldly as before. George preceded him.

"He is quite insensible," said George, as he stepped off the ice. "Was he long in the water?"

"Not two minutes," replied Effie. "Alp held his head above water all the rest of the time."

"It is not the water," said George, when Gerard had been laid on the grass. "He has no appearance of drowning. We had better get him home. Five shillings to the first who brings Mr. Rogers, or any doctor, to Prior's Mount."

"The boys have gone for Mr. Rogers," said Effie.

"Tell him to go to Prior's Mount, instead of coming here," cried George to the three or four messengers who had already started. "Who will help me?" he added, attempting to lift Gerard from the ground.

The bricklayer volunteered again, and the two started off with their helpless burden, Alp trotting on in front, and Effie and some stragglers following. Mr. Rogers reached Prior's Mount just as Gerard had been carried in; and Jessie and Effie were left in fearful suspense for nearly half an hour, whilst he and George remained upstairs. Jessie kept crying, and saying that she felt sure Gerard was dead. Effie only trembled. At last George came down, looking very grave. "He has spoken," he said. "He has asked for Harold."

"Is he sensible?" asked Effie, her teeth chattering so that she could hardly form the words.

"Yes, quite. Shall I telegraph for Yonge?"—to Jessie.

"Yes—but— How can he leave Davie? Had not I better go?"

"I don't think you had better leave now," observed George.

"I will go," said Effie. "You must stay here."

"I cannot—if Harold comes."

"I think you had better," said George. "But, Effie, there will be risk of infection."

"Never mind that," said Effie, impatiently.

"Shall I say that you are coming, then?" asked George, as he began to write for the telegram. "He need not wait, I suppose. How soon can you get there?"

"I will look in Bradshaw," said Effie, getting up as she spoke; but her legs trembled so that she could not stand, and she sank down again, saying faintly, "Tell me first what Mr. Rogers says."

"It is paralysis," answered George. "He thinks the seizure must have taken place directly he fell into the water. How did it happen? What made him venture on the ice?"

"He thought you were in the water—he jumped in to save you."

"Good God!"

"Does Mr. Rogers think he will die?" asked Jessie.

"He says it is a very severe seizure. All the limbs are affected; but his mind is quite clear, and his speech perfectly distinct."

"What did he say about Harold?"

"We thought he was insensible, but he called me, and when I went to him, said, 'Do you think Harold would refuse to see me now?' I said I would send for him, and then he said, 'Ask him to come quickly.'"

"Then he thinks he is dying?" said Jessie.

"Yes. I believe so. Effie, I think you must go down to Portsmouth this evening, and cross by the first boat to-morrow—that will be the quickest way of getting there. There is a train at seven. Can you go then?"

"Yes, if there is time."

"I will bring a cab—I am going out to send a messenger to the Telegraph-office with this. I have said that he may depend on your being with Davie early to-morrow. I have begged him to come without delay. Mr. Rogers will not leave till I get back."

When Goorge was gone Effie went upstairs to pack some necessary things. Jessie followed her.

"I think you ought to stay, Effie," said Jessie.

"He might want you. Do you know he loves you still—he told me so to-day."

"Don't, Jessie! I cannot bear that now."

"But won't you let me go to Davie?"

"No—you must not. You ought to stay here. You heard what George said. Don't say anything more about it, please."

The sisters were both silent as they almost mechanically put various articles into the portmanteau. They were just closing it when the cab drove up to the gate.

"I *must* see him," said Effie, in a hollow whisper. On the stairs she met George.

"Would you like to see him before you go?" he asked, noticing her wistful glance at the door of Gerard's room.

"Yes."

"I will ask Mr. Rogers."

Presently he beckoned her into the room.

Gerard's face looked much the same as usual, only rather flushed. He smiled feebly when he saw Effie.

"George has sent for Harold," he said. "I hope there will be time."

Effie could not say a word.

"Don't grieve about me, Effie. This is better than Borneo!" Gerard was silent for a few minutes, and then began again. "Ask George about the Communion. I should like it soon. Is George there?"

"Yes," replied George, signing to Effie that she must go.

"Will you give it me? There may not be time to wait tor Harold, and—perhaps he would not join in it."

"I will be back directly," said George.

"One moment, George. You were wrong in what you thought. Come nearer."

George bent down, and Gerard whispered something.

"Forgive me," said George, in a broken voice, and left the room. Effie was about to follow, in obedience to another sign from him, when Gerard spoke again.

"Effie, the engagement-ring you gave me back that—that day—I have always worn it lately—will you wear it again for my sake, when—after—after I am dead. It is on my finger now—I had it covered to look like a signet-ring. Will you? I don't think George will mind."

Still Effie could not say a word. She nodded.

"Thank you," said Gerard, tenderly. "My darling!"

Effie stooped suddenly, and kissed his forehead, and then went quickly from the room, and straight to the cab.

"Drive as fast as possible," said George to the coachman, and they dashed off at full gallop.

"Stop!" cried Effie, starting forward. She was

going to say that she could not leave Gerard; but George had turned away, and the cabman did not hear. She sank back with a feeling of utter helplessness, and was borne rapidly away.

It was just getting a little light when George heard a cab stop, and went down to meet Harold.

"Am I too late?"

"No.　He is still alive."

"Not sensible?"

"He has not spoken since seven o'clock—he took the Holy Sacrament then.　We do not know whether he is conscious or not.　Will you come up at once?"

Harold nodded.　As he followed George into the sick-room he gave one glance at Jessie, who was sitting by the fire, trembling violently; then he walked straight to the bed.　Gerard was pale now, and his chiselled features and large, deep-set eyes made his face look fearfully corpse-like.　Harold stood looking at him for some minutes, and then left the room abruptly.

"Go to him, George," whispered Jessie.　"I dare not."

Harold was standing by the passage window.　"He is not conscious," he said, almost fiercely, when he saw George.

"No; I think not."

"He will never know that I am here," said Harold, in the same tone as before.

"He gave me a message for you."

"I won't hear it! I *must* hear it from his own lips. He cannot be dying!"

"There is Rogers!" cried George.

The doctor bowed stiffly to Harold as he went into the sick-room. When he came out again, after about half an hour, he was not allowed to pass so easily.

"How is he, Rogers?" asked Harold.

"Very ill."

"Is there no hope?"

The doctor shook his head.

"Could no one do anything?"

"I sent for Dr. East last night. You heard his opinion, Mr. Monro."

"He quite agreed with Mr. Rogers," said George. "He would not alter the treatment at all. He said nothing more could be done; it was only a question of time."

"You said it was an accident--what accident?"

"He fell into the Steadham pond—plunged in, rather, noble fellow! to save me—thinking I had fallen in. It was a most deplorable mistake. I had foolishly sent my dog in after a stick. The poor animal could not get out again, the ice affording him no hold, and I ran for some means of saving him. Whilst I was away, Gerard and Effie came up, and, seeing the dog in the water, and on the ice near him my stick, and hat, and books—which I had thrown to attract his attention to parts of the ice where I thought he could break through—they very naturally concluded that I was in the water, and Gerard instantly went to my rescue. He sank directly, and Mr. Rogers and Dr. East both think that he was immediately paralysed by the shock."

" How could that be ?" asked Harold of the doctor.

" The system must have been predisposed. I find that he was in an unusual state of excitement previously, which might account for it."

" He was intending to go abroad," George explained, " and had been telling us all about his plans. He was certainly very much excited when I saw him about an hour before, and Effie remembers that it was the same just before the accident."

" And he must die ?" asked Harold again, still fiercely. " Will he never know me ?"

" There *may* be an interval of consciousness. You had better be at hand. If he is sensible at all it will be for a few minutes at the last. I will come again in an hour or two."

Harold went at once back into Gerard's room, and took his seat by the bed. There he remained immovably for many hours. When Jessie ventured to bring him a cup of tea, he swallowed it eagerly, without looking at her, but shook his head when she offered him bread and butter. A few hours later she brought him a glass of wine, and he took that in the

same manner as the tea, but again refused to eat.
At night he swallowed more tea, without appearing
to notice who was waiting upon him. All this time
there was no change in Gerard. The doctor looked
graver and graver each time he came, and Harold
grew more and more despairing. The night passed
like the day. Jessie sat by the fire, or moved noise-
lessly about the room. George lay down in the
adjoining dressing-room, ready to assist each time
Mr. Rogers came, or anything had to be done for the
patient. Harold still sat behind the curtains.

The dull December daybreak was just beginning
to make everything look cold and comfortless, when
the three watchers were startled by Gerard's voice.

"Have I been asleep?" he asked.

George was in the room in an instant, and Jessie
by the bedside.

"When can Harold be here?" asked Gerard,
without waiting for an answer to his former question.

"He is here," said George, and Jessie drew aside
hastily as Harold stood up.

"Will you forgive me now, Harold?"

"Don't, Gerard; I cannot bear that! Forgive *me!*"
and he fell on his knees by the bedside.

"But say it, Harold," persisted Gerard, with the
excitement of weakness. "Take off the curse. Call
me 'brother.'"

"Brother, brother!" cried Harold. "Dear, dearest brother!"

"Thank you for coming," said Gerard, feebly. "But I knew you would come. I knew I should see you again."

Harold got up and left the room quickly.

"Send Jessie to him, George," said Gerard.

Jessie shrank back in alarm, but at length yielded. She found Harold in the next room—little Bessie's bedroom, the children having all been removed to the next house. Harold was sitting on the low bed, with his hands clenched before him, his lips compressed, and his whole face working convulsively. As Jessie stood trembling at the door, not daring to go nearer, but unwilling to draw back, he raised his head, and said, almost in a whisper, "My wife."

Jessie sprang towards him, crying, "Yes, let me be your wife again. Oh, Harold, I have been so wretched! Give me back some of your love."

Harold stretched out his arms, and she threw herself on his neck. He pressed her vehemently to him, and the final melting of his strong, proud heart was shown in deep, convulsive sobs. Both started up when the door opened noisily. It was George.

"I think you had better come," he said. "He seems to be sinking. I have sent for Rogers."

"Harold," said Gerard's faint voice, as they entered the room.

Harold went forward, still holding Jessie, who hid shyly behind him.

"You know that I am dying; that the doctors say I cannot live. You do not believe that in a few hours there will be nothing more of me?"

"No, no—I cannot!" cried Harold.

"You believe that this death that is coming to me now is only the beginning of a better life?" asked Gerard, growing flushed and eager.

Harold hesitated.

Gerard grew still more excited. "Harold! you must believe it! When you think of me—when you think of little Isa—can you bear to think of us as gone, never to be seen again—never to *be* again?"

"No, I cannot," said Harold.

"Then you must believe in God—in His mercy."

"I believe in mercy—for you and Jessie have forgiven me."

"Jessie!" cried Gerard, joyfully.

Harold drew his wife forward—his arm still round her.

"Thank God!" said Gerard. "George, thank Him, and pray for us all."

George fell on his knees, and Jessie drew Harold down. When the prayer was ended Gerard began speaking again. "George," he said. "I want you to telegraph to Effie—have you a piece of paper?—just this: 'It is all right between Hay and the

Beauty. Gay is quite happy. It is best so.' Mind you are not so extravagant as to make it more than twenty words." He said this with a smile, which sent George from the room, and made Harold and Jessie turn quickly away.

" Harold, would you read a little to me ? Where is the coat I wore to-day, Jessie ?"

" In the wardrobe," answered Jessie, after looking puzzled for a minute. Gerard thought it was " to-day " that all had happened—she thought it was years ago.

" You will find in the tail pocket the little Testament aunt Elizabeth gave me. Read me some of the passages that are marked 'E' please, Harold."

When George returned Harold wished to give up the book to him ; but Gerard said, " Go on, Harold. It makes me think we are in Daddie's study on Sunday evening. We only want Effie. George, give her my very best love."

CHAPTER XI.

EFFIE received Gerard's telegram just as she was going out to get some new-laid eggs for Davie. A lady lodging in the same house was sitting with the boy, to whom she had taken a great fancy, so Effie was quite at liberty. She executed her commission —grasping the telegram in her hand all the time— and then, instead of going home, went on along the eastern cliff. The December sun, which looked so wan at Gateshill, was bright enough here, and made diamonds in the hoar-frost, and rainbows in the icicles that were festooned here and there upon the bushes. It was the first time Effie had been out since her arrival; but she now passed through all the wild beauty of this part of the Undercliff without any eyes for outward things. Presently she wandered from the beaten path, and after almost unconsciously winding in and out between great boulders of rock, and climbing over or stooping under top-heavy masses, she at last sat down to rest. Then she read the message again. It was just as Gerard had dictated it, excepting that George had added the words, "We fear the end is very near." She had that morning received a letter from George, telling of Gerard's protracted insensibility, and of Harold's despair. Most likely by this time the end had come. Oh, why had she consented to leave him? Perhaps at the last he might call for her, and feel her absence painfully. If she had only told him that she loved him—that she had always loved him—him only. But now he believed that she loved George—the tone still rang in her ears with which he had said, "I love you so passionately—so selfishly—that I cannot stay here to see you married to George Monro." Fool that she was! Why could she not speak then? Why could she not tell him that George was nothing to her—that *he* was, always had been, and always would be, everything. Did she not know it was so when she felt her heart die within her as he spoke of going to Borneo? If she was so dull as not to know it then, surely she knew it in those awful minutes— were they minutes or hours?—when she stood by the pond, and despaired of his life. Then why had she been dumb at his bed-side? Why, when he asked her to wear his ring after he was dead, had she not told him that she could not live after he was dead? Why, oh why, had she left him with only that cold kiss? She had always been cruel to him. What

dreadful words those were she said to him at Gourock.
He had always been so gentle and loving, and she
had been so hard and self-sufficient. She had thought
herself so immeasurably superior to him. Even when
she had loved him the most, there had been something of contempt mixed with her love. But now
how did they stand? How had she stood comparison
with him at her aunt's death-bed—in all the attendance on her? How with regard to Harold and Jessie?
She had driven them asunder; *he* had brought them
together again. He had thought of others always—
even at the moment when Death had struck him
down—she had thought only of herself. She had
been struggling to preserve her own calmness—to
maintain her selfish dignity — when, if she had
thought of him instead of herself, she ought to have
cast aside everything, and unsaid those wicked, lying
words she had said at Gourock. Were they lying?
She had believed them at the time. But if they were
true then, they were not so now—it was acting a lie
not to unsay them now. Gerard had said he would
not ask her again to "revive a corpse"—how pained,
but how tender he had looked as he said it! She
ought to have told him that it *was* revived—not
revived only to its former life, but to a life far
superior to that life. And how could it be otherwise? She had loved Gerard formerly because, in
her presumptuous self-conceit, she had believed her-

self necessary to him—her support necessary to keep him from falling. She had been humbled since then. She herself had failed in every relation of life, and now, so far from attempting to support others, she felt unable to stand alone. And the help she looked for was from him—from him who had fallen once, and so nobly redeemed his fall. From the time when he had come to Gourock to try and make amends for his former fault towards her, and when she had spoken those cruel words, there had been growing up in her a deep respect for the man she had once almost despised. All that she had seen of him since then had encouraged this new growth, until it had spread so as to obscure every other feeling. It was only when he spoke of going away, per-haps for ever, that she became at all aware that respect was only the root of a love far deeper than that which she had for so many years striven to eradicate.

As Effie sat thinking over all this, she was suddenly startled by a voice close to her.

" You are in grief, my dear." An elderly man, looking something between a Quaker and an English clergyman, was standing in front of her. A plain man, but with a beauty of expression which at once inspired confidence, and made his abrupt address, instead of the impertinence it might have appeared, the genuine expression of a fatherly

sympathy. Effie felt it so, and answered at once,
" I am in anxiety about a very dear friend." ·

" I also am in anxiety about a very dear friend.
Perhaps we may be able to comfort one another. I
will tell you of my sorrow, and, if you like it, you can
tell me of yours, and then we will tell each other of
our comfort. Shall it be so ?"

" I shall be grateful for any comfort," said Effie,
strangely drawn towards the friendly old man.

He seated himself on the rock beside her, and
began in a low, sad voice : " My friend lies at the
point of death—if, indeed, he has not already left
this world. He has been struck down suddenly, in
the morning of his life, and just when I was looking
to him as my right hand in a work which I have
much at heart—but it is not for that I grieve, selfish
old man as I am—I try to persuade myself that it is
for the loss to the good cause that I mourn; but in
my heart I know it is not that—it is that I shall lose
one who is as dear to me as my own son could have
been, had he been spared to me."

He stopped for a few minutes to subdue his
emotion, and then went on more cheerfully.

" Now I will tell you of my comfort. It is that I
believe the summons has come to one who is ready
for it—as ready in his bright manhood as if his life
had declined into old age like mine. It is that,
having dedicated his youthful vigour to the service of

God on earth, the sacrifice has been accepted before
its consummation.   It is, above all, that he has given
his life for another, and that his death, like his life, is
full of faith and love.   This is my comfort, and,
were I not naturally the most selfish of men, it would
be comfort enough to turn all my grief into joy.
Now would you like to speak of your sorrow, or would
you rather not ?"

"My sorrow is the same as yours, except that it is
all selfish."

"And your comfort ?" asked the old man, as she
paused.

"I do not know," whispered Effie, ashamed to
remember how little she had thought of such comfort
as her companion's.

"Do you doubt your friend's safety ? Remember
the penitent thief.   It is never too late for repentance."

Effie was silent, and the stranger went on.   "*My*
friend was not always what he is now.   He once lived
a selfish, worldly life.   But the good seed had been
early sown ; and of late years it has sprung up so
vigorously that the tares have dwindled away before
it. The good seed may be in *your* friend's heart, and
this blow may have come to break up the hard soil,
that it may spring up, and bring forth fruit.   Yes,
fruit, even on a death-bed.   I believe that my dear
young friend on his death-bed has shown as noble

fruits of repentance and faith as he would have done
had he lived to enter upon his chosen work as a
Missionary."

" A Missionary !" cried Effie, a sudden light breaking upon her. " Who—who are you ?"

" My name is Joseph Eden," answered the old
man, looking rather surprised.

" And your friend is Gerard Yonge !" The discovery was too much for Effie, and she burst into
tears.

" Our grief is the same," said Mr. Eden kindly,
putting his arm round her in a fatherly manner, and
making her rest her head upon his shoulder. " Your
friend is also Gerard Yonge. But who are you, my
dear ?" he asked, when Effie was a little more composed.

" Did he ever speak to you of Effie Garnock ?"

" Are you Effie Garnock ? I have heard much of
you, my dear. Your father's was the hand which
first sowed the seed that has now sprung up into
Everlasting Life."

Effie sobbed. " He has been like a brother to you,
poor child. You are mourning for him as a sister."
The old man looked at Effie with a peculiarly search-
ing expression as he spoke. She felt the colour rush
to her face.

" He has told me how he wronged you once, and
how generously you forgave him. And he has told

me of his punishment too. But that punishment
was a blessing in disguise, for it taught him to fix
his hopes higher than earthly happiness. We all
need something of the sort to tell us this is not our
rest."

" And he has learnt that ?" asked Effie, timidly.

" Do you not see it in him ? No—it is shown
more in works than in words. Do you know that for
more than two years he has spent nearly all his
hard-earned money, and all his spare time, on the
veriest outcasts of society, and especially in trying to
save from the lowest degradation one who deeply
injured him."

" Mrs. Price ?" exclaimed Effie, involuntarily.

" Yes. He was seeking her out when first I met
him. She has proved unworthy of all his persevering
efforts for her good. But others have made him a
better return. Many a poor creature, restored to
hope and self-respect, blesses the hour that brought
her under the notice of Gerard Yonge."

This only was wanting to complete Effie's humilia-
tion. She had made so much of *her* good works,
whilst *he*, without a word, or probably a thought of
any merit in it, had outstripped her beyond the
possibility of comparison. And George Monro,
whom she had so exalted over Gerard, what were
his easy labours, in a pleasant village, compared to
this trying and often discouraging work of which

Mr. Eden had spoken. Had she known how George had misjudged that work, his long fidelity to herself would not have saved him from the loss of her friendship.

"But how is this?" asked the old Missionary, with his straightforward simplicity, after a long silence, broken only by the sobs which Effie could not check. "He told me that the Effie he loved was indifferent to him—that she loved his friend, the friend for whom he has given his life. But this is more than grief for a husband's friend. Perhaps he was mistaken?"

"Yes—quite wrong—about that," said Effie.

"And about the other? Surely this is not indifference?"

"He thinks so—I thought so once."

"When he met with what he calls his punishment?" asked Mr. Eden.

"What was that?"

"When he asked for your love a second time, and learned that he had forfeited it beyond recal."

"He did not love me then," whispered Effie. "He only wanted to atone for the past."

"I think you are wrong, my dear. I believe that he loved you deeply, and was severely pained by your rejection. He may once have shown a boy's light fancy, but he loves now with a man's true heart. But," added the old man, solemnly, "why should

I talk of earthly affection, when perhaps he now
knows something of the mystery of Eternal Love.
Nay, my dear, we cannot wish it otherwise. If he
were spared to us it would be as a helpless cripple.
Should that be God's will we must believe that
there is a purpose in it, but it will be sad to see. It
is best so."

These words reminded Effie of the telegram she
had received, and she gave it to her companion. In
spite of Mr. Eden's submission, his hand shook violently as he took the paper, and when he had read
it the tears ran down his furrowed cheeks.

" He has learnt to say it at last," he murmured.
" Yes, my dear, he is right. It is best so. We must
not wish it otherwise."

A strange solemnity came over Effie as the old
man talked to her, and she reached home in a very
different frame of mind to that in which she had
come out—the bitter, despairing feeling had gone, and
she almost thought she also could say, " It is best so."
It was the first time that she had ever met affliction
with humble submission, instead of proud endurance.

Her newly-acquired calmness was put to the test
that evening, when another telegram arrived. Then
it was all over! She might enter at once upon the
life of widowhood which she had planned. She had
prepared herself for this—she had known it must
come—she had even persuaded herself that she did

not wish it otherwise. Then, why could she not summon courage to look at those few words which would end all suspense? Oh, if she might only have five minutes more of that precious suspense! There was hope in that, but this would bring despair.

"Please, miss, the man says will you sign the paper," said the maid-of-all-work, appearing at the door.

Effie was forced to rouse herself, and as she complied with the request, her eyes fell upon the words: "He is better. Rogers acknowledges it, though he does not say there is hope. He has had a quiet sleep."

The next morning's post brought a letter from Jessie, despatched just after the telegram:

"Gateshill, Tuesday Afternoon.

"DEAREST EFFIE,

"Harold says I am not to give you too much hope, for fear of a disappointment, but I do really think Gerard is much better. Perhaps I am too happy myself not to be hopeful. But even Mr. Rogers allows that he *may* recover, and you know that is a great deal from him. I am afraid Harold will be quite knocked up. He looks dreadfully ill. It seems ages since yesterday morning, when he came, and Gerard was insensible. It was so terrible to see his face as he sat by the bedside. I thought there was no hope for me—I thought it would be like it

was when little Isa died. I did all I could for him—
George said I had better—but he never took the
least notice. You cannot imagine the relief it was
when Gerard spoke this morning. I hardly heard
what he said to Harold, but it made Harold cry out
to Gerard to forgive him, and then he went out of
the room, and they made me follow him. Oh, Effie!
it was so dreadful to stand before him, and expect
that he might send me away again! But he was
very kind. We could not say much then, but since
we have been happier about Gerard I have told
him everything—about my not caring for him properly at first, but how I have got to love him really
now, and how unhappy I have been; and he has
told me that he never ceased to love me, but he says
he was so angry when I left him that he vowed to
himself he would never see me again, and he
should have kept the vow if Gerard had not sent for
him when he could not refuse to come. He has
been very miserable too. But we shall be happier
now than we ever were before. Gerard said it
would all come right, the very day of his accident.
We little thought then how, or how soon, it would be.
Harold does not seem to dare to hope about Gerard,
but George and I feel very sanguine. I think, even
now that I have got Harold back, it would break
my heart to lose Gerard. When Harold began to
read to him this morning, he said it reminded him

of the Sunday-evening readings at Pixycombe, and
that we only wanted you, and then he told George
to give you his very best love. He was so pleased
about Harold and me. You cannot think how
beautiful he looks lying there, and when he was
talking solemnly to Harold, there was something
quite unearthly in his face. I thought then that
he would die. But I am sure now that he will live,
and we shall all be happy. George says it is post-
time.

"Give my love to my boy. The others are quite
well, and very good.

"Ever your affectionate Sister,

"JESSIE."

Effie could not share Jessie's confidence. Her
mind had been so strung up to hear the worst,
that it would not now readily open to take in hope.
Every moment she dreaded some reversal of the
good news. But none such came. The day after
Jessie's letter arrived a note from George, told of the
patient's continued improvement, and after that came
a still better account from Harold.

"Prior's Mount, January 1st.

"MY DEAR EFFIE,

"I would not let Jessie give you too much
hope about Gerard, but I think I may now safely

say that he is decidedly better. The circulation is in some measure restored on the left side, and he himself declares that he shall soon be quite well. Mr. Rogers thinks a complete recovery impossible, but he considers that a great improvement has taken place, and that there is now room for hope. Gerard's spirits are marvellous. He never loses heart or patience, in spite of his utter helplessness, and occasional acute suffering. Rogers says that if he recovers, it will be entirely due to his own happy temper— any other man would have died of mere impatience of such a death in life.

"I may thank you now for your last letter; I could not do so at the time I received it, for you desired to have no intercourse with me. You were quite right, and all that you wrote was most true. But I should never have yielded to anything less imperative than such a call as Gerard's. However, the submission is now made; and l suppose I may reckon as one of my rewards the restoration to your favour.

"Should Gerard continue to improve I would come and release you from your attendance on Davie; but l am afraid it would not be safe for you to come amongst the others after being with him.

"I remain,

"Your affectionate Brother,

"HAROLD A. YONGE."

When, a few days later, Effie heard that Gerard was pronounced to be out of all immediate danger, she no longer felt so impatient of her enforced absence. Davie was soon quite well; but both he and his aunt had to endure a long quarantine before they could be considered free from infection. Mr. Eden had left Ventnor three days after Effie's first meeting with him, and a week later had started for Borneo. From London he wrote to Effie.

"333, New Oxford Street,
January 7th.

" MY DEAR EFFIE GARNOCK,

" One word of farewell before I leave England, which will be to-morrow morning. I have seen Gerard Yonge, and my mind is very easy about him. I had feared, from his brother's letter, which you showed to me the morning I parted from you, that he might be over-sanguine about himself. But I had some quiet talk with him, and I find he is quite aware that if his life is prolonged it will be one of helplessness and suffering. He bears this knowledge with noble fortitude, and his only anxiety is to save those about him from sorrow on his account. He was greatly pleased to hear of my meeting with you, and was eager for all the most minute particulars of our intercourse. I did not think it well to gratify him entirely in this respect. One whose life hangs by such a feeble thread is none the better for having his earthly ties strengthened.

"God bless and preserve both him and you—whether in death or in life—is the earnest prayer of your sincere friend,

"JOSEPH EDEN."

When Effie and her charge had removed to another house, and had remained there for a month, which they spent almost entirely on the Downs, and the beach, it was considered safe for Davie to go home for a few days, before returning to school. It was evening when they reached Prior's Mount. As Effie walked up the little garden, with Harold by her side she felt choked with agitation, and when she got into the light drawing-room her head swam so that she could see nothing. She knew that Jessie came forward and kissed her, and she heard the children's voices, as if at a great distance, though they were close to her, and then she felt that her hand was in Gerard's, and heard his voice saying, "Poor little girl. She looks fagged. Give her a cup of tea, Jessie."

Jessie obeyed promptly, and Effie drank the tea with eager readiness.

"I told you so," cried Gerard, in a triumphant tone. "I knew she would like that better than dinner."

" And do you mean her to have nothing to eat?" asked Harold. "Because you are an old washerwoman are these unfortunate travellers to be starved? Oh, I see you are taking care of yourself, Davie. You don't mean to starve. How well the boy looks!"

" We have had such jolly fun," said Davie, with his mouth full. " Climbing over the rocks, and scrambling about the Downs. Auntie is such a capital climber."

Effie turned crimson, and the tears rushed to her eyes. She could not bear any mention of activity before Gerard. The mist of agitation had cleared from her sight sufficiently to show her his strong muscular form stretched on a sofa in utter helplessness.

Gerard understood her feelings, and said, lightly, " What nonsense, Davie! An old woman like Auntie climb! Why, I would race her with my crutches."

" I will go and take off my things, Jessie," said Effie, hastily.

"Go to my room," answered Jessie. " You need not go next door yet. Mrs. Mortlake is dining out."

When Jessie followed her sister in a few minutes, she found her crying bitterly.

" You are shocked to see Gerard, Effie. You would not feel so if you had seen him when he first got up. We think him so much better now. But it must be sad to any one who has not seen him

before. I forgot that. He is always so happy himself that he makes us almost forget there is anything
to feel sad about. But do try not to cry. He cannot
bear to see any one grieving about him, and he is so
quick he is sure to notice if your eyes are red."

Effie bathed her face diligently for some minutes.
But Jessie was right about Gerard's quickness. His
troubled look at Effie showed at once that he saw she
had been crying, and knew the cause of it.

" I thought Mr. Eden would have kidnapped you,
Effie, and carried you off to preach to the Dyaks," he
said, laughingly. " And then a native chief might have
taken a fancy to you, and decked you out in feathers
and pearls. Would not she make a capital squaw,
Harold ? A blanket and three feathers would do it
in an instant. Why, you are browner than ever, little
woman. Have you and Davie been living in a
gipsy encampment ?"

" Very nearly, only without the shelter of an
encampment," Effie managed to say now, for Gerard's
careless talk had restored her composure.

" I suppose you told fortunes and stole spoons—by-
the-by, it never struck me before how admirably
adapted those little quick fingers of yours are for some
such profession as that. And Davie is exactly like
the wild-looking boys who ride horses away with more
regard to possession than rightful ownership. I
would recommend you both to try the effect of

Rowland's Kalydor, and a comb would not be a bad institution for either of you. I suppose Mrs. Mortlake will compliment you on 'that rich olive tint, which really, my dear Miss Effie, quite strikes me dumb with — and that charmingly negligent chevelure. Diana herself could not attain any such delightful union of consummate art with Nature's free grace.' Poor little girl!" he cried, with sudden remorse. "It is a shame to quiz you—just after your journey too. Harold, make her eat something—if Davie has not quite cleared the table. You must eat, Effie. If you don't I shall have you casting envious eyes at my beef-tea presently, and I can't stand that."

"I am too tired to eat," said Effie, with a faint smile. "I would rather go to bed before Mrs. Mortlake comes home, Jessie."

"It is very jolly to have the old brown face to look at once more," said Gerard, as she offered him her hand to say "good-night." He held her for a minute with his left hand, of which he had now quite recovered the use, and looked earnestly in her face. Presently he looked down at his right hand, which lay helpless on his knee, and said, almost in a whisper, "My finger is so swollen the ring will not come off, Effie. I thought George was coming to-night," he added, suddenly, in a louder tone; and Effie was vexed to feel the hot blood rush to her cheeks. Gerard let go her hand, and said, quietly, "He will be down here the first thing in the morning, I suppose.　There is a great deal of illness in the village.　I dare say he was detained by some one."

Effie tried to look indifferent, but she only succeeded in looking embarrassed.

" Here comes my supper !" cried Gerard. " Martha, don't let Miss Garnock see it.　Bring it here, quick !"

" Do you think he looks very ill ?" asked Jessie, as Effie was wrapping up to go out.

" No, only thin.　I expected to see him looking much worse.　And you are very happy, Jessie ?"

" Yes, very," said Jessie.　" I did not know it was possible to be so happy.　Harold is so changed.　He is like he used to be years ago, only more lively, and less confident in himself.　He is getting more like Gerard, I think."

" Good-night !" cried Gerard, as Effie passed the door on her way out.　" Ask Mrs. Mortlake what she uses for her complexion."

" What do you think of him ?" said Harold, coming out with her.

" He looks pretty well."

" I wish he would not be so unnaturally lively. He tries to cheat us all out of our sorrow for him."

" Do you think it is forced ?"

" No.　I think he is really happy. It is wonderful. I am trying to learn the secret, Effie.　Gerard is teaching me.　Good-night."

CHAPTER XII.

"AUNTIE, you are to come in with me directly; we want to ask you about something," cried Freddie, bursting into the room where Mrs. Mortlake and Effie were just finishing their luncheon, one afternoon in April.

"What is it, Freddie?"

"I'm not to tell you till you get there. Come along. She may come, mayn't she, Mrs. Mortlake?"

"Here is the brave young Mercury come for the fair Pandora, and he asks permission of one of the humblest of Minerva's handmaids. Oh, fie! Mr. Freddie, you must learn to play the part of the winged messenger with greater— Farewell, Miss Effie. Pray, do not let these regions remain long in shade. '*Bonum magis carendo quam fruendo cernitur.*' Adieu, Mr. Freddie, you bearer of the gloomy pall of night. Present my warmest and most deferential regards to all the inmates of——"

Freddie had hurried his aunt away so fast that Mrs. Mortlake's further flow of words was lost.

" Auntie, couldn't we manage a party capitally ?" cried Davie, as Effie went into the room where all the family were assembled. " Say we could. You know we could. There wouldn't be the least difficulty about it. It's for Walter's birthday, you know, next Tuesday."

" What sort of party do you mean ?" asked Effie.

" Oh, a regular jolly party—a dance, of course, like we went to at Todd's, last Thursday. We are always going to fellows', and we never have any one here except just in a slow sort of way, that's not half fun."

" The most perplexing question is, Effie," said Gerard, who was looking as eager as the boys, '· would it be possible to stuff thirty or forty people into Jessie's bedroom for supper, or must we have Harold bound over to keep the peace, and then do our worst with the studio ?"

" At your peril !" cried Harold, shaking his fist at his brother.

" Wouldn't all the furniture out of these two rooms go easily into uncle Gerard's bedroom, Auntie ?" asked Davie.

" I have a better idea, Davie !" cried Gerard. " That shall be the supper-room. We have only got to get rid of the bed, and then it will be the old play-room again, which was a most spacious apartment always."

"Oh, uncle Gerard, such a wee little room!" said Bessie.

"Yes, that would be much the best," pronounced Walter; "and then Mamma need not be turned out —it would be a shame to turn Mamma out of her room."

"Never mind that, Walter," said Jessie. "But I cannot see how it is all to be managed."

"Let's pound old Mortlake, and knock a way into next door," suggested Davie.

"I'll do that," said Gerard, quickly, with a conscious look at Effie.

"Then we must pound Auntie too," cried Freddie, gleefully.

"No, Auntie isn't worth a pound—she's so small; she's only worth a penny," observed Gerard.

"Why don't you clap? uncle Gerard has made a pun. Papa, you mustn't go—we haven't settled yet."

"It appears to me that your object is to *un*settle. I only hope you will spare the foundations of the house, but I think they are in considerable danger."

"Then before you go say we may, Papa."

"May knock the house down? What do you say to their scheme, Jessie?"

"I should like it, if it would not upset everything too much."

"Then settle it as well as you can, boys. I give you *carte blanche.*"

"And Jessie will give us *blanc-mange,*" said Gerard.

"Uncle Gerard's made another pun!" shouted Davie.

"May we use your *carte* blanche to move the furniture, Harold?" asked the incorrigible Gerard, as his brother left the room.

"Perhaps Mamma would like it to *blanch* the almonds."

"Bravo, Walter! Follow in your uncle's steps always, my boy, and you will never go wrong."

"But this is not settling a bit," said Davie. "Uncle Gerard, I wish you and Walter wouldn't be so awfully witty. Let's be serious. Auntie, do help. How *can* we manage?"

"Need it be a dance, Walter?" asked Effie, who had been looking very grave during all the discussion.

"Take her to the pound, Davie!" cried Gerard. "She is one of those dangerous movers of amendments, who, under pretence of an innocent little improvement, put in a wedge which upsets the whole thing. Of course it need be a dance, and the only question is whether you and Mrs. Mortlake are to dance a galliard, as Queen Elizabeth and one of her ladies, or the Highland fling, with bare feet and short petticoats."

"Auntie, it must be a dance," said Walter, piteously. "Mustn't it, Mamma?"

"Yes, I think so. I don't see how else we are to amuse the people."

"What people are you going to have, Jessie?" asked Effie.

"Oh, I suppose all the old set."

"Not only children, then?"

"No, not children only — we must have some grown-up people whilst we are about it."

"Why do you look as if you didn't like it, Auntie?" asked Davie.

"She is thinking what she can wear," said Gerard; "whether she must go up to Abbot's, and buy a new white frock, or whether the old one will do, with fresh ribbons; and whether it will be an occasion for new, or for cleaned gloves. Be just like you were at Clara's party before Christmas, Effie—nothing could be better."

"I was not thinking of that important subject, for a wonder," returned Effie.

"What is it makes you look so grave then?" asked Gerard.

"That old Mortlake has been bothering her with Mercury, and all that rot," said Freddie.

"Has she been salivating you, Effie?" cried Gerard, laughing. "Is that what you mean, Freddie?"

"I don't know what that is, uncle Gerard, but I know it has made Auntie look dismal."

"'O'er the lake of the dismal swamp she paddles her white canoe,'"

sang Gerard. "That's the Mort-lake, you know, Freddie. Give me a piece of paper and a pencil, Walter, and I will make a list of the company. First, Butterfields—shall I put down two, or three, dozen ?"

"Mr. and Mrs. Samuel are sure not to come—there will only be the three boys from there—then there are Sarah and Emily——"

"Those horrid old maids," cried Davie.

"And Clara and her husband—and Mr. and Mrs. Joe—that will be all the Butterfields. Then there are the Rogerses, and the Kents, and the Crashawes, and the Blunts, and——"

"Where will you put them all, Jessie ?" asked Effie.

"Oh, they will put themselves somewhere," answered Gerard. "I have got ten Butterfields. How many of all the others ?"

"It would do very well if you were not to attempt dancing."

"Aunt Effie, what a bore you are !" cried Walter, and immediately had a sofa-cushion in his face.

"Well, she is, uncle Gerard. She opposes everything. She is not a bit of good. She had much better not have come."

" Would you rather not have come, Effie ?" asked Gerard, anxiously. " Was there anything else you wanted to do ?"

" No, nothing," said Effie, feeling very much inclined to cry. The idea of this dance was distressing to her for Gerard's sake, and he was the most eager of all to promote it.

" We must have George Monro," said Gerard, bending over his list. " Look there, Effie, have not I got on capitally with my writing ? You would never know that was done with the left hand."

" We haven't settled about the rooms yet," remarked the practical Davie.

" I am sure my plan is the best," said Gerard.

" Do you like uncle Gerard's plan, Mamma ?" asked Walter.

" You know the bed would not have to be put up again, Jessie," pursued Gerard, " for I am going to set up my own establishment on Wednesday."

" I don't like *that* plan," said Jessie. " I think it is very unkind of you, Gerard."

" How many Rogerses am I to put down ?" asked Gerard, paying no attention to Jessie's remark. " Of course not Minnie, Davie ?"

" I don't care," asserted the boy, colouring crimson.

"I suppose we must have the old doctor to flirt with Effie."

"That's why aunt Effie doesn't want us to dance—she wants to sit all the evening talking to Mr. Rogers."

"She can do that in spite of the dancing."

"No; she'll have to play."

"That she shall not!" cried Gerard. "Jessie, you will have a man to play? Effie is not to be sticking at the piano all the evening."

"The Butterfield girls would play, and the Miss Kents."

"Once, perhaps, and Effie would do all the rest. I shall invoke the thunders of the Church if you don't engage that little musician—what is his name?"

"Mr. Hope."

"Of course— Just think how inspiriting it is to dance to the music of Hope—and, I am sure from Effie's face now, that hers would be the music of Despair. Effie, I know you are sick of all this. Now, confess that you are longing to be off to a meeting of District Visitors, or School Teachers. Say it out:

'My heart's in my parish; my heart is not here;
My heart's with my curate, his labours to share.'"

This was sung in a very low voice to Effie, and with a shy, wistful glance. Effie coloured angrily,

and the tears, which had been very near her eyes all
the morning, suddenly overflowed.

"Effie! I didn't mean to hurt you. I didn't
think you would mind."

Gerard let his pencil and paper fall, and caught
Effie's hand.

"Poor little girl! We have bored you terribly. It
was a shame to send for you in such a tyrannical way."

"Can I write any invitations?" asked Effie, making
a great effort.

"Yes," said Jessie. "You may write to all in
Gerard's list."

Effie wrote away industriously till dinner-time.
As she got up to go Gerard said in a low voice to
her, "You don't half like the idea of this party, Effie
—why is it? you used to be so fond of dancing—and
how well you did it! What famous waltzes we have
had together!"

This was too much. Effie's only safety was in
flight. But she would not leave the house without
one more effort to put off the proposed dance.

"Harold," she said, entering the studio, "don't
you think this scheme of the boys is rather ill-timed.
It seems so horrible to be having a dance whilst
Gerard is in this state."

"But the whole thing is Gerard's doing. He put
it into the boys' heads, and he is quite as much bent
upon it as they are."

"That is because he never thinks of himself. But he *must* feel it when it comes to the point. You know what an indefatigable dancer he used to be."

"But what can be done, Effie? Gerard would be annoyed beyond measure if the thing were to be given up on his account."

"I wish it had not gone so far——"

"I did not oppose it," said Harold, "because I think it is as well all Gateshill should come and see that we are no longer such fair game as we have been for ill-natured reports."

"I did not think of that," rejoined Effie. "I suppose it must be then. Yes; I see that you are right."

For the same reason Effie saw that she could not escape the party. Her presence was necessary to complete the evidence of restored family peace. So on the Tuesday evening, after giving her most zealous help towards the preparations—to make up for her previous coldness—she dressed herself as Gerard had requested, and went in early, to be ready to dispense tea and coffee to the guests.

Gerard was already established in a corner of the dancing-room, on a light chair, to have as little as possible the appearance of an invalid, and Freddie and his sister were pirouetting about on the white cloth.

"Here she is!" cried Gerard, as Effie appeared at the door. "That's right. Good little girl, to do as I told you. I wish you had a few flowers, though.

It is a bore for some reasons to be such a pauper as I am."

"I would much rather be without flowers when I have to help in the management of a party—they are in the way then."

"What a swell you are, uncle Gerard!" cried Davie, at the door. "Who tied your choker? I can't get mine right a bit—do see to it, Auntie."

"My usual valet," answered Gerard.

"Who, Harold?"

"I say, uncle Gerard, you *are* an awful swell!" cried Davie again, when his necktie was arranged to his satisfaction. "Doesn't he look awfully jolly, Auntie? Won't all the girls fall in love with him?"

Gerard coloured like a boy, and glanced shyly at Effie.

"With his beard, you mean, Davie. That was my doing, was not it, Gerard? Would not it have been sacrificed, but for my entreaties?"

"Yes; that it would, Effie. Then I shall owe my conquests to you?"

"It is such an awfully jolly beard," said Davie, "so soft and smooth! Just come and feel it, Auntie."

"Just leave my beard alone, Davie," cried Gerard, "and fetch me the engagement-cards—they are on the piano. Have you got a card, Effie? Take one then, and put me down for—let me see, I must not be greedy— for two dances."

Effie stared.

" Is that too much to ask ?"

"What *do* you mean, uncle Gerard ?" said Davie, putting Effie's wonder into words.

"Not that I am going to dance, Davie. I shall not attempt that till *your* birthday party. Will you spare me two dances, Effie ?"

"I have all to spare," said Effie, hurriedly. "I am not going to dance at all."

"Not going to dance! Why, surely— You don't disapprove of dancing. George does not object to it ?"

" I don't know at all what Mr. Monro thinks on the subject," said Effie, coldly, telling an untruth in her desire to show indifference about George's views. Gerard looked anxiously in her flushed face.

" There is an arrival, Effie," said Jessie, as she and Harold came into the room together.

" *Here* is an arrival—of the belle of the evening," said Harold, proudly.

" *There's* the first bell of the evening !" cried Gerard, as a coachman's loud peal rang through the house.

The guests came flocking in quickly now, and soon the rooms were nearly full, and the dancing began. When Effie's duties at the tea-table were over, and she made her way into the drawing-room, a waltz was just beginning. She stoutly resisted all solicitations to join in the dance, and devoted herself to the amusement of a knot of boys whose feet refused to perform anything more intricate than shuffling through the figures of a quadrille. Presently Freddie came to her.

"Uncle Gerard wants you, Auntie."

"You have not promised me my dances yet, Effie," said Gerard. "You must not cheat me."

Effie gave him her blank card.

"May I do what I like with this?"

"Here is my pencil," said Effie. "What shall I write?"

Gerard put the card down on his knee, and taking her hand in his made her write G. A. Y. all across the space left for engagements. "Will that do?" he asked, looking at her with laughing, but eagerly excited eyes.

"Yes," said Effie, quietly.

"Are you sure, Effie? Will you keep to it?"

"Yes, as far as I can. But I must see that everything goes right amongst the dancers. Now I must set them to work again. Neither Harold nor Jessie have any idea that a party will not go without driving."

When another dance had begun, and Effie came back to her place beside Gerard, it was occupied by Nathaniel Butterfield, and several others were standing round. Gerard was a great centre of attraction for the non-dancers; and it was impossible to penetrate through the crowd that surrounded his chair till a movement was caused by Clara going to the piano to sing. Effie, in the midst of several of her boy-admirers, was standing against the wall just opposite to Gerard. During the first song, a brilliant display of Clara's exquisite voice, it was hard work to make the boys listen quietly; but when a plaintive little German air followed there was a perfect silence. Effie's heart beat quickly, for this was one of the songs that Clara had sung on that evening, eight years ago, when the first doubt of Gerard arose. As the remembrance struck her she involuntarily looked in his direction. The space between them was clear now, and her eye caught his, fixed upon her with yearning tenderness.

As Clara sang,

"Ich habe gelebt und geliebet,"

Gerard's look said that if he were not a cripple he would be by Effie's side; and that look drew Effie irresistibly to him.

"Thank you, Effie," he said, in a very low voice. "Did you know how I was longing to have you near me?"

Effie did not answer this question; but when the song was over, and the buzz of conversation began again, she said, "Clara's singing is certainly quite perfect."

"Yes, it is very beautiful," returned Gerard, thoughtfully. "I can bear it now; but a year or two ago the sound of her voice was more hateful to me than the screech of a hurdy-gurdy, for it always reminded me that it once made me throw away all my happiness."

"Effie, where can George be?" asked Jessie, coming up, whilst Effie was trembling with the emotion excited by Gerard's words, and the tone in which they were spoken.

"Has he not come yet?" asked Effie, with studied indifference.

"No. I wish he would come. I am sure Nathaniel Butterfield would like a game at whist, and we cannot make up four without George—there are only Mrs. Mortlake and Harold to play."

"Shall I play?" asked Effie.

"No, you cannot be spared. I could not manage the dancers. It is very tiresome George is so late. Ought not some dance to be set going now, Effie?"

Effie went off to her duties. When she came back Mr. Rogers gave up his seat to her by Gerard's side, saying, as he did so, "You don't deserve to sit down, Miss Effie. You have been very idle to-night. I don't at all approve of young people not dancing. I shall speak to George Monro about it—we must not let him make an ascetic of you."

The old gentleman went off before Effie had time

to answer him, and just as she turned to Gerard with an indignant protest against Mr. Rogers' conclusions, George himself appeared at the door.

"Give me that card, Effie !" said Gerard, hastily.

Effie hesitated.

"Do not let George see it, then,—he might not like what I have written," said Gerard, in a rapid whisper, as George approached.

"I am afraid my offering comes very late," George said, holding out to Effie some beautiful flowers.

"That's right, George! Flowers were all that was wanted to complete her," cried Gerard, after a momentary struggle with himself, shown by a sudden pallor and a tight compression of his lips.

Effie gave an appealing glance at Gerard, and rather an angry one at George. "I am very much obliged to you," she said, stiffly. "But,—may I put them with the other flowers in the next room? I should spoil your beautiful bouquet if I were to rush about with it in my hand."

"Oh, certainly," said George, in a mortified tone.

"Do you disapprove of dancing, George?" asked Gerard, when Effie had gone away with her flowers.

"Certainly not. I highly approve of it. I don't dance myself, because I think if there are two sides on which any conduct can be viewed, it is the safest plan to keep on that side where one's inclinations do *not* lie. But I would not on any account apply this theory of mine to any one but myself."

" Then it is not at your request that Effie has given up dancing?"

" Has she given up dancing? Certainly it is not at my request. I should have no right, had I any inclination to make such a request."

" She will not dance to-night, and the blame has been laid on you by several people—and I must confess that I was one of them."

" Then I will say to you, ' Look nearer home.' "

" ' Nearer home!' Who at home is likely to influence her in such a matter?"

" I do not know for certain, but I think I can guess what it is that influences her. Cannot *you* guess?"

" I have not the slightest idea, if you are not the culprit. She has been a puzzle to us all for the last few days—putting every obstacle in the way of this party, when she is usually the readiest to forward every scheme of the sort."

" And you have had no suspicion of the reason?" asked George, looking searchingly into Gerard's face.

" What suspicion could I have?—excepting that you had become more strict in your notions, and that Effie took her tone from you."

" Did it never strike you that there might be a reference to yourself in her conduct?"

"To me! Why, I should like nothing better than to plunge into the thick of this mad galop."

"Exactly," said George, looking very much confused, and turning his head away as he spoke. "That is the very reason, I imagine, of Effie's conduct. It would be painful to her to enjoy what you cannot share. At least, that is my idea as to her feelings."

Gerard did not say a word, and presently Effie returned.

"Jessie wishes to know if you would mind taking a hand at whist, Mr. Monro ?"

"'Mr. Monro,' Effie !"

"I beg your pardon. But what answer shall I take to the whist-players ?"

"I will take them my own consent," said George, walking towards the other room.

Effie glanced at Gerard, and his grave face made her also move away.

"Stop, Effie, one moment !"

Effie laughingly pointed to her engagement-card, and sat down.

"No, I release you from that," said Gerard. "I have found out now why you will not dance, and why you opposed the idea of this party. It was very kind of you ; but, indeed, the sacrifice was quite uncalled for. I am not such a dog in the manger as to grudge pleasures to others which I cannot enjoy myself. You must not think so badly of me, Effie."

"It is not that, Gerard. It is for my own sake— not for yours."

"Do you mean that your pity for me destroys your own pleasure? Little woman, what a kind heart you have!"

"Give me that card, Effie," Gerard said, sadly, after a long silence.

"I cannot spare it," answered Effie, trying to smile.

"Please give it to me. I cannot owe anything to pity. It is very good of you; but, Effie, I cannot bear pity from you!"

Effie thought her heart would burst. She felt as if she must cry out before all the company that it was not pity, but deepest love, which made it impossible for her to have any pleasure unshared by him. Indeed, this impulse had been her torment for many weeks. It never gave her any rest. When trying to occupy herself with reading or working at Mrs. Mortlake's, or with active duties in the village, she was unceasingly possessed with a longing to see Gerard, to make sure that he was not worse, or to seek in his constant fun and merriment evidence that he was not unhappy. But as soon as she was with him, witnessing his helplessness and his patience a still stronger impulse would seize her—the impulse to throw herself at his feet, and to pour out the confession of her admiration and love. This now became so overpowering that she could hardly have resisted it, had there not at that moment been a general move to the supper-room.

A select party of Gerard's admirers, incited by Effie, brought their supper into the drawing-room, to keep him company, and he roused himself to entertain them, in return, with every kind of nonsense.

Effie was obliged soon to leave this merry set to attend to the rest of the guests, and after supper she was occupied for some time in getting off the younger children. When she returned to the dancing-room she thought that Gerard looked weary and depressed. Little Lily Rogers had fallen asleep with her head on his shoulder, but there was no one else near him.

" She will tire you, Gerard," said Effie.

" No, oh, no. Poor little thing ! Minnie and Charlie will not give up dancing. She has just confided to me that she wishes she was in bed. I suppose we are a good way into to-morrow morning ?"

" It is nearly one o'clock. I think the children ought all to be packed off. Most of them are gone."

" The day of my move has come then," said Gerard.

" Oh, Gerard ! what a foolish move that is !"

" My dear Effie, would you have me *sorn* upon Harold all my life ?"

" Harold would desire nothing better."

"It is not that only. There are many reasons why it will be much better for me to be independent."

"But to live in such a wretched lodging. And you will be so dull."

"No, no. Mrs. Potter is a first-rate melodrama. I know I shall never be tired of being her audience. I have stipulated that the door between my room and her laundry shall be opened, so that whenever I like I may have a front stall, and witness the whole performance to perfection. It would not be possible to be dull. Then I shall be able to come here whenever I like, and I shall have plenty of visitors. You will come and see me sometimes, won't you?"

"Will you give me a free admittance to the stalls?"

"I don't know about that. I must not make the entertainment common. When you are very good, perhaps I will admit you to the shilling gallery—but not on any grand occasion, such as ironing or mangling day. I have once had the honour of being present at the 'Thrilling Tragio-Comic Performance with One Italian and Three Flat Irons,' and I consider it a privilege not to be lightly dispensed to the vulgar herd. Well, Lily, you are not in bed. Here is Freddie wants you to dance with him."

Lily departed, and then Gerard's manner changed. "Effie, will you do me a favour?" he asked.

"Yes—anything in the world that I can do."

"You can do it. Dance this waltz. I have been so counting on seeing you dance?"

"Davie," said Effie, "will you dance with me?"

"Why, dearest little Auntie!" cried Davie, "I should have liked to dance with you all the evening, but you said you would not dance."

"I have altered my mind," said Effie; and the two whirled away.

"And you thought I was such a selfish old curmudgeon that I should mind seeing you dance?" asked Gerard, when Effie came back to him, flushed and breathless.

"I did not think so, Gerard. But I thought, and think, that my next dance shall be with you."

"How do you know that I shall ask you?"

"I shall ask *you*."

"How forward and improper!"

"If you are backward and ungallant, and won't take broad hints, what am I to do?"

"Whatever you do, Effie, don't pity me again. Don't think to spare me by sacrificing yourself."

"Gerard, this is such a trifle, and you take it as if it were a serious matter."

"This is one proof of something which I have suspected for some time, and am now certain of."

"What is that?"

"It convinces me that I am right in going away

from here. Effie, do believe me : it will be no kindness to me for you to sacrifice yourself to spare my
feelings. I can bear—I do not say it boastfully—
whatever has to be borne. I have prepared myself
for it. But I cannot bear to stand in the way of your
happiness. It would have been better far that I
should never have come out of Steadham pond."

"Gerard, how dare you talk so ? *Then* you would
have stood in the way of my happiness."

Gerard shook his head. " It won't do, Effie. I
know you would have been sorry for me, little woman ;
but you would soon have been very happy, notwith-
standing. You would have given a few tears to
' poor Gerard,' and some one else would have wiped
them away. But now, Effie, don't make me wish
that I had died !"

" What is it you want me to do, Gerard ?"

" To think of your own happiness, and not of me
at all."

" I cannot," whispered Effie. " I cannot think of
one without the other."

But Gerard did not hear this, for as Effie spoke
there was a general leave-taking, and their talk was
interrupted. Effie's last sight of Gerard that night
was as George was carefully wrapping her up in the
hall, preparatory to leaving.

CHAPTER XIII.

"I HOPE I have not compromised you very deeply in the eyes of Mrs. Mortlake's servants, Effie, by asking to see you alone ; but I have neither time nor inclination, at present, to stand on ceremony."

George Monro had been shown, in compliance with the request to which he referred, into the room in Mrs. Mortlake's house corresponding with the "play-room" next door, and here Effie had joined him.

"No ; I think the servants understand that our interviews are about nothing more interesting than parish matters," answered Effie.

"Parish matters have not brought me here to-day," said George. "I want to consult with you as to what is to be done with Gerard. I am not at all easy about him."

"Don't you think him so well?" asked Effie, anxiously, every tinge of colour leaving her face as she spoke.

"He is certainly not so well as he was three months

ago; and Mr. Rogers is most decided in his opinion that, unless something be done for him, he will soon be very much worse."

"What *can* be done?"

"That is the question. His present mode of life is most unfit for a person in his state of health. Mrs. Potter is a very good woman, and he could not have more devoted attention; but nothing can make up for the dirt and discomfort of that house, and I am sure that Gerard suffers from these annoyances, although he is so determined to make us all believe that he has nothing to complain of. Then, Rogers has great doubts whether he takes sufficient nourishment—he suspects that Mrs. Potter does not make his food palatable enough to tempt the appetite of an invalid. In short, Rogers says that as the winter comes on his remaining in that ill-built, draughty, and unwholesome house would be nothing less than suicide."

"He will never be persuaded to leave it," said Effie, in a tone of despair. "He, who used to be so yielding, is now as firm as Harold ever was, in all matters of principle—and this is a matter of principle with him."

"It is a matter of feeling, also, Effie, and that complicates it. I do not wonder that, considering his brother's increasingly expensive family, he will not accept aid from him; and it is certain that, with his own very small means, it would be quite impossible for him to procure the comforts which he ought to have."

" Then what *can* be done ?" asked Effie again.

George got up and walked to the window, in evident agitation.

" Effie," he said, presently, turning towards her, but remaining at a distance, " you alone can save Gerard."

" I !" cried Effie, beginning to tremble violently.

" ' Yes. You once told me that, though you no longer loved him as he then was, you could never cease to love the memory of what he had been. Will even that shadow of a warmer feeling allow you to see him sacrificed for the want of help which you alone can give him ?"

" Oh, George, tell me how ?"

" He needs happy companionship, careful attendance, and the means of obtaining luxuries, which to him, at present, are necessaries. Rogers assures me that with these requisites he might be entirely restored to health—without them, he must soon sink into hopeless disease."

" I know what you mean, George," whispered Effie, as distinctly as her trembling lips and chattering teeth would permit. " I have thought of it again and again. But how can I do anything ? What can I possibly do when he says nothing ?"

"He *can* say nothing. Can he—a cripple, and almost a pauper—ask you to be his nurse, and his support?"

Effie was silent. This difficulty had never struck her before.

George went on : "I should not say all this, Effie, if I had not seen enough to convince me that your feelings are changed since you told me that you no longer loved Gerard, and since you told him the same. I feel all the more bound to speak, because he believes me to have gained the place in your affections which he fancies himself to have lost. Am I not right, Effie, in my conviction that he has not lost that place."

"That is what makes it so impossible that—" began Effie, then finding herself unable to finish this sentence, she tried another. " If I could ask him to let me be his nurse, for the sake of—for the sake of old times, and—and of what we once were to each other— I could do that; but—it is different now—I—I——"

" I know," said George, kindly, though not without an effort. "You love him too well now to let any other consideration actuate you. I believe that his feeling is much the same—it is that which makes him so shrink from receiving pity from you."

" Are you sure about his feeling?" asked Effie.

"I am sure of his loving you deeply," answered George, with quiet self-control. "I will tell you what proved to me that I could no longer answer it to my conscience to forbear speaking to you as I have done now. This morning I met Gerard in his chair. He then asked me to call upon him as soon as I was at leisure, as he had something particular to say to me. I went to him at three this afternoon. He immediately began by saying that he felt compelled to speak openly to me on a subject which had long greatly distressed him. He knew that for his sake— to spare him suffering—I was sacrificing my dearest hopes, as well as your happiness. He went on to beg me most earnestly to lay aside this mistaken conduct. He told me that he had long schooled himself to bear the loss which his own folly had brought upon him, but that what he could *not* bear was to be a second time the cause of suffering to you. He said, also, that from selfish considerations, he wished to dissuade me from what he called my ' Quixotic generosity,' as, if the blow had fallen, he could endure it with much more fortitude than was possible whilst the sword was hanging over his head. In fact, he declared that the suspense caused to him by the unsettled state of things between you and me kept him in such continual mental excitement as to retard his recovery, and endanger his life. He put all this to me in the most forcible manner—evidently combating an imaginary resolve on my part to sacrifice my own hopes, in return for his sacrifice of himself with the idea of saving my life. I am afraid that he gives me credit

for greater magnanimity than I could have displayed
had I had any hopes to sacrifice. As it is, it requires
no very great generosity to bestow on another what is
already his, and has never been within one's own
reach. However, I could not undeceive him in any
satisfactory manner, as all my evidence must have
rested on mere suspicion, and, as far as I myself am
concerned, I could not arrogantly renounce the happiness which he believed to be mine. So it remains with
you, Effie, to put an end to his suspense— and to mine
also, for I think that I, like Gerard, am induced to
push matters on, in order to put an end to a state of
uncertainty, which is a continual trial of my resolution.
Not that I have ever been in any uncertainty as to
my fate," George added, with a melancholy smile, as
he got up to leave. "But when I have said the
'Amens' at your marriage I shall be better able to
feel that it is good for me to abide as St. Paul advises.
God bless you, Effie, and direct you to the best course
in this matter. Remember that Gerard can *ask* you
nothing, however much you have it in your power to
give him. Remember that, in some cases, conven-
tionalities must be set aside ; and, at all events, the
responsibility rests with me rather than with you."

"Oh, George, how good you are ! I have been in a
miserable state of doubt and uncertainty for months.
You have cleared it away a little—but how can I get
the courage to do what you advise ?"

"Go and see Gerard—see how ill and worn he looks, and how comfortless everything about him is. Don't let him blind you with his jokes and his assumed spirits; remark how rapidly his smiles die away, and what a weary tone there is in his voice, even whilst he is talking the most lively nonsense. Think how you— and you alone—could change all this, and the courage will come. Good-bye. I have done to-day what I always highly reprehend—interfering in the affairs of others. I shall find my just reward, I suppose, in a ceremony performed by the Rev. J. Crashawe, *assisted* by the Rev. G. Monro." George went out of the room as he spoke, and Effie was left to her own thoughts.

The result of these thoughts was that in half an hour she was walking rapidly up the hill. Knowing it to be Mrs. Potter's washing-day, she made her way round to the laundry, and found, as she expected, the good woman at her wash-tub. The door into Gerard's room was shut, and Effie was not sorry for an excuse to delay her visit to him.

"How are all the children, Mrs. Potter?"

"Pretty middling, I am thankful to say, Miss Effie. My blessed infant is suffering sadly with his teeth. It is a severe exercise to see a helpless innocent so afflicted."

"It must be very trying. Your children suffer a great deal."

"Indeed they do, miss. But every pang that rends their beloved little frames only makes them more precious to their parents' hearts. Ah, Miss Effie, Dr. Rogers had no sympathy with a mother's feelings when he said I should be thankful if my darling Jemmie was taken, after the poor little sufferer had had twenty severe convulsions in a quarter of an hour. I confess, miss, that my feelings were deeply wounded by his words. 'No, Doctor Rogers,' said I; 'if it is the will of the Almighty to take this blessed innocent, I hope I may have grace given me humbly to submit; but the children of our poverty are as dear to us—and perhaps far dearer—than the heirs of his wealth are to the lordly possessor of millions; and to lose one of these angels, who cheer the gloom of our lowly and afflicted state, would be like losing the life-blood from our hearts.' And my feelings on this, as on every subject, are shared by the partner of my woes—my beloved James."

The force of Mrs. Potter's eloquence was heightened by the most emphatic flourishes of various dripping articles of clothing, fresh from the soapsuds. Effie could hardly help laughing at the thought of the appropriate name of "Mrs. Siddons," which Gerard had bestowed upon his landlady.

"And how do you think Mr. Yonge is, Mrs. Potter?"

"Very bad, Miss Effie," answered the tragedian, in

a hollow whisper. " His strength is ebbing from him, drop by drop, as I wring the water from this sheet. *I* see it, Miss Effie. Other people may be blind, but eyes that watch him day after day, as mine do, see all. I said to Dr. Rogers only yesterday morning, 'Dr. Rogers,' said I, 'I love him like one of my own precious infants, and the quick eye of affection shows me that he is going fast.' But Dr. Rogers is blind to the truth, miss. 'Yes, Mrs. Potter,' said he, 'I hope that he is going—to a milder climate for the winter.' 'No, Dr. Rogers,' said I, ' my eyes do not deceive me —he is sinking into his grave, and before the winter comes, climate will make no difference to him." What with tears and soapsuds the soft-hearted laundress's face was in a sad plight now ; but Effie no longer felt any inclination to laugh.

"I shall mourn for him like a mother for her first-born," continued the good woman, between her sobs. " And my beloved James feels just as deeply. He has been like a ray of the blessed sun in our course through this gloomy vale ; and when his corpse is carried from our door, and laid in the dark grave, all the light will depart from this afflicted house. You will see for yourself, Miss Effie, how fast he is sinking. He has not half the strength he had a week ago."

"May I go in to him now ?" asked Effie, rather affected by Mrs. Potter's gloomy forebodings, though she knew that excellent woman was given to exaggerated views both of joy and sorrow.

"I have been obliged to put the wash-tub against this door to-day, miss. Perhaps you would not mind going through the other way. His door is open. You will excuse my coming with you."

Effie went so gently into the room that Gerard did not hear her. He was gazing intently before him, evidently in deep and troubled thought. Effie was certainly struck with the thin, haggard look of his face.

"Effie," he exclaimed, turning pale as he caught sight of her, "have you seen George?"

"Yes; he has been with me nearly all the afternoon," answered Effie, shutting the door, and coming towards Gerard with her hand out.

"And you have come to tell me," he said, hurriedly. "Stop a moment! It is best so—but——"

He grasped a chair which stood before him, and the veins in his hands stood out like cords. He breathed fast and heavily, and his face was deadly white. As Effie started forward in alarm at his appearance, he looked up at her with a ghastly, attempt to smile, and said, "Come and tell me all about it to-morrow, Effie,—I—I cannot stand it now."

Effie threw herself on her knees before the chair which he still held, and looking up in his face, cried,

"Gerard, dearest Gerard, it is not that—it is not what you think. George is nothing to me! We are nothing to each other!"

"Effie," gasped Gerard.

"I respect and like him—but that is all. I have never had any other feeling for him."

"Effie!—Gourock—you told me then that you cared for him."

"I never told you that, Gerard. I was foolish and unkind. I said you had no right to ask what you did. I was hurt that you should think it possible I could care for any one——"

"And you did not care for any one then? You do not care for any one now?"

"I cannot say that. I *do* care for some one. Gerard, you must know who it is that I care for—that I have always cared for——"

As Effie spoke the blood rushed to her face, and the tears to her eyes.

Gerard looked fearfully agitated. "How can I know, Effie? You told me I had no right to ask."

"Do not remind me of the wicked words I said that day—I have repented of them ever since. I hate myself for having been so cold, and hard—and—and false."

"False, Effie! Take care! Think how I might understand your meaning!"

"Why will you not understand my meaning,

Gerard? Why will you force me to humble myself any more ?"

"Oh, Effie, you are torturing me! Speak out plainly—I cannot bear this."

"Speak out ?—must I speak out plainly what most women only whisper? Gerard, why will you not understand that it is you that I care for—that no one else is anything to me—that you are everything —everything." Having managed to get this out, Effie burst into tears, and hid her face on the chair, sobbing violently. Gerard was so perfectly silent, that, after a few minutes, Effie looked up in alarm.

" My darling," he said, softly, as his loving eyes met her timid glance. " Is it really so, Effie ? Say it again. I cannot believe it. You told me it was all over."

"Gerard, I was mad that day. I thought you said what you did out of pity—and that you wanted to make up for the—for the mistake that happened so long ago."

" I did want to make up for that—to myself. I did say what I did out of pity—to myself. Then you thought I did not love you, Effie? I did not love you as I do now "—he could not go on for a few moments—" I did not then feel that your love was the only thing in the world worth living for—I did not then know what an awful struggle it would be to give you up. But I loved you truly, deeply, Effie—much more deeply than when I was fool enough to mistake vanity and selfishness for love. But, Effie, it was true what you said at Gourock, that you did not care for me. I felt that it was true. Do you remember you said it was impossible to revive a corpse ?"

"Gerard, do forget all that. You reminded me of those words once before—and oh! how the remembrance of them made me suffer afterwards !"

"When I was ill, Effie ? Did you suffer then ? And yet you went away."

"I was obliged to go away, to send Harold to you —you wanted Harold."

"Not half so much as I wanted you. Effie, it gave me an awful stab to think you could leave me then. But it was best so, for when I thought that you had left me like a dying dog by the road-side, it was much easier to give it all up. And it was not so, Effie ? You really did suffer for my sake ? I cannot make it all out. I have just sent George to you ; and I thought you had come to tell me that it was all right between you ; and, instead of that, you tell me— What is it that you tell me ? Say it again, Effie."

He pushed away the chair against which Effie had been leaning, and she then rested her clasped hands upon his knee ; a position which she had been used to take with her father, and sometimes with Gerard during their engagement. Gerard laid his hand over hers, and looking up in his face, she made her con-

fession : " After—after all that happened eight years
ago last spring, I determined that I would not be
weak and foolish, and I tried very hard to forget
—to forget everything. I did manage to get sensible
at last, and when you came to Gourock I felt almost
angry with you for trying to undo all my work."

" I knew it, Effie! I knew you did not care for
me then."

" I thought I did not, Gerard. But afterwards,
when you were so good to aunt Elizabeth, and when
I began to understand all your goodness, all the old
feelings came back stronger than ever—oh, so much
stronger !"

Gerard leant forward as if he would have drawn
her to him, but Effie held back. " I must confess
all," she said. " I used to be such a conceited little
fool, I thought myself much better than you——"

" Quite right," muttered Gerard.

" I thought myself so strong, and you so weak, that
I must always uphold you, and you encouraged me
to think so. And even when—when I thought most
about you, I was full of absurd pride in myself, and
distrust of you—no wonder you got tired of me——"

" Effie, I never got tired ! I was bewitched for a
time, but——"

" Let me go on, Gerard. What happened then
brought me a little to my senses, and afterwards
there came other things to bring down my pride ; and

now, Gerard, these last few years, when I have seen you, instead of being weak, so strong, and good, and noble, and have known myself to have done nothing but harm all my life, whilst you have done nothing but good——"

"Effie, not that! I have done more harm than good. I——"

"I must finish! All that I hear and see of you raise you higher and higher, and all that I know of myself sinks me lower and lower. My pride is all gone now, Gerard. I am thoroughly humbled. Oh, I have so longed to tell you this for so many months!"

"Tell me something else, Effie. You almost said it just now. Make me quite happy for a little while. Say that you love me."

"Must I say more than I have said? Have I not disgraced myself enough?"

"Would it be such a disgrace to love me?"

"A disgrace? No. But a disgrace to force the confession upon you, as I have done. No," she added, vehemently, rising to her feet, and looking almost as tragic as Mrs. Potter. "It is an honour to love you, Gerard. I glory in it! There would be more glory in loving you ,without a hope of return, than in being loved devotedly by any other man in the world."

Before Effie knew that she was within reach of Gerard's arm he had flung it round her, and dragged her to him. As he kissed her passionately, she hid her face on his shoulder, and her violent excitement ended in another burst of tears.

When Effie asked Mrs. Potter the next day how she thought Mr. Yonge, the gloomy forebodings had all vanished.

"He is getting on nicely, Miss Effie. As I said to my beloved partner this morning, 'I feel a lightness in my heart, dear James, which tells me that a joyful future lies before us;' and half an hour after, before James left the house, miss, who should arrive but Mr. Crashawe, to appoint him to the office of pew-opener at the church. It is a grand step on fortune's ladder. I have no doubt now that the tide of our fate has turned, and that blessings will now flow in upon us instead of afflictions. Yes, Mr. Gerard is as brisk as the soaring lark, and I can see the glow of returning health upon his face."

CHAPTER XIV.

MRS. POTTER's cheerful anticipations seemed likely
to be realized as far as her lodger's health was concerned. Gerard improved rapidly in strength and
spirits after his explanation with Effie. But there
was no other result of George's scheming. The
marriage which he had done so much to promote did
not seem likely to take place, for Gerard said no
word of marriage, and had apparently no intention of
making any change in his mode of life. As the
winter advanced, Mr. Rogers grew urgent that some
change should be made, and Harold determined to
try what his straightforward tactics could accomplish.

"I suppose you and Effie consider yourselves
engaged again," he said, abruptly, as he sat by his
brother's side one morning, having greatly surprised
Gerard by his appearance at such an unusual time.

"How can I think of an engagement, Harold?"
answered Gerard, sadly. "Should I say to Effie, 'I
have fifty pounds a-year to live on, and I want a

nurse, will you marry me?' No, Harold, I cannot think of marriage. I know that Effie would sacrifice herself if I asked her, but I will never ask her."

" It will make her position very awkward if you do not. I think already that she feels it. Have you never mentioned marriage to her?"

"Never. I thought she would understand that it would be the basest selfishness in me to propose such a thing."

" I think you should explain that to her, if you are quite resolved. But I believe you are wrong. She would think it no sacrifice to be your nurse, and marrying her would enable you to take the measures necessary for your recovery."

"I could not marry her for that, Harold. I wish I had a kingdom to lay at Effie's feet, but I will not lay my crutches there."

" But you have no chance of getting rid of your crutches if you go on living as you are living now."

"I am much better. I am another man to what I was a month ago—before I was happy about Effie. I am sure I shall get on now without taking any desperate measures."

" Well, you will explain to Effie."

" Yes. I will. Here she comes."

"Then I will go. Good-bye."

" Harold is a mercenary old match-maker, Effie," said Gerard, when his brother had left the house.

"Is he?"

"What do you think he wishes me to do?"

"What?"

"To ask you to marry me, that you may maintain and nurse me."

"Well—why not?" asked Effie, turning very red.

"Why not, little woman! Because I want your love, not your charity—because, if I had 'got houses,' and I had 'got lands,' if 'half Northumberland' belonged to me, it would not be enough to give in exchange for your love."

"Then you think houses and lands are all that I care about, Gerard?"

"Of course, you are well known for the most mercenary of little women. Now, it is of no use. You are not going to force me to marry you. You were quite forward enough in proposing to me as you did. I claim the right of refusal. I don't see why an unfortunate man should be entirely without appeal if a small but resolute woman takes it into her head to make him the object of her charity. Get me into an almshouse—there would be some work for your benevolent energies. The worst is that you have got that mischievous curate as an accomplice; and there is no telling in what unguarded moment he might do the deed. Why, before I knew what he was about, I might be a married man! It is awful to think of!"

"Yes, we could manage it most comfortably," re-

turned Effie, laughing. "We have only got to tell
Mr. Potter to turn into the church some morning,
when he draws you out in the chair, and if we were
all ready there, with the licence and the ring, you
would have no possibility of escape."

Gerard shuddered. "I could take refuge in some
'just cause or impediment.'"

"No, you could not, for George would not listen to
you."

"It is terrible to think of a bachelor's defenceless
position. The law ought to do something for us.
When there are women at large who stick at nothing
—not even at making love to a man when he is alone
and helpless—some means ought to be provided for
the defence of the subjugated sex. Why should there
not be a 'Society for the Protection of Unmarried
Men?'"

Gerard went rattling on with all sorts of nonsense
till Effie got up to go, and then his manner suddenly
changed. "Effie, it is terrible to see such happiness
so close, and not to be able to grasp it. Promise me
one thing—that I may have hope to live upon. Promise me that as soon as this ring will come off my
finger I may put it upon yours, and that we shall be
engaged. I will not marry you till I can put another
ring upon your finger with my right hand. I want a
wife—I do not want a nurse."

More than a week later, when there had been a

touch of wintry weather, and Mr. Rogers was becoming very angry that Gerard was still in England, Effie was summoned to Harold one morning by little Bessie. Harold and Jessie were together in the studio, Jessie looking very bright and eager.

"We want to hold a consultation, Effie," said Harold. "I have had the offer of an engagement, similar to the one which took me to Rome five years ago—only that this is to visit all the principal Italian galleries. I should decline it at once—for it would be too great a sacrifice to leave my home now—but it has struck me that we might make this a means of moving Gerard. My idea is that we should all go to Italy, or, if Rogers prefers it, to the south of France, and that, having established you all comfortably somewhere, I should go on to my work, which I could get through in a couple of months. I should then be free to return to you, and to spend the rest of the winter working at my book, for which I am very anxious to get some quiet time."

"Is not it a delightful idea, Effie?" cried Jessie, as soon as Harold paused.

"Yes, it sounds perfect. Would you take the children?"

"Only Bessie, I think. The boys could remain at school, and we should find some one to take pity on them in the holidays. What do you think, Jessie? Would you like to have them, or not?"

"Poor little fellows, it seems a shame to leave them," answered Jessie. "But I suppose it would not do to take them from school for so long. The Butterfields would be very glad to have them in the holidays, or Mr. Rogers, or George Monro."

"Yes, we should have no difficulty about that. The only difficulty that I foresee will be with Gerard. I will go at once, and see if I can bring him to reason. There is no time to be lost, for if I accept, I must be at Florence by the middle of December."

There *was* some difficulty with Gerard. He objected that he could not afford to travel, and refused to believe in the pretence that his presence would be necessary to enable Harold to feel easy in leaving the rest of the party, when his duties called him away. His objections, however, were not proof against Jessie's persuasions, Effie's wistful looks, and Harold's firmness, and he at last yielded. Harold accepted the offered engagement; and on the 1st of December the travellers started for Cannes, Mr. Rogers having recommended either that place or Mentone, and Cannes being considered preferable on account of the shorter journey there.

The ladies and their invalid companion travelled by easy stages—spending three weeks on the road. Harold parted from them at Paris, and went forward as rapidly as possible, that he might lose no time in getting to his work. The earlier part of the journey,

though easy, was not particularly enjoyable, as from
Paris to Toulon the travellers had constant mist or
rain, which shut out every glimpse of the distant
scenery. But the two last days, across the Esterel
Mountains, were perfectly charming to them all—
especially as Gerard had already so greatly benefited
by the change that he was hardly at all fatigued by
the drive. Harold had fixed their winter quarters
in a sunny house half-way up the wooded hill on the
western side of Cannes. Here Gerard soon made
rapid progress towards the full use of his limbs; and
in three weeks Effie persuaded him to let a mule be
his help in exploring the beauties of the neighbourhood. Their first excursion with this useful but
intractable quadruped was to the brow of the hill
from whence the Maritime Alps were to be seen.
There Effie had her second view of the snow-mountains, as she stood silent a little in front of Gerard
and his steed. The sight of these white peaks
sharply defined against the clear blue sky affected
her in much the same manner as the sight of the
Bernese Oberland had affected her. But with this
difference : those mountains spoke to her of the
sovereign justice of God—these told her of His
mercy. Then the eternal snow pointing heavenward,
led her heart to the acknowledgment—"The Lord
God omnipotent reigneth." Now her whole being
joined in the hymn of Nature—" For His mercy

endureth for ever!" These solemn thoughts were interrupted by Gerard's voice, in a tone of glad excitement.

"Effie, don't look round, but take off your glove!"

Effie obeyed.

"Now give me your left hand."

Effie felt something slip on to her third finger; and her overwrought feelings overflowed in tears of gratitude when, on drawing back her hand, she saw on it the ring which it had once cost her such a pang to return to Gerard.

"Oh, Gerard!" she cried, "I was just recalling the time when I first saw snow-mountains; and now——"

"Now the snow-mountains stand there as emblems of our eternal union. My darling!" Gerard added, passionately, as he drew her back, and kissed her. After a pause, he asked, "Were you very unhappy when you first saw snow-mountains, Effie?"

"*Before* I saw them I was, but afterwards—it was such a strange feeling—it seemed to me that in such a beautiful world everything *must* be right."

"I know what that feeling is," said Gerard, thoughtfully. "Do you remember that evening at Gourock when you told me you did not any longer care for me? Well, I was terribly cut up then. I had been working so hard for your sake, and then to find it all in vain! If that had happened in the winter, in a dull street in a town, I believe the disappointment would have made me quite desperate. But after we parted that night I walked along the banks of the Clyde for hours, in the glorious moonlight, and all my rebellious feelings were calmed. I felt, as you say, that the Maker of such a world *must* be right."

"And how right it all was!" exclaimed Effie. "For me, at any rate. I should never have been so happy as I am if I had not been as miserable as I was."

"I can't quite think that, little woman. It cannot have been good for you that I should have made you suffer so cruelly. *You* did not need punishing. Now *I* did. I am like this mule. I must be kept right by hard blows."

"The old story, Gerard! Are you going to begin that again ?"

"No, not quite the old story. Do you remember when we started this morning we had grand ideas of being merciful to our beast, and using no stronger persuasion than soft words ? By the time we got to St. François' shrine he had found out our weakness, and did his best to kick me off. Then I belaboured him soundly, and he has been manageable ever since. That has been the way with me through life. At first everything was easy to me—I did not think there was such a thing in the world as a rod for *me*. Then I became restive, and so the rod fell, and I got blow after blow, till I had learnt that there was a Hand over me against which it was in vain to struggle, and which was ruling me for my good. There is no fear of my struggling to any purpose, now that *you* have got the reins."

" I have not got them yet."

" You will have them very soon. See, it will not be long before this hand is ready for its work." He stretched out his right hand as he spoke, showing that the fingers were no longer helpless.

Four months later Gerard and Effie were again looking at the snow-mountains from the same spot. No mule was with them now, for Gerard could walk quite well. Another sign of the improvement in him was that he was sketching.

" I am a horrible hand at landscape," he exclaimed, impatiently, as he looked at his work. " If there were any chance of Harold being back in time I would leave this for him to do. But I don't expect he will have a day to spare, and we must have something to remind us of our good old friends here."

" I don't think I shall ever need any reminder," said Effie. " Their shapes seem to be printed on my eyes."

" We have been very happy here, have not we, little woman ?"

Effie's only answer was a smile—so bright that it told of worlds of happiness.

U

" Uncle Gerard, here's a letter for you," said Bessie, approaching in a breathless condition. " And Mamma has heard from Papa, and he will be here at the end of next week."

" He had better not be later, or he will be too late," said Gerard, glancing triumphantly at Effie. " I shall not wait for any one beyond Monday week. Now let's see what George has to say. Effie, what do you think ?" he exclaimed, when he had read a few lines. " What living do you think Mr. Monro has bought for George ?"

" Pixycombe," said Effie, calmly, but an excited flush came into her face.

" Yes. How did you guess? He is going to take possession at once. His father bought the next presentation years ago, but kept it a secret from George ; and now the vicar is dead, and George is vicar. The old rascal! He has stolen a march upon me. I meant to be Vicar of Pixycombe."

" You ! You can't be Vicar of anything for years to come."

" Not so many years, Mistress Impudence. I shall be in full Orders before this time two years."

" I wonder what sort of clergyman you will make, after all," said Effie, looking at Gerard, with something between a laugh and a sigh.

" Nothing to compare with George, I am afraid,"

said Gerard, answering the sigh, which he attributed to some doubt of him.

"George is very good," remarked Effie. "But he is not perfect. Of course he is not perfect in practice —no one is; but I do not think he is perfect in theory. His views of duty are very exalted, but they do not satisfy me."

"*I* have no right to say that any one's views of duty do not satisfy me," said Gerard, humbly, still haunted by Effie's sigh. "But I agree with you, little wisdom, in finding fault with some of his theories. He and I have often fought over several matters. For instance, I think he is inclined to over-exalt his office. Of course, from one point of view it cannot be too highly estimated. But as it relates to other men—I hardly know how to explain my meaning; but it seems to me that there is a sort of presumption and arrogance in any man setting himself apart from others. Do you understand what I mean, Effie?"

"Yes, I think so. But does not it make a difference when a man sets himself apart from others for the sake of his office, not for the sake of himself."

"I think it really comes to the same thing. 'Stiggins' exalts himself, and Father Ambrose exalts his office; and silly girls like poor little Miss Leafe worship them both, and they both like it. It is not for the sake of George's office that Miss Leafe is always running after him."

" That is not George's fault."

" No, poor old fellow ! But he is inclined to take all that sort of thing rather as a matter of course. I don't think that it *is* his fault, though. It is the fault of his school. He is the priest — not the pastor."

" And do you mean to be a pastor—a Stiggins?" asked Effie, in affected alarm.

" Yes," answered Gerard, " and you must mix my hot gin and water for me. You see the great advantage of hot gin and water is that a man who was tipsy over night cannot call himself a saint, and other people sinners."

" But that is just what Stiggins does," said Effie.

" True. Well, I won't be a Stiggins, then. In fact, I could not. I shall never have Miss Leafes running after *me*, Effie. I have not got it in me to be either petted as a shepherd, or worshipped as a priest."

" That is just as well," said Effie. "It is much better for you to be kept down. But I must say I would much rather you should be a priest than a shepherd."

" You are wrong, Effie. If by a priest you understand one who is to enter alone into the Holy Place. We have no such priest now—at least, not on earth.

What we want now is one who, by study and self-discipline, can lead others into the Holiest, which has been thrown open to all. That is what Mr. Eden taught, and that is what I believe."

Gerard so seldom showed by his conversation that he had given much thought to serious subjects, that when he did so Effie was always surprised to find that he *could* think deeply. She generally found, also, that he thought not only deeply, but justly, as she readily confessed in the present instance.

" I think you are right, Gerard. Then would you claim no especial sanctity for the priestly—or clerical office ?"

" For the office, yes—for the man, no. Do you remember, Effie, when I was a boy, I turned aside from the path your father had marked out for me because I thought I was not worthy to follow in his steps. I should not do that now. I am no more worthy than I was, but I believe now that it makes no difference. One cannot escape from responsibility. A layman is just as much bound to do his duty as a clergyman is, and he has more temptations to resist."

"Then do you think there is no difference ?"

" None whatever. Excepting that, of course, any one who pretends to lead others is more open to blame if he does not go straight himself."

" And you would have a clergyman just the same as other men ?"

"Exactly. What is right for them is right for him; and what is wrong for him is wrong for them. How can a man lead others if he does not go the same way that they do? But I have preached you a long enough sermon, Effie."

"I see what you mean," said Effie; "and I think now that you are quite right; though I never saw it in that light before. It was not that I meant about George. What I complain of is a sort of coldness which he used not to have. His first sermons at Gateshill were all that one could wish."

"Poor fellow!" cried Gerard. "No wonder he is cold! His life has been a very dreary one, and we know whose fault that is. We must not grudge him Pixycombe."

"We!" repeated Effie, in a defiant tone. "I don't grudge him Pixycombe."

"Yes, we. We for ever, after next Monday week."

On this important "next Monday week" a very simple but very pleasant-looking bridal party walked past St. François' road-side altar, and down the hill to the pretty little English Church. Effie's face was perfectly calm and peaceful as she leant on Harold's arm, with Bessie clinging to her other hand. Jessie, following with Gerard, looked younger than the bride, and wonderfully beautiful. Gerard was quiet and agitated; but when the service was over, and he and Effie stood for a moment alone, side by side in the church-porch, his fervent "Thank God for this," was full of intense happiness.

It was certainly a most unorthodox wedding. But then English people abroad are freed from many of Mrs. Grundy's restraints, which are all-binding at home. And especially in this intoxicating climate, with its flood of sunlight, Mrs. Grundy's sceptre is gone. So our party were able to dispense with the trying formality of a wedding-breakfast, and, instead of sitting down, with forty or fifty more or less unsympathising friends, to a meal which everybody wishes at an end, to listen to speeches which nobody wishes to hear, they sailed across the beautiful blue bay, to a cool landing-place in a little pine-wood, and there they had a quiet pic-nic. When the fast-increasing shade of the trees warned them that it was time to separate, Harold and Jessie sailed back to Cannes, and Gerard and Effie drove on to Mentone, on their way to Genoa.

CHAPTER XV.

It was just such a May morning as that on which, twenty-five years before, George Monro, then a boy fresh from Eton, had been awakened by the bells of Pixycombe Church. Now, as then, the beautiful chimes rang out merrily through the sweet morning air ; and now, as then, a traveller had slept at the little inn near the river, and at the first sound of the bells was ready to walk up the hill to the church. As the guest passed out, the landlord, who was standing at the door, called his attention to a tall, red-haired man, who was also hurrying up the hill.

"There goes Mr. Lang, sir, our doctor, to Northerby."

Hearing himself named, the doctor stopped, and bowed to the stranger. "A fine morning, sir."

"Yes, very fine. I think we ought to know each other, Mr. Lang—my name is Monro."

"Indeed. Very glad to make your acquaintance, Mr. Monro. I have often heard of you, but never before had the pleasure of an interview. You'll be going up to our friends at the Vicarage ?"

" Yes. It is five years since I have seen them. I only reached Pixycombe late last night, and, as I am not expected, I did not like to make my appearance at the Vicarage at such an hour."

"All hours are alike at the Vicarage for receiving a guest," said Alexander Lang. " The doors stand open night and day—figuratively speaking, of course. We Scotch folks pride ourselves on our hospitality ; but Gerard Yonge and his wife beat any one *I* ever met with."

" 'Given to hospitality,' " said George to himself, but not to his companion.

" You are no stranger at Pixycombe, Mr. Monro."

" No, I was here for three years. It seems very much like home."

" You left on account of some preferment, I suppose."

" Hardly preferment. But I wanted a more stirring life. I could not find work enough here."

" Yonge has made himself work enough, I think. You know we have a model parish, Mr. Monro."

" I don't know much about it. Gerard Yonge was never fond of telling of his own good deeds."

" No, you are right, Mr. Monro, quite right. I know as much of his good deeds as most men, and something more."

" What do you think of his health, Mr. Lang ?"

" Oh, that's all right. Nothing ever ails the Vicar. But it is this country life has set him on his legs. I did not think much of him when he left St. Matthew's."

" No ; he worked much too hard there, and a London parish is very trying to a sensitive nature like his. It suits *me*, but I can stand a good deal of wear."

" You have got St. Matthew's now, I believe."

" Yes, I was presented to the Incumbency whilst Gerard was curate there, and then he stepped into my place here."

" Pixycombe is in the gift of your family, I think."

" My father bought it for me fifteen years ago. But St. Matthew's gives me much more congenial work."

" Gerard Yonge seems equally pleased with the change. He is exactly the man for this place. You should hear the people talk of him and Mrs. Yonge."

" I suppose Mrs. Yonge is very active in the parish ?"

" She is just the Vicar's shadow. Wherever he leads she follows. I believe that she has more independence than most people give her credit for, but it is impossible to imagine either of them without the other."

" And what are the works you spoke of in the parish ?"

"More than I can tell you of. Church matters don't come within my province, but I must say I think Yonge a little overdoes it there. All his services, and his church open at all times, seem to me to smack of Popery. But nobody can find fault with his work amongst the old and sick people. He comes on my ground there, and I could tell you something of his patience and kindness. I am not much of a religionist myself, but Yonge's way of practising what he preaches forces one to own that there may be some truth in what the parsons say. I beg your pardon, Mr. Monro! I forgot you were one of the cloth yourself."

"I have heard something of this sort at St. Matthew's. Yonge was very popular there."

"He could not be otherwise than popular anywhere. Now, to show you the sort of thing he does: you know what severe weather we had last winter? Well, on the very coldest night, when the snow was lying thick on the ground, the Vicar walked all the way to Northerby—twelve miles there and back—to fetch me to the child of his only enemy in Pixycombe."

"Then I suppose the enemy was converted into a friend?"

"A fast friend. It was Lee at 'The Bells.' He had taken offence at the Vicar for drawing away the men from his tap, by the cricket, and the reading-room, and such things, and so he revenged himself by keeping his children from school, and his wife

from church. Well, on the day I am speaking of,
Lee's little girl had a fall on the ice, and hurt her
head. The news of the accident did not reach the
Vicarage till ten o'clock at night, but down comes
Yonge at once. The child was raving in delirium
then ; but no one thought of sending six miles for a
doctor, when no horse could get along the roads.
Besides, Lee had not been over-civil to me, and he
fancied I would not come out on such a night for his
sending—not, of course, that I should have refused.
However, the Vicar knew I could not refuse *him*, so
off he came, and knocked me up as the clock was
striking twelve. I did not get there a bit too soon
to save the child, and I took care to let Lee know
that he owed her life to the Vicar. But that was
not all. Yonge soon found out that the little girl
had no chance of quiet at home, so what does he do
but have her and her mother at the Vicarage, and
there they lived on the fat of the land for two months,
till the child was well again. I only tell you this as
one example in many. My patient lives here. Good-
morning, Mr. Monro. You will be too soon for the service, but I suppose you are going to the Vicarage first."

But that was not George's plan. He sat on a stile
till the first comers began to drop into the church ;
and, after speaking to one or two acquaintances, went
in with them. The self-denying Incumbent of a
populous London parish had passed the age of sentiment,

but he felt an unwonted excitement when the Vicar's wife came up the church with her three children. How little changed she was from the Effie Garnock he had first seen in front of Eton College! And yet she was changed. No one would have called Effie Garnock a pretty girl, but Mrs. Gerard Yonge was a very comely woman. The thin face had filled out; the anxious brow had grown smooth and placid; the mouth, which George had so often seen compressed with inward trouble, had now got something very like a dimple at each corner. As she sat in the peaceful church with her pretty children, George knew the change he saw in her was the result of ten years of almost untroubled happiness.

The rising of the whole congregation as the Vicar entered roused George from his reverie. The first glance sufficed to show him that Mr. Lang was right about Gerard's good health. He had seldom seen a more vigorous man, or one who, in middle age, had retained more of the joyous look of early boyhood. As the service proceeded, George could not keep his thoughts from dwelling on the extreme beauty of that face, which he had seen first in the brightness of happy youth, then overclouded with conscious error, and then haggard and worn with disease and suffering. He was thinking too much of the Vicar himself to pay undivided attention to the Vicar's sermon, which was very characteristic—straightforward and earnest, but not in the least eloquent—there were none of the elements of a popular preacher in Gerard Yonge ; but the reverent self-forgetfulness of his manner during the whole service was better than the highest eloquence.

Stepping round to the Vicarage-gate as soon as the service was over, George seated himself on a grave-stone, and waited for his friends. He had some time to wait, for the congregation also waited for their Vicar, who, instead of leaving the church by the vestry, came out through the western door, where his flock were all drawn up in array, ready to shake hands with him. This, with the necessary talk, naturally took a good while, and even when the Vicarage party turned towards their own gate there were still some stragglers to be noticed. On they came, however—the wife clinging to her husband's arm, and the children hanging round them. As they drew near to George he could plainly distinguish the Vicar's words.

"Georgie, you rascal, do you want to pull my shoulder out of joint? Well, little woman, did the texts do better to-day? There you are, Rowe "— to an old man who was creeping along the path. "What do you mean by staying for the sermon, you troublesome old fellow? Did not I tell you that I would give up having a sermon at all, if you would not leave the church after the prayers? Now, you know, you are quite done up. You are coming to the Vicarage, of course ?"

"No, Master Gerard, I don't like to be always intruding."

"You are not to go toiling home in this sun, you obstinate man ! Come, come along with us," and the Vicar laid his hand affectionately on the old labourer's shoulder.

"Well, Master Gerard, there never was any refusing you."

"Don't hurry. Come on at your own pace. The children want to hear the story of the mutiny that you used to tell me when I was a boy."

"God bless you, sir, and them too," said the old man, fervently.

"Lizzie, the book-markers were capital; they carried me through in triumph. There is Rowe just behind, Mrs. Shaw ; you had better wait for your admirer. Well, Nancy, so you have got your boy home. How well and manly he looks !"

"Yes, sir, I have got him home—praise be to God, and thanks to you !"

"Eden, my boy, if you go to sleep in church I shall be obliged to put you back to the children's service. You may read the Bible during the sermon, if you like, but you *must* keep awake in church."

"Yes, Papa, I will always. Let me come to grown-up church."

"Very well. But grown-up people don't sleep in church. Nash, I shall see you this afternoon—five o'clock, remember."

This interrupted progress had at last brought the party nearly to the gate where George was sitting, and in another moment the Vicar had shaken off his family, and was grasping his friend's hands.

"I thought you were never coming away from the church," said George. "I have been out this half-hour."

"What a shame not to tell me you would be here! I should have cooked up a swell sermon. It is not fair to come down upon us poor rustics in this sudden way. I say, old boy, how good it is to see you! Effie, has not he grown a venerable old gentleman, with his grey hair?"

"Venerable old gentleman yourself!" cried George. "I am a year younger than you are."

"I defy you to find a grey hair in my head! And is not Effie young and beautiful? She is growing quite handsome in her old age—if she were not so very fat."

"Mamma is not fat, Papa! What a shame!"

"This is our son and heir, George. Georgie, this old gentleman is your God-papa—I don't think he ever gave you any plate, though. I suppose he has got some little present for you in his pocket."

"Papa, how rude you are!"

"This is our daughter. You see she is already following in her mother's steps, and tyrannizes over me. This fellow bears a name which ought to bear *him* up very high—he is ' Joseph Eden,' but as we object to Joseph, he is supposed by most people to have some connection with Paradise. We have several more children in-doors. Here we are. I need not introduce the house to you. Welcome, old fellow ! Take him in, Effie, whilst I go and look after the rest of the company."

George was a little startled when he saw "the rest of the company." A long table was laid in the dining-room, and two or three old people were already seated at it. Gerard soon came in with Rowe and two other visitors, and the party was completed by the arrival of Mr. Lang, and the descent from the nursery of two noisy boys. What with the children, and the old pensioners, most of whom were deaf and half-blind, the meal was a scene of strange confusion : but both the Vicar and his wife seemed quite in their element, and George was ashamed to let it appear that his nerves were not so strong as theirs.

" Will you walk with me, George ?" asked Gerard, getting up from the table at last, to George's great relief. " I have got to go down the village before the afternoon service."

" Mr. Lang gives me a grand account of your works," said George, as they left the house.

"Lang is a good fellow. I was his first friend when he came to London, a raw Scotch boy, and he never forgets that."

"How came he here ?"

"There was a practice to be disposed of at Northerby, and he bought it, to be near us. Who do you think is his wife, George ?"

"Any one that I know ?"

"I only tell you under the seal of confession, mind, Mrs. Price."

"Mrs. Price !"

"Yes. It is a strange story."

"By what means has she been made a respectable member of society ?"

"I thought you would be surprised," said Gerard. "It does seem a wonderful transformation, certainly."

"How *did* it come about ?"

"You know that villain Culmer soon cast her off. Some years ago I found her out in a wretched condition. I always felt that the unhappy woman's engagement to me had been one cause of her elopement with that scoundrel, so I was obliged to do what I could to save her. I interested Mr. Eden in her, and he got her, at last, to go to a sister of his, living near York. She went on quietly enough for some time with this old Quaker lady, but just at the time Miss Garnock was in London—you remember that time ?"

" Perfectly."

" Well, just then I had a letter from Mrs. Abel to say that she should be sorry to entertain unjust suspicions, but she could not help fearing that her young friend was not quite so steady as she might be. I knew that if the innocent Quakeress suspected evil it must be very glaring indeed, so I went off at once. There was no doubt of the fact that Mrs. Price was at the old work with little notes and secret meetings ; but it was necessary to investigate the matter very cautiously, and then came the summons back to aunt Elizabeth's death-bed. The day after I left, my interesting penitent went off with a poor singing-master. I heard nothing more of her till the winter we were at Cannes. Then I ran against her in a shop at Nice. She was again in the lowest depths of poverty, and the poor man whom she called her husband—though it turned out that after all she was never really divorced from her original husband——"

" What an escape you had !" exclaimed George.

" Yes, had I not ? Well, I found the unhappy singing-master dying in a miserable lodging in the town. He was in the last stage of consumption, and in an awful state of remorse and despair. He refused to see a clergyman, but he let me read to him, and I was with him pretty often till he died. At his earnest entreaty, the poor woman, who really seemed to have a sincere affection for him, went to live with some relations of his in Wales. Again I lost sight of her for a few years; but at last I heard from the Welsh Methodist parson that she had fallen into such a habit of drinking that he could no longer reconcile it to his duty to his family to keep her in his house. As the poor wretch had mentioned me as her only friend, Effie and I thought we would give her a chance, so we had her here."

" Well, you *are* a Quixotic pair !"

Gerard laughed. " It *was* rather rash. But she behaved very well in every respect but one—it was impossible to keep her from the brandy-bottle. At last Effie suggested that we should treat the habit as a disease, and call in the doctor. Alexander Lang took up the case with great ardour, soon made a marked improvement, and in less than a month, proposed to marry his patient. She had had positive information of her husband's death before she left Wales. I did all I could to dissuade Lang. He knew something of her previous history, and I told him more, but without the least effect, and they were married two years ago. It seems to be all right. He speaks with the utmost respect of his wife, and, as you see, looks very well satisfied. We don't see much of her, for Effie cannot get over a strong aversion to her voice, and I don't care to be reminded of the worst and most unhappy period of my life—even for the sake of coutrast with the present. I shall not be long in here. Will you go and see old Palmer next door in the meantime?"

" And the Gateshill people are all flourishing?" asked Effie of George, as they were all walking from church after the evening service.

"Yes, all, I think. You know the Potters have got Mr. Samuel Butterfield's lodge?"

" Hurrah!" cried Gerard. "No, we did not know it. ' Fortune's beams have illumined this gloomy vale ' then. Dear old Mrs. Potter! I should like to see her."

" You know we had a visit from Mrs. Mortlake last winter," observed Effie.

"I never appreciated Mrs. Mortlake before," said Gerard. "She is such a good woman, besides being such capital fun."

" She is an excellent woman—she has the largest heart and the largest mind of any one I ever met with."

" Is Clara at all altered?" asked Effie.

" She has grown very matronly, and Nathaniel is quite patriarchal."

" And how does old Harold look? and Jessie?" asked Gerard.

" Extremely well. Of course you heard what a good degree Walter took?"

" Yes. Harold wrote to me in high spirits about it. He is a clever boy. It is very cunning of old

Hay to make a barrister of him, considering the intimacy with the Butterfields. Jessie says there is a great flirtation between the future Lord Chancellor and Cissie Butterfield."

"Something more than a flirtation, I fancy. The great *flirtation* is between Fred and my little niece. Clara tells me that Katie was quite inconsolable when Fred went to sea."

"And old Davie—does he do nothing in that line?" asked Gerard.

"A great deal of play-work, but nothing serious. He makes terrible havoc of all the young ladies' hearts, I believe."

"He is a very good-looking fellow."

"Your Georgie is just like him."

"Is not he?" cried Effie. "They are both like Gerard."

"How has Bessie grown up? We have not seen her for four years."

"She is a fine girl, but not pretty. She is as like her father as Walter is like his mother and Davie like his uncle."

"And Jessie is as handsome as ever," said Gerard, "at least she was when we saw her last year."

"Quite as handsome, I think, and Harold seems more in love every time I see them together."

"I don't wonder at his being in love with Jessie as she is now," said Gerard. "She is a different creature from what she used to be. Trouble was a great blessing to her."

" Did you hear what Harold had put on little Isa's tombstone ?" asked George.

" No."

" ' She is not dead, but sleepeth.' ' If we believe that Jesus died and rose again, even so them also which sleep in Jesus will God bring with him.' "

" That is very good," said Gerard, thoughtfully.

" You remember the seed from which that sprang, Gerard ?" asked George. " It was the text on which you preached when we all thought that you were dying. You see Harold has not forgotten your words; they have borne good fruit. I have long ceased to regret that you leaped before you looked that day on the Steadham pond."

" So have I. It was the luckiest leap that was ever taken. But how stupid it was of me, to be sure." As he spoke the Vicar threw his arm round his friend's neck, in the old boyish fashion.

" It was not very wise, but it was very noble," said George.

" Noble ! I believe I did it in a kind of rage because I had settled to go to Borneo, and did not like the idea."

" You see he is as fond as ever of depreciating himself," remarked Effie, as the party turned into the Vicarage. The look of pride in her husband which accompanied Effie's words recalled to George's mind a certain walk in Gateshill Lane, when Effie had told him she despised Gerard, though she could not cease to love him.

"What is your recipe for popularity, Gerard?" asked George Monro, as the three friends were sitting in the Vicar's study after the children had gone to bed.

" Do you remember your first sermon at Gateshill?" asked Effie, before her husband could answer George's question.

"Do *you?*" exclaimed George, with a gratified look.

"Yes, perfectly. The text you took for that sermon is the key-stone of Gerard's popularity. It is the text not only of his preaching, but of his practice."

"Nonsense, little woman. *You* are my recipe for popularity."

" Don't believe him, George."

"Then you think love is a more powerful stimulus than duty," said George, thoughtfully. "I thought that was your theory from your sermon this morning."

"My dear fellow, I have no theory. I leave all that to Effie."

" If it is not your theory, it is your motive, then. What makes you do so much for your people here?"

"Tell him, Effie. I am sure I don't know."

"Duty, perhaps," said Effie, with one of her old impudent glances.

"My dear little woman! You know I never in my life did my duty."

"Then it is as I said—love."

"Well, they are 'an awfully jolly lot of people,' as Georgie says."

"And the St. Matthew's people, were *they* 'awfully jolly'?" asked George.

"Poor wretches! How I did pity them!" cried Gerard. "I knew so well what it was to have got all wrong, and to despair of ever getting right again."

"'Pity is akin to love,'" said George. "Well, I only hope I may never have to succeed you again," he added, laughing. "Theory, or no theory, you are a trying man to be compared with. I suppose the secret is what you say, Effie. I wish I had kept closer to the text of that first sermon of mine. I have somehow got to regard Obedience as higher than Love."

"How can they be separated?" asked Gerard.

"I suppose they cannot be separated. I thought they could be. It seemed to me a glorious thing for a man to give up his will—not for love, or for hope, but for duty. And I believe I got too fond of preaching this."

"That is all very well for you, who can do your duty," remarked Gerard. "But how about us reprobates?"

"I have heard something of your reprobate condition," said George. "Effie, don't you dislike mock modesty? And this was the 'reprobate' who taught me my duty so powerfully this morning!"

"You don't mean to say that *I* did anything powerfully! Effie says I am the tamest of preachers."

"I don't mean to say that you were eloquent. But there is always power in one who goes right down to the root of the matter. And, after all, that text of which you spoke, Effie, *is* the root of the matter. All we really want is to make men believe that ' God is Love.' "

"That is it, George!" cried Gerard, with a burst of enthusiasm, which proved that he had, at any rate, *one* theory. "The only thing really worth living and working for is to teach poor starving and suffering wretches that all *must* be right which comes from Perfect Love and Perfect Wisdom!"

"How to teach that?" asked George, wearily, thinking of many failures.

For all answer, Gerard pointed to a wooden Cross, which stood on his mantelshelf.

"Half my congregation would cry 'No Popery!' if they saw that in *my* study," said George.

"Mr. Eden gave it to me," continued Gerard, "when he had brought me by Its teaching to see that all is for the best. And having once seen that—having once learnt that pain, and disappointment, and sorrow are things rather to rejoice in than to grieve over—my own love of comfort forces me to try and make others learn it too, that I may escape the horrid sight of any hopeless suffering."

"You are luckier than most people if you do not find it a lesson which men are very slow to learn," said George.

"It certainly is that," replied Gerard. "I will tell you what it is like. When any of the children are out of sorts Effie administers a most unpalatable dose, which she calls 'Tonic Bitters.' Of course the children hate it, though she tells them, over and over again, that it is for their good. Just so we try to persuade people that pain and suffering are for their good. And as Effie occasionally takes a dose herself, that she may tell the children how much better and stronger it has made her, those who have gained strength through suffering are the best able to speak in favour of suffering. Now I have done my sermon. And now, Effie, by way of illustration, and for the improvement of his smoke-dried complexion, suppose you give George a good dose of 'Tonic Bitters.'"

THE END.

LONDON

PRINTED BY WILLIAM CLOWES AND SONS, STAMFORD STREET
AND CHARING CROSS.

www.ingramcontent.com/pod-product-compliance
Lightning Source LLC
Chambersburg PA
CBHW060539030726
47498CB00004B/1257